The
Godmothers

ANGELA HARTLEY

The Godmothers

This book is a work of fiction. Names, places, characters and events are all based on the author's imagination or are used fictitiously. Any resemblance to actual persons, living or dead, or actual events is purely coincidental.

November 2023

Cover design by Aubrey Labitigan Jai Design

Angela Hartley

Acknowledgements

Special thanks to all those who have supported me throughout the process of writing and publishing The Godmothers.

To Sue Vendy, Melanie Sibborn-Kay, Carol Marriott-Clayton and Roisin Robertson for their invaluable support in the editing process.

To Barry, my husband and number one supporter and critic.

To Alex Philipson, for giving me the confidence and encouragement to publish my first novel. Without you, Alex, the character of Alexandria in this book would never have seen the light of day.

I dedicate this book to the many godmothers and godchildren in my life. You don't know how much you're all loved.

Also by Angela Hartley

Finding Home - Published March 2022
Forever Home - Published October 2022
After the Rain – Published March 2023

Available to purchase or download from Amazon.co.uk

The Godmothers

By Angela Hartley

The Godmothers

Chapter 1

The Present

"For pity's sake, that's the last thing I need, today of all days! Blue Monday, where on earth has that concept come from? What will they think of next?" Mel questioned herself, already feeling quite desolate. She was driving the short distance home from Heathrow Airport in her silver Audi TT having just dropped her daughter, Sarah, off in plenty of time to catch her flight to Hong Kong. From there she was flying into Sydney, Australia, before an internal flight to Adelaide. And now, Mel was returning home, to the prospect of an empty house, and what was more depressing, an empty nest.

Mel was carefully navigating the last couple of miles of the journey, slowly picking her way through the rush hour traffic. She was trying to avoid all the yummy mummies as they darted between parked cars, or dashed along the wet pavements in order to collect their precious little ones from the local primary school. It was obvious from the way they ran, or fought with their umbrellas, they were desperate to get back to the shelter and warmth of their cars; no intention of dawdling in the playground today for a gossip. They would be in a hurry to start their short drives home, or more likely the drop-offs at whatever after school clubs, or events their child was signed up for that afternoon. "Children nowadays appeared to have more hectic social lives than their parents," Mel thought to herself. Mothers run off their feet, trying to keep up with the demands of their offspring, or more likely the competitiveness of the other mums. Mel knew all about that, constantly hearing the cries and moans of the women who called into her coffee shop on a daily basis.

It was mid-January, and according to the local radio station today was 'Blue Monday', the most depressing day of the year. With the weather and the mood she was in, Mel could see where they were coming from. Christmas was over for another year, the decorations all boxed up, the tree dumped on the recycling pile, and the freezer and cupboards still full of all the food bought and never used over the festive period. The days were short, the nights were long with the cold and dark doing nothing to foster a healthy frame of mind.

This year, it seemed worse than ever. Christmas had been okay — a relatively quiet and sober affair in comparison with previous years, with New Year turning out to be a damp squib. A quiet night out with friends, nothing particularly special. Mel had not felt like celebrating, but had gone along anyway, feeling like a spare part among a group of 'happy couples', and although there were a few single guys in the party, there was no one of interest.

She had no love in her life, having just finished the latest in a long line of disastrous relationships. Her nineteen-year-old daughter was about to fly the nest, and to top it all, she was forty this year! Forty — where had that come from? It seemed only five minutes since she was the same age as Sarah, with her life ahead of her. Where had the years gone, and more importantly, what had she done with her life?

Chapter 2

The Present

As Mel was pulling into the driveway of her detached four-bedroom property in Chelsea, Jenny was packing away her classroom, after a difficult lesson with Year 9. Getting them to concentrate today had been more difficult than usual, and sensing she was struggling, they had not made it any easier. It was the last session of the afternoon, and all most of them wanted was to hear the bell and head home to their PlayStation, or consoles or whatever they played nowadays. A mixed ability group of thirteen and fourteen-year-olds was never going to be an easy gig. Whoever scheduled a double Maths session for the end of the day needed their heads examining, in Jenny's humble opinion.

"Mum, are you giving me a lift home tonight, or do I have to catch the bus again?" Emily asked, popping her head around the classroom door on her way back to her own classroom. Having just finished a P.E. session, she was still wearing her tracksuit, although there was little evidence she had exerted herself much during the lesson. Sport was not her bag at all. Emily was always happier with a book in her hand or a keyboard in front of her.

"If you can wait half an hour, I'll give you a lift. I've just got to return some things to the staffroom before I leave." Thankfully, Monday was the only night Jenny could escape as soon as lessons ended, with no staff meetings or after school activities to delay her. Every other evening there was something that meant she had to hang around for at least an hour after the bell had gone. "What's your brother doing?" she asked, continuing to pile the books up.

Harry was fifteen, Year 10 and two years older than Emily. He, unlike Emily, was sports mad and had joined every team or club that would have him.

"I think he's got football practice tonight, so he's probably getting the bus home with his mates when it's over. I saw him at lunchtime in the canteen, but he didn't talk to me," she added, disgruntled that she had been ignored, again.

"Well, why don't you wait for me outside the staffroom? I won't be too long." Jenny smiled at her daughter. Emily was a quiet girl and Jenny knew she had not settled at high school anywhere near as easily as her brother had, having made few friends. Jenny often wondered whether her being a member of the teaching staff at the school made that more difficult, or not for her daughter, having heard many a story from others in the staffroom about their own experiences. Some chose to send their children to different schools, even pay to go private to avoid any possible conflict, or to at least keep their private and personal lives separate. However, that was not an option for Jenny. The local state school was all she and her husband Jason could afford; on a teacher's salary private education was out of the question. And as this school was in their catchment area that was all they had been offered. The way things were going though, keeping up with the bills was becoming more of a challenge every day. Jenny often wondered how soon it would be before she needed to look at taking on extra tuition, just to help make ends meet.

As she made her way to the staffroom, seeing Emily sitting outside playing on her phone and looking quite forlorn, she wondered where her life was going. Or more precisely where it had gone in these last twelve months. It had been just before Christmas the year before last, when Jason had dropped his bombshell, informing her he was leaving home, to move in with another woman – an affair that, unbeknown to her, had been going on for over six months.

After sixteen years of marriage, most of which had been happy, Jenny recalled, and at the grand old age of forty-five, Jason had decided it was time for his midlife crisis. He was shacking up with a younger woman, who just happened to be a single mother of one of the boys at his school. A quiet little boy in Year 2, according to one of her sources. With Jason Headteacher, that had not gone down at all well with the governors, or parents alike. Whilst he had not been directly asked to tender his resignation, it was made abundantly clear he was skating on thin ice, his position remaining precarious. The affair soon became the talk of the playground, the more the news got around.

Jenny had felt like the wounded party, distraught and completely hoodwinked by her husband's behaviour. She was also the one left to pick up the pieces with Harry and Emily. Once they realised the full extent of their dad's behaviour, keeping their spirits up had proved a challenge, especially as she was trying hard not to badmouth him, at least not within their earshot. Who knew how it would all end, or if he would ever decide to come back home? So, for now at least, Jenny had decided to keep her options open. Separation was temporary, whereas a divorce would be final, as well as stressful and expensive; both of which she wanted to avoid, at all costs.

"Come on then, sweetheart," she said thirty minutes later, her bag and coat in hand as they walked to the car park, digging out the keys to the ten-year-old Ford Focus she was driving these days. "Why don't we call in and see Grandma and Grandad on the way home? We've not seen them all week, and I know Grandad wanted you to help him with something on his iPad. You can do that while I have a quick chat to Grandma."

Emily smiled, knowingly. Grandma would have some baking to hand, and after having to run around during P.E. to keep warm, she was starving.

Chapter 3

The Present

As Jenny was leaving her parents' home, heading two miles down the road towards hers and Jason's three-bedroom semi-detached house in the middle of a 1970s housing estate just outside Manchester, Heather was stoking up the fire. It was six o'clock and she was putting extra logs into the log-burner, in a vain attempt to keep her cottage warm. Living out in the wilds of Scotland was beautiful and idyllic in the summer months. However, once the winter arrived, lowering the temperatures to well below zero most evenings, with gusty winds and heavy snow making some of their roads impassable, then living suddenly got much more difficult. Shopping became something that needed to be planned well in advance, the larder and freezer being frequently re-stocked whenever a trip to the local supermarket ten miles down the road was doable.

Heather had a beautiful traditional cottage situated in a small Scottish village, just north of Stirling and not far from Loch Lomond. It was set in a pretty landscaped garden with views to die for; the hills and mountains stretching for miles in the distance. In the summer, it was a haven for tourists, many a car or campervan was to be seen driving around the Highlands in search of the infamous monster. In the winter months it was all but deserted, just a handful of hardy locals who had been born and bred in the area, and had never found the need to move.

Nowadays, a lot of the properties were rentals or second homes, with fewer and fewer indigenous Scots choosing to live with such remoteness. Consequently, the average age of the population was rising year-on-year, with fewer families and younger people opting to stay. The primary school now had under twenty pupils, with talk that once the current headmistress retired in a year or so, it may need to close. The children would then be forced to catch the bus to a neighbouring village each day, the idea of which no one supported. Getting staff was proving more difficult each year, not just at the school, but in the village stores, the post office and the doctor's surgery too. Young people wanted to live where there was more life, more opportunities, better jobs. And as beautiful as the village and its surrounds were, it did not tick any of those boxes.

Heather was originally from Edinburgh and had moved to her current home when she married Bruce, twelve years ago at the age of twenty-eight. She had met him one weekend at an art and crafts exhibition in the city, being hosted at the gallery where she worked. Bruce had been spending the weekend visiting his friends, who just happened to be the owners of the gallery. He had been invited along in an attempt to boost the numbers. Bruce was a publisher by profession and also an interested collector of art. He had a keen eye for what would sell and what would, in his view, languish on the shelf forever, either because it was overpriced, or was just not marketable. His friends valued his opinion.

Heather was displaying some pieces of jewellery she had made, along with other artwork she had produced; pieces of pottery and stained glasswork. She enjoyed crafting on every level, and could turn her hand to making most things. Her bright display had initially caught his eye, but when he saw the pretty brunette behind the desk, her smile lighting up her face, he was instantly smitten, and wanted to find out more about her.

Bruce, in his early forties, was nearly fifteen years older than Heather, so knew he had to tread carefully where she was concerned. He had been widowed several years previously, when his wife had passed away suddenly. Since then, he had very much lived a bachelor's life, content in his remote cottage, immersed in his books. Although he travelled occasionally on business, by and large he was happy to work from home. He had no particular need for company, other than his own and his cat's, Misty. He had an eclectic mix of friends who occasionally visited the cottage, and who he visited from time to time, although no family to speak of. He and his wife had never been blessed with children, and as they were only children themselves, their line died out with them.

Having been introduced to Heather, he found her both easy to talk to, as well as easy on the eye, reminding him almost of one of Raphael's cherubs with her curves and pretty features. Over the following weeks, he would regularly call into the gallery, simply on the off chance she would be working. He could see there was an intelligence about her, with a creativity and sensitivity that he found appealing. Being artistic himself, they found they had plenty of things to talk about. Heather was not your usual 'twenty something', whose life was controlled by the latest fashions, the latest gadgets. No, she liked the simpler things in life, and in time that included Bruce and the lifestyle he lived.

After several months of old-fashioned and chaste courting, Bruce taking Heather out for dinner or drinks, the occasional show or exhibition, she was eventually invited to visit his cottage for the weekend. There was no expectation on either side, other than a growing realisation that their friendship was perhaps developing into something deeper. For Heather, though, on arriving at the cottage, and seeing Bruce standing in the doorway to welcome her, it was almost a nirvana moment. She felt at peace, as if she had come home.

That was nearly twelve years ago, she reflected, wondering where time had gone. They had married shortly after her twenty eighth birthday, neither seeing any sense in a long engagement. It felt right, with their love being perfect for them. It was not the type of romance some women would have dreamed of, passionate encounters, or lusty moments, with each ripping the others clothes off at the slightest provocation. No, theirs was a profound love, both deep and meaningful and built on the basis of friendship, trust and shared passions. They had lived in harmony in their cottage, each occupying their own space, but always as one. They were happy whenever they were together, and equally content when they were working alone; Bruce in his study, Heather in the converted barn that had become her workshop.

Who would ever have known Bruce had a heart defect, or that one day, whilst poring over his latest manuscript, his heart would just decide today was the day it had done its last? That had been two years ago now. Two years since she had found him slumped over his desk when she had been taking an afternoon cup of tea up to him, having come back into the house to start to prepare their dinner.

Since then, Heather had lived alone in the cottage, with just the cat and her memories for company. She was surrounded by everything Bruce had stood for; the peace, beauty and tranquillity talking to her every day. Whilst it was reassuring to feel his presence wherever she walked into the house or in the surrounding countryside, it did leave her wondering how she would ever be able to move on. A widow by the age of thirty-eight, childless with no idea what, if anything, life had left in store for her.

"Oh well, come on up Misty, let's get settled in for the evening. It's going to be a cold one, so I'm glad I've got you at least to snuggle up to." Heather patted the settee next to her and smiled over at the cat, purring contentedly in front of the fire.

Chapter 4

Freshers' week – 1998

"Now are you sure you don't need me to help unpack your boxes, Amy?" her mum asked, fussing over her daughter, whilst trying to disguise the sadness she felt deep in her heart. "Dad and I don't need to leave for another hour or so, so there's plenty of time to get this sorted for you. Then we could all head out for something to eat, if you'd like? There looked to be a nice pub across the road." The thought of having to leave her daughter alone in the halls, was something Jean had really struggled with over the preceding weeks. Now that it was actually here, the reality was even more difficult to deal with.

"Come on love, let's leave our Amy alone to get herself settled. She'll be right as rain, and she can ring us if she needs us, can't you love?" Ron asked, knowing how much his wife was struggling. He sensed that it was time for them to go. He had seen three other girls in the adjoining rooms when they had arrived half an hour earlier, and could now hear laughter coming from the direction of the kitchen. His daughter had heard it too. "Let's let Amy unpack and go and meet her roommates. You'll be alright, won't you love?"

"I'll be fine Dad, and thanks for the lift," Amy replied, before adding, in an attempt to soften the pain her mum was obviously feeling, "Mum, I'll ring you tomorrow night and let you know all about my first day. Don't worry, it won't be long before I'm home again."

"Well, if you're sure then, okay." Jean reluctantly sensed she had lost the battle. "Remember though, if you need us, or if you want to come home at any time, just ring. Your dad will be straight over to collect you. It's only a few hours on the motorway, so you don't need to stay if you're not happy, do you?"

Amy was the first member of their family to go away to university, and Jean was struggling with the thought of her daughter being so far away from home. She was worried there would be no one to look out for her, to protect her or keep her safe. She knew her daughter was a bright and sensible girl, raised to be independent, so, in reality the risks were minimal. However, that did nothing to stop her from worrying about her baby, worrying about who she might meet.

"Come on Jean, let's get going before the traffic gets too busy. We can always stop off for a drink or a bite to eat, if you'd like, on the way home." Ron, taking his wife's arm in an attempt to encourage her to move, knew it was time to leave. "Now, give us both a big hug Amy love, and we'll be on our way. And like your mum says, you know where we are if you need us."

A couple of minutes later, they closed the bedroom door behind them and headed to the car, Jean anxiously looking back all the time, conscious she had left something. Realising it was her daughter, and she needed to leave her behind, she trudged on. Once inside the car, Ron handed his wife the box of tissues he kept in the glove box, precisely for occasions such as these.

"Knock, knock," Melissa said, five minutes after she had heard the front door closing. "Can we come in, or do you want to be left alone for a while longer?"

"No, come in, please," Amy replied, wiping the tears from her eyes. She had tried to stay strong whilst her parents were around, although as soon as her bedroom door had shut, the enormity of what she had done had hit her for the first time. Seeing her mum holding back the tears had been difficult enough, whereas stopping her own once they had left had proved impossible.

The door opened and in walked three girls, the first carrying a tray of drinks, the second a plate of chocolate digestives and the third holding the door open to stop it banging shut.

"I hope you like tea, because we've made you a cup too – and Melissa had some biscuits in her stash, so we've opened them," said the girl carrying the tray. "I'm Jennifer Rafferty, by the way, from just outside Manchester. My friends call me Jenny, or Jen, whatever the mood suits."

"Thanks, I love tea – I'm from Yorkshire, just outside Sheffield, so I was raised on the stuff!" Amy replied, managing to control her voice, in an attempt to disguise she had been crying. "I'm Amelia Rawcliffe, although I prefer Amy."

"I'm Melissa Milton-Barker, and only my grandmother calls me Melissa. My friends call me Mel," announced the tall, willowy blonde confidently as she placed the plate of biscuits down on the small desk by the door. "I'm from London, well, Richmond really. Most people don't know where that is, so saying London is easier, I find."

"And I'm Heather, Heather McDougal, and I'm from Edinburgh. I was originally born in Ireland, that's another story though." The last of the three girls introduced herself in a broad Scottish accent. She was dressed, Amy noticed, in a hand knitted, loosely fitted jumper and baggy jeans, her dark hair pulled back off her face by a bright red headband, revealing a pretty, if slightly chubby face.

"Well, as it looks like we're going to be roomies for the next year, I suggest we spend some time, either now or later, getting to know each other. And we can work out a rota for who's doing what." Mel appeared to be taking charge of the group. "I, for one, can't cook for toffee. I can mix a mean cocktail though, and I've got a car for whenever we need to get around. I love to shop too, so I'm happy to volunteer to do the shopping, provided someone tells me what to buy, as I've got a bad habit of going off-piste whenever I'm let loose with a credit card!" Her clipped, upper-class accent did not go unnoticed.

"Well, I can cook a little," Jenny offered. "Sadly, on my allowance the menu's likely to be limited to beans on toast, or the odd poached egg, if we're lucky." She had sensed Mel's upbringing and financial status was a long way from her own working-class background. Funding the newly introduced tuition fees had been a struggle for her parents, her dad pointing out that 1998 was the worst year for their daughter to be starting her degree. They were determined though to give her the education she needed. They had saved up and forgone treats and luxuries for the last couple of years, with her dad working overtime at the factory whenever it was on offer, and her mum taking in ironing. Jenny had in addition worked part-time in a café during her sixth form years, managing to save the majority of her wages, with any money she was given for Christmas or birthdays squirreled away too. Even so, it would not stretch that far, not once books and other resources had been taken into consideration, she feared.

"I'm a clean freak, my mum always said," chirped in Heather, finally. "So, I'll be able to keep on top of the kitchen and do the washing up. Hopefully manage to keep the bacteria at bay, and avoid any nasty tummy bugs."

"Well, by the sounds of it, I'm in for an easy life." Amy laughed, feeling relaxed and a lot more chilled having now met her roommates. "By the sounds of it, you three have everything sorted. So, that just leaves me with the job of either cleaning out the loo or sorting out the socials, and scouting for boys! We're here to have some fun, as well as studying, aren't we?" she asked, sensing the others were pretty relaxed.

"I'll drink to that," proclaimed Mel, raising her almost empty mug of tea. "Then again, I'll drink to most things," she laughed to herself.

"Here's to us all, and to our next twelve months. Let's hope we survive it," Jenny raised her mug.

"To us," Heather added. "Let's hope we become friends, as well as roomies." A broad smile lit up her face as she spoke.

"Friends for life, no matter what life throws at us. Through thick and thin," Amy concluded, as they all clinked their mugs of tea together.

"Yuk, that's gone cold," Mel shrieked, almost throwing her mug down. "How about we quickly get ourselves sorted, then head out and have a look around.

We don't want to spend our first night in, do we? What kind of students would that make us?" she laughed, intent on making the most of Freshers' week.

Chapter 5

The Past

"So love, how did it go yesterday?" Jean enquired a couple of days later when Amy rang her from the payphone outside the Student Union bar, a bag of coins in her hand.

"Not too bad, Mum," she replied. "The girls I'm sharing with all seem really nice. One's from London – she's Mel. One's from Manchester – Jenny, and one's from Edinburgh – Heather. We all went out last night for a look around the town, and ended up having a drink and our tea at the Horse and Hounds across the road."

"That sounds very grand," Jean replied, unsure about her daughter going into bars unaccompanied.

"No, it was actually good fun. It's the pub across the road, where most of the students hang out – so the beer's cheap and the food's pretty basic. It was busy, given last night was everyone's first real night out, so there were loads of people around. Everyone was looking as lost as us!" she laughed.

"And are the other girls doing English, the same as you?" Jean enquired.

"No Mum, we're all doing something completely different, which will be fun. Mel's doing law and politics. Her dad's an MP apparently, so he wants her to follow in his footsteps. I don't think her heart's really in it though, but it's early days. Jenny's doing Maths and wants to go into teaching, eventually. Heather's doing something to do with art and design. I'm not quite sure exactly what she's looking to do. She loves making things and sounds really creative. She's made most of her own clothes too."

"That sounds nice, dear. Don't let them distract you though, will you? You've gone there to study and do well with your English. If you want to get into journalism, like you say you do, you're going to have to knuckle down and work hard."

"Don't worry, Mum. I'm really focussed. In fact, I've already been down to the Student Union to enquire about their magazine. I wanted to see if I could either help out with the editing, or at least contribute some pieces to it." Amy replied, conscious her mum was a real worrier. "I think some writing experience with them would help me a lot. It might even contribute as part of one of my assignments, if I'm lucky."

"Well, as long as it doesn't distract you, love," parroted Jean, again.

She and Amy's dad, Ron, had left school at the age of fifteen, going straight to work at the local steel factory, where most of the youngsters ended up from their town. They had met there, and eventually married in their early twenties, settling down in a working-class area of the town. Ron was now a foreman, so was not doing too badly, for a boy with a basic comprehensive school education and minimal qualifications to his name. He wanted more for his daughter though than simply working on the shop floor like him or her mother, or living in a terraced house all her life.

"Amy's a different kettle of fish from us," Ron had argued when the envelope containing their daughter's A Level results had dropped on the mat; followed shortly by several offers from universities throughout the country to study English. "We can't let her waste her time doing a menial or office job, when nowadays there's so much more opportunity for bright girls, like our Amy. She could go into management, or do anything she wants with those qualifications." He persuaded Jean to let her go and follow her dreams, whilst remaining realistic enough to know that those dreams could take their only daughter far away from them. Who were they to stand in her way?

Amy had been chatting for ten minutes. "Right Mum, I'm going to hang up now as others are waiting to use the phone. I'll ring again in a few days, shall I? And don't worry about me, I'm fine. Give my love to Dad too." She hung up quickly, before her mum could distract her with yet another excuse to stay on the phone.

The rest of the term flew by, and before long it was mid-December and time to return home for the Christmas holidays.

All four girls had settled into their respective courses, and with the exception of Mel, who really could not be bothered with the lectures, or spending time in the library pretending to be riveted by dry textbooks, they were enjoying their studies. On paper, Mel was perhaps the brightest of the four. She had a string of top-grade A levels from the public school she had attended in London, as well as an opinion, or argument, on everything. She was well read, and well connected, and from the way she spoke had more life experiences than the other three put together. Her manner was engaging and she was really likeable. She was neither pushy nor arrogant, simply easy going. And above all she was kind; with the most generous heart anyone could imagine.

"I'll run you all to the railway station in the morning, if you'd like." Mel had offered the previous evening as they were all packing up ready for their journeys home. "It's no trouble for me. I'm not in any hurry to get home anyway. In fact, I think I'd rather stay here, if that was an option," she confessed.

"Don't you want to see your parents?" Amy questioned, a surprised look on her face. Amy had phoned home religiously each week, but to her knowledge she was the only one of the four who had. Heather had occasionally rung her dad, and Jenny had received a few letters, whereas she did not recall seeing any delivered for Mel.

"Not really, if I'm honest." Mel replied frankly. "My father will be either tied up with his constituency stuff, or gallivanting around with his latest fling. Either way I'm unlikely to see much of him. My long-suffering mother will be fussing over everyone, worrying about everything as usual, completely stressed out. My home is never a particularly restful environment, I can assure you of that." As she spoke, she laughed in an attempt to hide some of the embarrassment she felt about her rather dysfunctional family.

"Won't your older brother be there?" Heather enquired. "I thought, from what you'd said, you get on really well with him."

"Oh, James. Yes, I do and yes I think he'll be around for Christmas. I guess he'll be avoiding the parents as much as me. Mum's desperate to get him married off, and keeps introducing him to daughters of friends, or acquaintances of hers. Girls, who in her opinion are the 'right sort of wife material'. James is having none of it though. He's determined to avoid getting married, or for as long as he can manage it. At least not before his thirties, is his view. As he's still only twenty-three, I imagine there's a few more years' worth of wild oats for him to sow. And they won't be with the sort of 'girls' Mother would approve of, I can assure you of that!"

Mel's brother sounded like a real ladies' man, and a character to boot, as far as the others were concerned. Although, as none of them had brothers of their own, they could not offer any real comparisons. Amy and Jenny were both only children and were doted on by their parents. Heather's mother had died four years earlier when Heather was in her early teens. Her father, Graham was still alive, living alone now that Heather was away at university. He was in his early fifties and still relatively fit and independent, working as a landscape gardener and out in the fresh air most of the year. She also had a sister, Ellen, who was six years older than her and already married. Heather had announced a couple of months previously that Ellen was expecting her first baby in March, so would be making her an aunt. The up-and-coming event was giving her creative juices something to think about in terms of what she could make for the baby. She and Ellen were close and she was looking forward to the baby's arrival, but they were sadly nowhere near as close as Mel and her brother sounded.

"Well, I'm looking forward to going home," chirped in Heather. "I've missed my dad. It's the longest time he's been on his own since Mum died, so I want to see how he's coped. Whenever I've phoned he's not said much. It'll be good to see how big Ellen had got too. I've designed some things for the baby's nursery, so hopefully if she likes my ideas, I'll be busy crafting over the holidays."

As Heather's ideas were not always to everyone's tastes, Amy and Jenny exchanged a wry smile.

"I'm sure she'll love them," replied Mel politely, trying desperately hard to disguise the fear in her voice at the thought of anything to do with a baby. Maternal was certainly not a word that would come to mind when describing Mel.

Chapter 6

The Present

Tuesday morning arrived and although there was a real nip in the air, Mel decided to walk the short distance from her home in Chelsea to the King's Road, where her coffee shop was located. It would have been so easy to drive, but this morning she felt like she needed some fresh air to blow away the cobwebs, as well as the exercise. After spending the previous day in the car, or scrunched up on the sofa feeling sorry for herself, she needed some activity. She had hardly slept, still worrying about Sarah. She worried whether she had navigated her way through all the airports without hassle, or if she had arrived safely in Australia yet. "As a mother, do you ever stop worrying?" she thought to herself, questioning whether her mother had worried about her half as much as she did about her own daughter.

When Mel had been in her teens, going to university was the extent of her separation from her family – not travelling to the other side of the world. Sarah was not her though, and yearned for a gap year before she got bogged down with the real world. She was bright, although not particularly academic, with the thought of three or four years studying for a degree simply something that did not appeal to her. Equally, she had no desire to do anything else, so was at a complete crossroads. Mel knew exactly how Sarah felt so put no pressure on her to conform, or do what her grandfather was strongly recommending. No, Sarah was to be allowed to do as she wanted. Unlike herself, Mel thought ruefully, regardless of the consequences.

James, understanding how his sister felt, had one evening suggested Sarah might like to visit him and Connie and spend some time working on their vineyard, before perhaps starting her touring from there. At least that way, he argued, she would be with family for most of the time, and would be making herself useful into the bargain. Mel thought that was the perfect solution, with Sarah taking no time at all to jump at the chance. Visiting Uncle James and Aunt Connie and using Adelaide as her start point sounded perfect.

"Good morning," Mel said to no one in particular, as she breezed into "*Just Brewed*" mid-morning, having called in to do a few errands en route. The shop was already busy, with most of the tables taken, and a queue of people waiting to order. It was eleven o'clock, one of their busiest periods, with people popping in for their morning coffees, or collecting food for lunch time. She smiled and passed the time of day with a couple of regulars she recognised, before making her way to her office at the rear of the building.

"Good morning," Maxine chirped happily five minutes later, coming into Mel's office with a latte in one hand and a cranberry and chocolate cookie in the other. "I've brought this for you to try," she announced, handing the cookie to Mel. "One of our regular suppliers left two dozen as samples this morning, and wondered whether we'd be interested in giving them a go. What do you think?"

"Not bad," Mel replied, after taking a bite. "They're different to our usual cookies, quite chewy. How have they been selling?"

"That was the last one, I saved it for you. The others went within the first hour," Maxine replied. "We've sold probably about half, and the staff sampled the rest. Everyone's been positive about them, though."

"Yes, we could give them a go. Give me the supplier's details, and I'll look at the costs and recommended selling prices. If they work out, I'll include them on the orders for the group. Good work Maxine, thanks."

Mel now had twenty *"Just Brewed"* coffee shops throughout the south-west of England. She was always looking to increase that number, with the potential of exploring the options for franchising the brand, as well as expanding into other parts of the country. The shops, and importantly the brand, were both proving successful, with profits exceeding what she had ever imagined when she had originally started out. From one small shop, a chunk of her inheritance and not much else, how had she come this far?

Mel now controlled a sizeable empire and still involved herself on a day-to-day basis. She was no longer front of house, which was one of the downsides, she often thought, recalling the early days when she had spent many a happy hour behind the counter, talking to the people who came in. Now, along with her office manager, Odette, she concentrated on dealing with the suppliers and stockists, the bank and any legal aspects; the less fun things, she knew. Keeping a keen eye on these elements was essential though if she was to remain successful and continue to grow, as her advisors were recommending should be her next move.

Mel had hand-picked a team of managers to run the individual shops, plus a host of sales assistants who all shared the company's ethos – 'be friendly, kind and caring'. To her, wrapping the right people around her and developing their talents was one of the most important parts of her role. She wanted an atmosphere that was welcoming to customers and staff alike. Not everyone could create that. In her mind, everyone needed to be treated with dignity and respect, regardless of what their background was, or their status in life.

It was a lesson Mel had learnt the hard way. Coming from a privileged background, with parents who made her feel she was someone special; entitled, someone others should kowtow to, had made her uncomfortable from an early age. Hearing the way her parents would occasionally talk to others, people who in their view were beneath them, made her cringe with embarrassment. Mel was determined that was not her. It was a lifestyle she was not prepared to follow. She had fought against the system from day one, going against her parents and out of her way, if necessary, to treat people as equals; regardless of where they came from, or what their backgrounds were. No, she would not allow any privilege, or lack of privilege, to stand in the way of the people she, or her teams, came into contact with.

By the end of the day, Mel's mood had lifted slightly. After she had finished her dinner, a simple chicken pasta dish that had become her go-to meal whenever she was feeling down, she walked through to the sitting room and switched on the television for company. She realised she needed to do something positive to lift herself out of her gloom; something she could look forward to and get excited about. Otherwise, this year was going to go downhill fast, the same way sadly so many other years had gone previously.

Looking around the empty room, with no prospect of anyone walking in any time soon, not for the first time, she felt lonely. For once, she had no partner or daughter to chivvy her along. "Right, what should I do?" she asked herself, as she reached for the bottle of chilled sauvignon blanc she had carried through from the kitchen, topping up the glass she had downed with her meal. She picked up her laptop and opened the browser in search of some inspiration. At the same time, she could hear the familiar voice of a celebrity chatting away in the background, fronting a travel programme. It was featuring somewhere a lot more exotic than London in the depths of winter.

The programme continued to play out in the background, and as Mel half listened to it, the seed of an idea started to germinate in her head.

Chapter 7

The Present

Tuesday night tea was usually eggs on toast, or something equally quick and easy as Jenny was normally late home from school, having to attend one of the regular staff meetings. Thankfully, tonight she only had herself to feed. Emily and Harry had already had their meals at her parents' house, which had the added benefit of reducing the amount of washing up, or tidying away she had to do after she had finished eating.

Since Jason had moved out, over fourteen months ago now, she and the children had fallen into a new routine to get themselves through. It was not a routine any of them particularly liked, or would have chosen. Out of necessity though it had to be endured. On the nights she needed to work late, the children went to their grandparents' house for tea, and got on with their homework there before she collected them. Her mum and dad had been supportive throughout, leaving Jenny clueless as to how she would have coped without them. Her parents loved their grandchildren, so for them it was a treat and an opportunity to spoil them. Some nights, after-school clubs or Harry's training meant they varied that routine, but by and large it worked. Jason had the children to stay over at his girlfriend's house alternate weekends, and at those times Emily and Harry went straight there after school, not returning home until Monday evening.

Initially Jenny had dreaded those times when she was alone, wallowing in self-pity, wondering what they were doing with Jason and his girlfriend. She wandered around an empty house, at a loss to know how best to occupy herself. As the months wore on, and the more exhausted she became, doing the job of both mother and father around the house for two demanding teenagers, she started to look forward to her weekends alone. She started to appreciate the brief respite it gave her. Whilst time to herself was a commodity she was unused to, it forced her to develop different interests. She would spend time at the local gym, even go swimming or cycling if the weather was fine. Activities she could do by herself, she realised, given she was no longer part of a couple, or had lots of single girlfriends locally to call on.

Her friends had rallied around, inviting her out for a drink or over for coffee, even suggesting dating web-sites she might want to browse. However, Jenny was not feeling especially sociable these days. She did not feel particularly good fun to be around, and the thought of finding another man at her age was a frightening concept. "Who'd be interested in my stretch marks?" she had asked one friend when the suggestion was made. "Assuming I'd ever have the nerve to strip off in front him, that is! Urgh, the thought sends shudders down my spine."

However, something needed to change, that was for sure. What though? Her teaching job, as demanding and stressful as it was, was all she knew how to do. Apart from which, she badly needed the income, so no change there. Add to that, two teenagers, who were generally adorable, but they did have their moments. Other than waiting for them to grow up, and to stop costing her so much, what options did she have? It was surely too late to offer them up for adoption, she laughed to herself – although that would help with her financial situation!

Finally, her estranged husband, currently going through what she could only describe as a midlife crisis. What did she think of that? Was divorce inevitable, and how did she feel about that? Her life was currently a recipe for disaster. "Perhaps that's why Jason's left me," she often thought to herself. "Perhaps being a boring, overworked, mum of two doesn't excite him anymore." If that was his reason, she could understand why. It did not excite her very much either.

"Right, you two. Time for bed, I think," Jenny said, popping her head around the lounge door. "It's almost nine o'clock and it's school in the morning." She realised she needed some time by herself to chill, and having the kids sprawled out on the floor, playing their games or messaging friends, was not how she wanted to spend the rest of her evening. "I'll be up in an hour or so, so lights out please," she shouted after them, as she heard them climbing the stairs. "They're good kids really," she conceded, with a smile on her face, as she returned to the kitchen to finish tidying everything away and prepare the packed lunches for the morning.

The staff meeting had done nothing to improve Jenny's mood. There were obvious conflicts developing between some of the staff members that she would do well to avoid. She needed time to reflect before the morning on a couple of points that had been raised, because the last thing she needed now was to get embroiled in the petty politics of the staffroom. That would surely be the last straw, and she could not trust what she might say if her opinion was sought. Diplomacy had never been one of her strongest characteristics.

When she eventually took her cup of tea into the lounge, ready for a mindless hour in front of the television, her mobile phone rang. She was in two minds whether to ignore it, but seeing who the caller was, decided to pick up.

"Oh hi, how are you doing?" The slightest glimmer of a smile returned to her otherwise exhausted expression.

Chapter 8

The Present

Heather had spent the day driving across the city, to visit her father at the residential home he had been living in for the last eighteen months. She tried to visit at least once a week, often taking him out to a local café, or the park for a change of scenery, if the weather allowed. On each occasion recently, she returned home feeling emotionally exhausted, as she watched her father slowly slipping away from her.

Graham McDougal was only in his mid-seventies, however over the previous couple of years his health had gradually started to fail him, to the extent that he no longer felt capable, or safe, to live by himself. He had always been a fit and active man, working outdoors in the fresh air, getting plenty of exercise as he maintained the gardens of the kind folk of Edinburgh. Since his retirement ten years ago though, it was noticeable how soon his faculties had started to fail him. First it was his eyesight; "the gradual deterioration is nothing to worry about for someone of his age," the optician had assured Heather when she had accompanied her father for his annual sight test. Within a couple of years though he had almost completely lost the sight in one eye, with the sight in his second eye no longer that clear.

Around the same time, his memory gradually started to go. Ellen and Heather would become increasingly concerned when he did not turn up for family occasions, or forgot birthdays or anniversaries. They accepted for a man living on his own that was not too surprising, although when they noticed more subtle things around the house that had been left undone, it became more worrying. Doors left unlocked when he ventured out to the shops, even the gas left burning after he had removed a pan from the stove, and medications missed, occasionally doubled up when he realised he still had tablets left to take in the packet.

Initially a local lady was employed to go in each day to prepare his meals and do some light housework. Over time that was not enough, with residential care eventually becoming the only viable option left for Ellen and Heather to take. A solution was agreed upon after a long discussion with their father.

Heather had offered for him to move out to the countryside and live with her. Her house was more than big enough for them, and quiet now that Bruce was no longer around. Her dad though did not want the upheaval of moving somewhere he did not know, or would struggle to get around. Living so remotely would also have been a worry should he require urgent medical care, Heather sadly recalled, her mind instantly going back to Bruce, and how helpless she had felt, waiting for the ambulance to reach him.

Ellen's house was a lot smaller and with her two girls still at home, not really a suitable place for him to live either. Graham McDougal loved his daughters and grandchildren dearly, but the thought of living under the same roof as either of them was not something he would entertain lightly. No, a nice residential home with people like him would suit him well. They might even let him potter around the gardens or attend to the weeds, if he was lucky and asked nicely.

Settling down again for another quiet evening in front of the television, Heather stoked the fire and pulled out her fleecy blanket, ready to wrap around her legs when she eventually sat down. The cottage's thick stone walls protected against the harshest of the weather, although its modern open plan design, with the picture windows that perfectly framed the view of the gardens and the hills beyond, meant the living space took some time to heat up.

When Heather had first moved in, Bruce had paid for extensive renovations to ensure the cottage felt like home for her. He had lived there for some years, enjoying a rather sparse bachelor existence after his first wife had died, never too worried about mod cons or fancy furnishings. He was surrounded by his books and his art work, both giving him more pleasure than all the electronic gadgetry most men filled their homes with. Computers, flat screen TVs, sound systems held no fascination for him. He was attuned enough to know that his was not a woman's taste, the hard lines and dark furnishings providing no softness at all. Heather was given carte blanche to do whatever she wanted to stamp her identity on the cottage. After all, it was her home now as much as his and she needed to feel comfortable in it. Money was not an object, he assured her, allowing her to design a space that she would love to live in. A proper home for them both. One where they could not just relax, but entertain family, his friends or colleagues, the authors and artists he mingled with in his field of work. A welcoming space was what they needed.

The Godmothers

Although it was very much her design, as Heather now looked around the room, remembering the work she had overseen and the countless tradesmen who had been involved in what seemed a never-ending project, she realised how much inspiration she had taken from Bruce for her ideas. The room was stunning, a strange formality to its cosiness, so no matter what the time of year or occasion, the design worked. It was not at all girly, or full of craftwork, as one may have imagined given her passion and eclectic tastes. Simply a stylish and sophisticated space that they loved and felt able to relax in.

As she now sat back, with her latest novel in her hand and the small glass of red wine she allowed herself during the week sitting on the occasional table beside her, her mobile phone began to ring. Its high-pitched tune disturbed the peace and tranquillity of the room.

"Oh, Misty, who on earth is phoning at this time of night?" Heather often spoke to the overweight cat who was sprawled out on the rug, enjoying the heat of the fire. She moved the fleece from her now warm knees to reach for her phone. "What do you think, shall I just ignore it, and hope they go away?" She was not feeling particularly in the mood for talking this evening. Although seeing who the caller was, she decided to pick up.

"Hello there, lovely to hear from you." Heather was more than happy to have her peace interrupted.

Chapter 9

The Past

"Happy New Year everyone and happy new millennium too." Jenny shouted, as she threw her bags down in the middle of the hallway of the house they were now renting. She slammed the door behind her to keep the cold out and flicked the light switch on, all in one seamless action. "Where's everyone – is no one home?" As she walked through the house, she began to get worried that perhaps she was the only one back.

It was almost the middle of January and the first day back to university after the Christmas break. The four girls had moved from the halls of residence at the end of their first year into a small terraced property, ten minutes' walk from the university. It was close enough to attend whatever lectures they needed to, and nearer to the city centre, where the nightlife and shops were to be found. The halls had been convenient as newbies, but they had soon outgrown them and had been eager to branch out on their own.

"Hi, we're all in here," Amy shouted back, her voice coming from the room at the rear of the ground floor that doubled as the kitchen and dining area. "Come on through, I'm just brewing – unless you've got something stronger in your bags left over from Christmas?"

"Not for me." Mel almost groaned in reply. "I've drunk enough alcohol over the last few weeks, especially

New Year's Eve to last me a lifetime. I've almost forgotten what it feels like to be sober. Driving up today meant I didn't drink last night for the first time in weeks. I probably should try to dry out a bit. Give my liver a break!"

The other three exchanged a glance. None of them were big drinkers, whereas Mel was known to enjoy her drink. She could normally function better than the rest of them, even after a few too many beers or wines, or whatever it was she was drinking at the time.

"Sounds like you've had a great time," Heather observed, in an excited voice. "Anything good to report?" She was always fascinated by Mel's grand lifestyle. It seemed to be a million miles away from the quiet existence she enjoyed in Scotland.

"Not really. James and I did our best to avoid the endless round of parties our parents held at home, or tried to drag us along to. They were all loved up for a change, which felt weird. Apparently, my father's no longer seeing that other women, according to my mother. I'm not convinced." Mel had told the others in glorious detail about her parents, and their many foibles and indiscretions. She made them appear colourful characters, if not perhaps the most perfect, or role model parents. "Instead, James took pity on me and dragged me along with him to meet some of his friends. Most of whom were a rum bunch, I'd say."

"Oh, tell us more," encouraged Amy. "Did you meet any girls, or boys for that matter, who your mother would classify as 'suitable marriage material' for either of you?"

"Certainly not." Mel cringed at the memories. "In fact, quite the opposite. I'd hate for my mother to ever learn what we got up to, or with whom – especially New Year's Eve. The least said about that night, the soonest mended, I think!" She gave the others a look that clearly said 'don't even go there!'.

"Well, how about I finish brewing the tea and we can then discuss what plans we've all got for this term," concluded Amy, keen to get focussed.

"Okay. I'll just take my bags up, and then I'll come back down and help you, Amy," Jenny replied, glad to be back among her friends.

Whilst Heather was a little starstruck with Mel, and the world she seemed to occupy, Amy and Jenny were more circumspect about it. They had both been brought up as tough northern girls, with strong working-class roots. Neither was likely to have their heads turned by the thought of champagne parties, or flashy cars. No, they were here to work and graduate, with the type of degrees their parents would be proud of.

By the middle of February, it was apparent to the rest of the girls that Mel was not feeling herself, and that the charade she was putting on was simply that, an act. They had witnessed her eating and drinking, and her frequent trips to the toilet, as well as her change in behaviour. She no longer wanted to go far in the evening, was constantly tired and any desire to go to the library to study, or complete her assignments was non-existent.

"Mel, are you going to tell us what's the matter, because we're worried about you?" Amy asked one morning after Mel had turned her nose up at her breakfast once again. "You're not eating, you're not drinking and you're constantly tired. Anyone would think you were pregnant, if we didn't know better!"

Mel looked up and across the table at her friends, a panicked expression on her face - a face that was drained of colour.

"Mel, you're worrying us now." Jenny's voice was becoming concerned too. "Whatever it is, you can tell us. It's nothing serious, is it? Do you need to see a doctor?"

"I've seen a doctor. I had an appointment yesterday afternoon, and Sherlock over there," now looking directly over at Amy, "is right. I'm apparently six weeks pregnant. I'm going to have a baby early September."

"Shit, Mel, how did that happen?" Heather asked, completely confused and shocked by Mel's admission. As far as they were all aware, Mel had never shown any great interest in the lads around campus, or spoken of anyone at home who she was interested in. And in terms of dating, well, to their knowledge she'd not had a serious date for as long as they could remember.

"Unless it was the immaculate conception, I presume sex played a part in it, don't you Heather?" Jenny's tone was more sarcastic than she intended it to be. Then looking directly at Mel, she added bluntly "the question is, who's the father? Is it anyone we know, and have you any idea what you're going to do about it now?"

"It's no one you know, and frankly I haven't got a clue yet in terms of what I'm going to do. One thing's for sure though, I can't see me getting my precious politics degree next year, as my father expects, can you?" Mel sighed, tears now starting to run down her cheeks, as she faced the enormity of what she had just admitted to. "I don't expect he'll want me following in his footsteps, pushing a pram two steps behind, do you?"

"Well, we're here for you, no matter what you decide to do. Friends for life was what we signed up for, if I recall correctly. Through thick and thin," chirped Amy, a supportive smile on her face as she reached for Mel's hand.

"Yes, through thick and thin," repeated Heather and Jenny as one. The three girls then all got up from the table and came round to give Mel a hug.

"Thanks. You don't know how much I appreciate that," Mel smiled, wiping the tears from her eyes. "Well, I suppose I should have a slice of toast at least, before I head out and face this morning's lectures. After all, I am eating for two now, and I don't want to collapse in the lecture hall, do I?"

Chapter 10

The Past

By the time May arrived, and the end of year exams were on the horizon, Jenny, Amy and Heather felt prepared, albeit a little nervous. They had studied hard, knowing how important it was to get the grades they needed, so they could continue into their third and final year.

Mel, on the other hand, had neither prepared nor felt nervous about sitting her exams. For her the outcome was rather less important, and somewhat irrelevant in her mind, as she had no intention of coming back after the end of term to complete her final year. Politics was not something that had held any interest for her anyway, so what was the point of putting herself through another year, especially with all the added pressure of a baby to worry about?

She had eventually returned home at Eastertime to inform her parents about her condition, having put it off as long as she felt able. Now three and a half months pregnant, her health was good and the morning sickness had passed, just leaving her at the stage where clothes were starting to feel snug. With careful planning, she could just about manage to get away with it. None of her fellow students knew of her condition; Mel deciding it was not something she was prepared to bandy about. So, other than her housemates, it was 'Mum's the word' if anyone asked how she was feeling.

Driving back to London she had prepared herself mentally to take the onslaught of their denunciation, knowing they would hurl both abuse and blame in her direction, demanding to know who the baby's father was at the very least. Her father was likely to get the proverbial shotgun out of his cupboard once he learned the culprit's name. That however was a secret Mel had vowed to keep to herself, whatever the cost. The implications, should her parents ever find out, were something she was not willing to think about. A sudden shudder went straight down her spine at the mere thought of it!

Her mother, Julia Milton-Barker, was surprisingly supportive, once she had got over the initial shock. Rather than get stressed out, as Mel had anticipated, or scream and rant about how her daughter had ruined her life, she approached the situation with a degree of maturity that caught Mel completely off guard. They had talked relatively calmly in the plush surrounds of the formal sitting room, in which Julia conducted most of her entertaining, over a civilised cup of tea with some delicate sandwiches and cakes the housekeeper had prepared ahead of her arrival.

Mel felt almost as if her mother had invited her around for afternoon tea, as if she was one of the ladies she usually associated with, and not her daughter returning home after three months of being away. Whilst her words were conciliatory, Julia's face clearly spelled out the disappointment she felt; disappointment no doubt that she could no longer boast about her clever daughter, or arrange that perfect match for her. Thankfully for Mel though, her mother's usual histrionics were kept at bay, leaving her to ponder what strength of medication she was currently on.

Her father, Lawrence Barker, was by comparison outraged when he returned home from one of his constituency meetings later that evening. He was tired after a series of discussions with disgruntled constituents, banging on all day about their problems. What did they seriously think he could do about it, he asked himself? When Julia calmly told him of their daughter's condition whilst Mel was upstairs in her room, it was almost the last straw.

"Mel, get yourself down here, immediately!" he screamed up the stairs. "Your mother and I need to speak to you, this instant."

For what felt like an eternity her father ranted, threatening to cut Mel off unless the issue was resolved immediately. He was unable to even mention the word 'baby', or register the concept it was his grandchild he was talking about in such harsh tones. His embarrassment was obvious, his precious daughter now 'up the duff!' he said, his vocabulary reverting to the usual slang he used whenever he was lost for words.

"What low-life has done this to you, has ruined your life?" he questioned, intent on not letting the subject drop. "Tell me his name now and I'll get him to pay for the abortion, at the very least. Julia, you can make the appointment in the morning as it will need sorting fast, so you can get back to your studies. I don't want them impacted, or for the last two years to have been wasted. Just for a sprog to ruin your career."

"Lawrence may consider himself upper class now, a respected member of parliament," Julia thought to herself, as she watched the way her husband handled himself, a large tumbler of whiskey in his hand, his face becoming even pucer the higher his blood pressure became. His youthful good looks were long behind him now, and beneath his polished exterior, there was no hiding his working-class roots.

"If you've finished," Mel replied, once she sensed her father had finally run out of steam. "For one, I'm not having an abortion, and in terms of who the father is, that's none of your business. It's my body, so if I choose to have this baby, then that's my decision. And as far as the rest is concerned Dad, politics is not for me. I've wasted two years following your dream – not mine. So, as far as university is concerned, I've no intention of going back next year, or graduating."

"So, what are your plans then, dear?" Julia enquired, quietly proud of her daughter and the way she had stood up to her father. Lawrence was a bully, Julia realised not for the first time, regretting how she had never had the strength to stand up to her husband as her daughter just had. His behaviour had got noticeably worse over the last few years, the occasional comments from both friends and relatives never going unnoticed by her. She had always batted them away, even put up with him and his countless affairs for the sake of appearances. Divorce was not an option she had ever seriously considered, until now. Leaving her to wonder whether at her age it was not perhaps too late to rebuild her life.

"Well, Mum, the baby's due sometime around the end of August. So, it looks like I've got until then to sort myself out." As Mel replied, she smiled at her mother, sensing at least the support of one of her parents. "And by the sounds of it, Dad, as the baby and I wouldn't be welcome here, I'm going to need to sort out somewhere for us to live, as a priority. And given what you've just said, I might as well start now." Turning towards Julia, Mel added, "I'll go and pack what I need, and then come back for the rest another day, if that's okay with you, Mum?"

Chapter 11

The Present

"Oh, hi Mel. How are you doing?" Jenny asked, as she put her cup of tea to one side, in order to answer her mobile phone that was ringing on the table beside her.

"Hi Jenny, just hang on a minute will you, whilst I patch Heather in," Mel replied once her friend had answered the phone. "Heather, are you there now too? Good. I've got Jenny on the line. Can we all hear each other?"

"Hi Jenny. Yes, what's this all about Mel?" Heather enquired, turning her novel over and picking up her nearly empty glass of wine. "Is everything okay? It's after nine o'clock, so it's quite late for a social call, isn't it?"

"Yes, everything's fine, I suppose." As Mel replied, she desperately tried to keep the sadness out of her voice. "Sarah flew over to see my brother James in Australia yesterday, and I'm at a loose end. It's been a shitty sort of day, so I just thought I'd give you a call and check in on you. Is that okay?"

The three often spoke on the phone and usually met up a couple of times a year, particularly if there was a special birthday, or an event they wanted the others' support at. However, given everyone's busy diaries, phone calls, or more recently Skype calls, were generally at a prearranged time.

"That's fine by me. I was just reading in front of the fire." Heather put her book down and made herself comfortable.

"Fine by me too," Jenny added, happy for the distraction. "The kids are upstairs, so I'm just de-stressing before going up to bed. I've had a rough day, topped off by an excruciating staff meeting, which seemed to go on forever. It all got quite heated at one stage, which I suppose did make it a bit more exciting for a while. Watching the Head of P.E. squirm when some of his exploits were being discussed. Apparently the headteacher's received a complaint from a parent, although he didn't go into all the details. By the end of it, I was starting to feel quite sorry for Mr Jones. It's awful how sometimes a petty, innocuous and innocent comment can have such nasty connotations, when someone's of a mind to stir up trouble." Jenny tried to disguise how tired she was with it all. "I was glad to get home, although, in truth this place doesn't feel much like home at the moment. Not since Jason walked out. Just a building, where me and the kids exist. So, whilst yours might have been a shitty day Mel, mine's more of a shitty life at the moment," she concluded, in her usual acerbic tone.

"Well, if we're playing top trumps then, I can't say I've had a great day either," chirped in Heather, not wanting to be outdone. "I've been visiting Dad today at his residential home, and each time I go it gets more difficult. I hate leaving him there. I then spend most of the drive home crying, wondering whether I should turn around and break him out, and bring him home with me. I know that's not a real alternative any more, which doesn't help me feel any better," Heather sighed. "He hardly knows who I am nowadays, which is soul destroying. The carers are really kind, but they're having to do more and more for him each day. I don't know how much longer he's going to last, or whether he's any fight left in him. It's heart-breaking to see how much he's deteriorated over the last few months."

"We're all having a tough time at the moment, aren't we?" Mel felt for both of her friends and the difficult circumstances they found themselves in. Sadly though she could not empathise with either. Having never been married herself, the concept of a husband walking out and abandoning her, as Jason had done to Jenny, was something she could not really comprehend. There had been many men in Mel's life over the years, but largely they had stayed around on her terms, and when she felt the relationship had run its course, she had felt no compunction in showing them the door. Whilst the odd man had moved in for a few months here and there, she had never 'lived' with anyone long-term, or moved out of her own home to share someone else's life. No, for her own, and her daughter's sakes, her independence had been hard fought for, and was paramount; a principle she was not prepared to compromise on, for anyone.

In terms of Heather, and her obvious devotion to her ailing father, well, that was something else Mel struggled to identify with. Her relationship with her own father had been testy for years, ever since the day she announced her pregnancy, and gave up on 'his' dreams for her to follow him into politics. Any respect for him was lost, and following the inevitable divorce from her mother a couple of years later, there seemed to be no road back. Over the years, he had tried to offer the occasional olive branch, and on the rare occurrence their paths had crossed they were polite and cordial. However any trust, or importantly love, had long since gone.

"Yep, and although it's only January, is it too soon to say I can't wait for this year to end? At least that way we'll miss the dreaded 40! The thought of spending that in a classroom full of spotty teenagers is not something I'm looking forward to at all." Jenny laughed, the tone of her voice becoming lighter for the first time since their conversation began.

"Oh god, I'd forgotten that!" Heather replied, the shock evident in her voice. "At least I won't have any spotty teenagers to contend with, although what I will be doing is anyone's guess. No doubt Ellen, or one of my nieces will be making me a cake, or something equally memorable." Whilst Heather loved her sister dearly, and had great respect for the way she ran her household and balanced the pressures life threw at her, she did feel over the years motherhood and marriage had sucked all life and sense of fun from her. Now, only in her mid-forties, Ellen was practical, dependable, and ever so dull.

"Well, you'll be delighted to know that I haven't forgotten about that particular milestone at all. In fact, that's partly why I've summoned you both tonight," Mel began. "I've had an idea, which I wanted to run past you, to see what you think."

"Sounds intriguing," Heather replied, genuinely excited. Mel had always been the most sociable of all of them, the glue that held them together, and the one that generally lifted their spirits when the going got tough. "What's your idea, Mel?"

"Well, I've been looking into villas in Greece, on one of the Greek Islands perhaps, and I was thinking we could hire one over the summer. It would give us a chance to get away and have some fun, with a bit of ouzo thrown in for good measure. What do you think?"

"Sounds great to me," Heather replied without hesitation. "I'd need to square everything with Ellen first, to make sure Dad was okay whilst I was away. I presume you've not booked anything yet?"

"No, not yet. I wanted to check with you two first, to make sure you're both onboard."

"It sounds good to me too, and I don't want to stop either of you from going, but I'll not be able to make it, sorry," Jenny replied, forlornly. The idea of spending a couple of weeks, relaxing in the sun with her two best friends, without any of the stresses or demands of everyday life was something she would give her eye teeth for at the moment. Alas it was not meant to be. "Even if it's over the school holidays, I've still got the kids to consider," she added, realising the line had gone quiet at the other end. "Apart from which, I don't think my budget would stretch that far. Whilst Jason's contributing to basic bills, I'm finding it difficult managing on my salary. Holidays sadly fall into the luxury bucket that I just can't afford right now."

"Can't your parents, or Jason have Emily or Harry for a week or so? They are his kids too. Why don't you ask him? After all, it's not every year we turn forty, is it?" Mel knew how difficult Jenny was finding everything. "And in terms of the cost, well it's my birthday treat to us all. I'll pay for the flights and the villa. I'll even hire a housekeeper to organise the food, and make sure we don't run short on wine. All you'll need to buy is a couple of glamorous new bikinis, and perhaps a sunhat for the beach."

"I'm not sure, Mel." Jenny found her resolve weakening the more Mel spoke about what she had been looking at online, describing the types of villas she had been researching, with even the option of hiring a yacht for a few days sailing around the islands a possibility.

Mel had come up with the idea of Greece earlier that evening, while searching the internet looking for a fun experience they could all take part in. Something that worked around Jenny's work and budget, and Heather's remoteness and need to travel. Escape rooms were all the rage, or spa days at a country hotel. Nothing however sparked her imagination, or seemed a suitable way to celebrate a milestone birthday.

The travel programme, playing out in the background, suddenly caught her attention. The dulcet tones of the presenter washing over her, as she marvelled at the clear blue seas, the picturesque towns and villages, the seafood, the constant sunshine. Mel recalled a holiday she had taken more than ten years ago to Greece, with a particular man friend at the time, his name she could no longer recall. They had spent their days lounging around the pool and their nights drinking, before making love under the stars. The holiday was memorable, if not the man, and it had got her thinking. Okay, it was extravagant, but she could afford it, and what was better than sharing her good fortune with her best friends?

"Come on, Jenny. Can you have a think about it at least, please?" implored Heather. "We all need something to look forward to, don't we? This could be just the tonic to put some sparkle back into all our lives. By the sounds of it, we could do with that at the moment, couldn't we? And as much as I love Mel, going without you, just wouldn't seem right."

"My thoughts entirely, Heather," Mel agreed. "After all, who better than us to know how important life is, or how easily it can be lost. We should grab what opportunities we have to celebrate life. We should not hold back at any cost, is my opinion, for what it's worth."

"Okay, okay. I get the message," Jenny relented, the excitement of an adventure eventually taking hold. If only she could manage the logistics. "Leave it with me for a couple of days and I'll see what I can sort out."

"Great," said Mel and Heather almost in unison, their bags mentally already packed.

Chapter 12

The Past

"Hello, may I speak to Amy please?" Julia asked, speaking to the young lady who had answered the phone after she had carefully dialled the number her daughter had given her.

"Yes, I'm Amy. Who's speaking, please?" Amy replied politely, unsure who the caller was. She was still at home with her parents, standing at the bottom of the narrow staircase answering their phone, having just rushed down when she heard it ringing and no one answering it. Her parents must have popped out. Amy was finishing off her packing, in preparation for moving back into her student accommodation for the final year of studying. Her dad was driving her down later that week and she was looking forward to it. The summer holidays had been fun, but she had missed her friends.

"It's Julia Milton-Barker, Melissa's mother. She's asked me to telephone you, to let you know that she has delivered a baby girl this morning. I'm to let you know that mother and baby are both well, and that the baby is called Sarah. Melissa asked if you could kindly let Heather and Jennifer know please."

"Oh, how wonderful, thank you for phoning. Give Mel our love and let her know we'll all try to get down to see her and the baby as soon as we can. Do you mind me asking if she's going to be living at home, or with her grandmother when she gets out of hospital?" Amy asked, as diplomatically as she could.

"They will be living with my mother for the time being," Julia replied, unsure what else to say. "I presume you have the address?"

"Yes, thank you. And thanks again for letting me know. Congratulations by the way!"

As Amy replaced the phone back into its cradle, she wondered whether offering congratulations had perhaps gone a little too far, particularly given Mel's parents' reaction to the news they were to become grandparents.

Amy recalled how Mel had returned to their empty house from London after telling her parents she was pregnant. She and the others had gone home for Easter, leaving Mel alone in the house for four days. By the time they had all returned it was obvious Mel had done little else, other than cry; unsure what her options were now that she had effectively been cut-off by her father and felt distanced from her mother.

From that point, Mel changed. Gone was the dutiful, if somewhat privileged daughter, and in return a strong-minded and independent young woman was born. Someone who was determined not to be bullied into doing anything, just because her father said so.

Over the next few weeks, Amy, Heather and Jenny banded around Mel to provide the support and protection she needed, cocooning her from the outside world. Mel no longer had any interest in attending lectures or completing assignments. Remaining at university however felt the right thing for her to do, for the foreseeable future at least. The house gave her shelter, and her friends provided the love and support she so desperately needed.

They talked long into the night, mulling over her options. They knew time was not on their side with the end of the academic year fast approaching, as was the due date for Mel to deliver her baby.

The breakthrough came one Sunday in late May, when Mel's maternal grandmother arrived unexpectedly, knocking at their door, her highly polished, chauffeur-driven car looking incongruous outside their small terraced house. The size of it almost filled the narrow street, with the grey-haired driver not knowing where to look as he waited patiently for his mistress to return.

Mrs Milton had come to collect Melissa, she announced, with the intention of her granddaughter staying at her home for the duration, making it quite clear that she and her baby were welcome to stay as long as they wanted. She clarified, for the avoidance of any doubt, that under no circumstances would Lawrence be admitted, or allowed to interfere in any way. She was a formidable lady, and rather than put up any argument, Mel packed her bags, knowing the option Granny presented was the right one, for now. She hugged all the girls, assuring them she was happy with the plan and would be in touch, before making her way to the car. All her belongings had been stowed in the boot, making it abundantly clear she would not be returning to university any time soon.

The final year of university began, and the remaining girls needed to find a new roommate to take Mel's room. Without the fourth income they would not be able to afford the rent, and none of them could contemplate not sharing. Although the concept of introducing another person into the mix was not one they relished either. They had bonded so well and they would feel the loss of Mel deeply. They did not want another girl, or anyone else for that matter, to come in and in any way threaten the balance of their friendship.

"There's a guy on my course, who last term was struggling to find accommodation. He's called Craig, you've probably seen him around. Shall I give him a ring and see if he fancies sharing with three girls?" Jenny suggested one day. Craig was a nice enough guy, a straight-talking Yorkshire man, who appeared to keep himself to himself – so provided he chipped in with his share of the costs, and helped out with jobs around the place, what was the harm, Jenny argued?

"I've no problem with that," Heather replied with a shrug of her shoulders.

"Me neither," Amy agreed. "Having a man around the house could be useful after all, especially if he's handy with a screwdriver. The door on the bathroom is almost falling off its hinges, and even reaching to change lightbulbs is a struggle for me."

"Well, let me ring him now," Jenny offered. "I think he's bunking down on a mate's floor at the moment. So, if he's interested, I presume he'll be over in the next day or so, to check us out."

By the end of the week, Craig had moved in and soon became a fixture around the house. He proved himself not only useful with a screwdriver, but particularly adept with a saucepan. Having grown up in a household of women, with two sisters and his mum, he had been taught to look after himself from an early age, and importantly was used to girls and their moods. He instinctively knew when to take cover if it was 'that time of the month' and not to take all the hot water if one of them was planning on it being bath night!

The girls all got on well with him, regularly recounting to Mel stories of their new housemate. He had a very caring and sensitive nature, and was unlike most of the young men they regularly saw or socialised with around the campus. He, like Jenny, was studying to be a teacher - with science as his specialism. And whilst their paths crossed occasionally, there were few lectures they attended together.

Craig hailed from Leeds and was a proud Yorkshireman, although he added that did not make him good at cricket – or sports of any description for that matter. "Not with my physique," he would joke, conscious that he carried a few extra pounds around his waistline, and at well under six feet tall would never be anyone's first pick for the basketball team. He loved to read, to cook and to listen to music and was a true family man at heart. Tales of his sisters' exploits often littered his conversation whenever he needed to keep up with Heather, Jenny or Amy as they discussed various topics over their cornflakes.

"I quite like him. I think he's nice," Amy admitted one day, when it was just the three of them together. "Do you think he's got a girlfriend, Jenny? I don't recall him ever mentioning one, do you?"

"I don't think so. I think he was interested in a girl in the first year. That didn't go anywhere, not as far as I recall. He's a bit of a loner and although he's relaxed with us now, I think he's actually quite shy. Do you want me to ask him, and see whether he's single or spoken for?" Jenny replied, a mischievous grin on her face.

"Heavens, NO!" Amy was astounded at how bold she had been by even admitting to fancying Craig in the first place. None of them had ever brought a boy back to the house, or confessed to seriously finding anyone attractive before now. It was unchartered territory, so, for her to fancy their new housemate could be a recipe for disaster. "Don't you dare, that would be too embarrassing!" Amy went so red her complexion suddenly resembled a pickled beetroot.

Heather and Jenny exchanged a wry smile, realising there was mileage in this one. They had noticed how Amy became giggly, or lost focus whenever Craig was around, and how his behaviour changed whenever she walked in. It was certainly one to watch, they thought to themselves.

In November, Mel phoned to invite Jenny, Amy and Heather down to London the first weekend in December, to attend Sarah's christening at the local parish church. She offered to collect them all from the railway station on Saturday lunchtime, before taking them back to Granny's house, where they were invited to stay for a couple of nights. She would then drive them back to the station, in time for the early train on Monday morning back to university. In her mind, it had all been planned and sorted.

"It will be great to actually see you all again," Mel said realising it had been six months since she had seen her friends. "It will also give us all an opportunity to get glammed up for a change, enjoy the highlife. And a chance to get me out of these sweatpants; I seem to be living in nothing else these days. Granny's getting caterers in, so the food should be good too, and there'll be plenty of champagne, hence the need to stay over! Plus, you'll get time to meet Sarah, she's a real poppet and is growing so fast."

Heather was delighted with the idea, agreeing immediately to the plan. She had always been fascinated by Mel and her lifestyle, so the opportunity to visit her home and meet some of the family she had spoken of, for her was a dream come true.

Jenny and Amy were a little less anxious to give up their weekend. Not for any other reason that it was so close to their finals, and neither could contemplate not passing with flying colours. Both were worriers, and no matter how many top grades they got for their assignments, or hours they put in at the library, it never seemed enough.

"Oh, come on you two," Heather begged in her broad Scottish accent, once she sensed their reluctance around the table. "A few hours break won't do you any harm, surely? You could read on the train, even take your books with you, if it's that important. We can't let Mel and Sarah down now, can we?" Heather's design course was less academic and more practical, with the majority of her course work already assessed towards her final grades.

"I suppose you're right. A couple of days won't make a difference," Amy conceded eventually. "I haven't a clue what I'll wear to the christening though," she added with a worried look on her face.

"Me neither," Jenny exclaimed, knowing her clothing budget had already gone for that term, the pair of jeans and the winter jacket she had bought the previous week taking her above her limit.

"Don't worry, I've already thought about that." Mel had already accepted that perhaps it would be a little daunting for her friends, or that they would have nothing in their wardrobes suitable for a formal do. "I'm going to pick out a dress for each of you, if you send me through your sizes - as a little present from me, because I've got a massive favour to ask you all ......"

"What favour?" Jenny questioned on behalf of the others, noticing the quizzical stares from Heather and Jenny as they all listened to Mel. Jenny was naturally suspicious of most things.

"Well, Sarah needs godparents, and I couldn't think of three better godmothers than all of you, if you wouldn't mind offering up your services, that is?"

"Oh, how wonderful." Heather was the first to respond, a broad smile lighting up her face. "I'd love to be one of Sarah's godmothers."

After a few seconds, Amy said, "on one condition." Heather and Jenny looked at each other, more than a little confused, whilst Mel remained quiet at the other end of the line.

"What's that?" Mel asked eventually, fearing her plan had backfired.

"Well, it's simple really. If I ever have children, that you will all agree to be their godmothers too."

"What a brilliant idea," seconded Heather. "It's a bit like the promise we made on the day we first met, to be friends for life. Let's make a pact now. To us, the godmothers. To always be there for each other's children, no matter what."

"The godmothers. I like the sound of that," agreed Mel, as the others simply smiled at each other across the kitchen table, knowing their lives would now always be entwined.

Chapter 13

The Present

"Hi James. How y'all doing?" Mel enquired, as her brother picked up the phone on the third ring, trying to inject a brightness into her voice – a brightness she was simply not feeling. It was an early spring morning in London and Mel was sitting at the granite island in her kitchen, still nursing the cup of coffee she had made over an hour ago. She was desperately trying to dispel the worrying sensation that had crept up on her from nowhere. For no logical reason, over the last forty-eight hours, something had been niggling at her. Call it mother's intuition or not. And until she'd been reassured everything was well with her daughter, she could not settle.

It was early evening in Adelaide, so a perfect time to phone her brother. She pictured him sitting on his veranda, quaffing one of his latest award-winning wines. James had emigrated to Australia over fifteen years ago, having met and married an Australian woman. Connie had been travelling on her gap year in the UK. She was ten years younger than James, and on the surface they had little in common, but for some reason they worked as a couple and were extremely happily married. They had built a good life for themselves and their two young children; both working on the vineyard Connie's parents owned, and from where they operated a successful business, producing and exporting wines around the world.

Before he and Connie had married, James' knowledge of wines and champagnes has been limited to what he bought in the bars and restaurants around London. The types of places he regularly frequented with some of his wilder friends; men his mother certainly did not approve of, even though most of them were well connected and came from respectable families. He had become a 'Hooray Henry' in his youth, intent on his own enjoyment, and living comfortably off his healthy allowance. Work for James was more of an inconvenience than a career, something to do during the daylight hours, when the bars or nightclubs were shut, or the party season was quiet.

A chance meeting with Connie one evening, in a swanky restaurant in London's West End, proved to be a real eye opener for him. She was dining with a chap James vaguely remembered from Eton; someone the year above him, to whom he had talked occasionally but did not know well. He went over to say hello and re-introduce himself, anything to pass the time while his friends turned up. It turned out his old school chum and Connie were cousins, with him hosting her for the few weeks she was visiting family in England.

James was invited to join them for a drink, and sat for over thirty minutes while waiting for his friends to arrive. He secretly hoped he would be stood up, so that he could stay where he was all evening. He was mesmerised by her, hanging on her every word, spoken in the softest of accents. Here was a young lady, barely a woman, who was not only bright and beautiful, with long blonde hair and clear sun-kissed skin that made her look more Scandinavian than Australian, but someone with a strong work ethic, and a clear view of where her life was going. She explained that wine was in her blood, and as her parents' only child was destined to take over the family business, once they eventually retired. She was intent on learning the trade from the roots up, she joked, and continuing the tradition her grandfather had begun of making some of the finest wines in the southern hemisphere.

The following day, James contacted his friend asking for Connie's details, arranging to take her out that same night, just the two of them. By the end of the next day, James knew he had found the woman he wanted to marry, thankfully without the help, or interference of his mother. She had been on his case now for some years to make a suitable match, and as willing as he had been to play her charade for as long as it suited him, he had no intention of allowing her to matchmake!

"Hi, Mel. Wonderful to hear from you." Mel noticed more of James' Australian accent each time they spoke. They had not seen each other for a couple of years, although they regularly kept in touch. Since Sarah had travelled over there, they had spoken often. "Yes, we're all fine, thanks. Connie's just in the office out at the back, sorting some paperwork before the morning. The kids are upstairs, probably watching Netflix in bed. It's been a relatively cool day here today, so we're all inside, with the air-conditioning on its warm setting."

"Oh, and I'd imagined you'd be outside, enjoying the evening sun. I keep forgetting it's almost winter there now." She laughed, knowing James' idea of a cold day was nothing like the same as hers. What Mel would give for some sunshine, she thought, looking out of the kitchen window at the ominous clouds, mentally counting down the days to her holiday. "Anyway, I'm glad I've not disturbed your evening meal. It's just I've been trying to get hold of Sarah for the last day or so. It's nothing urgent, just for a catch up. As she's not answering her mobile, I thought I'd give you a quick call, to check everything's okay."

"Yes, everything's perfect. Nothing to worry about at all. In fact, I've got an old friend staying with us at the moment. Sarah's taken him out for a spin around the vineyard in the jeep. I think she's feeling completely at home here now, even offering to do some of the guided tours when the tourists drop in unannounced, which gives us a break!" he laughed. "The kids love her being here as well, she's like the big sis they never had. We might keep her when her visa runs out. What would you say to that?" he joked.

"I'm not sure about that," she laughed in return. Sarah had been away now for over three months and Mel was missing her dreadfully; selfishly praying for her daughter to return home soon. And as there was still no firm date for her travel, Mel was finding the waiting hard. "Anyway, I'm glad everything's okay. I just hope you're not working her too hard, whilst you two put your feet up," she replied, enjoying the banter with her brother. "So, who's staying with you? Anyone I might know, by any chance?"

"Possibly, but highly unlikely. It's someone I used to know quite well, many years ago, at Eton. He's recently split from his wife, and is going through a tricky divorce, by all accounts. He contacted me out of the blue last month, with a view to calling in for a few days whilst he's over here on business. He'd heard from a friend of a friend that I was living here now, and as he didn't know anyone else in the area, thought it would be good to swing by and catch up. He only arrived yesterday, and is staying for a couple more nights."

"Oh, sounds great. It's good to have company, and nice of him to have made the effort. It's not that you're that accessible, is it? Miles from anywhere."

"It's not that remote, I'll have you know! We do have electricity and running water these days. No, he's a nice enough chap, and from what I've seen so far, appears to have calmed down a lot since I last saw him. He used to be a real wild child, that's for sure. I hate to admit it, but I'd go as far as saying he even put some of my antics to shame on the odd occasion. And given his father once trained to be a vicar, that's certainly saying something."

As Mel listened to her brother speak, her mind was whirling, trying to place the guy he was speaking about. All of a sudden, her heart began beating faster. The reasons for her concerns starting to become clear the more her brother described his visitor.

"And you say Sarah's taken him for a drive?" As she asked, she tried to keep her voice calm.

"Yes, they got on quite well over dinner last night. He's a real raconteur. He was talking a lot about London, mentioning some of our old haunts, and how they've changed over the years. I think it fascinated Sarah. I'd say she found him quite charming, actually. I have to admit, for a guy his age, he's aged rather better than I have. Still very trim, unlike me. Connie seemed to think there was definitely a hint of George Clooney about him," he remarked. "Which is quite funny given his name is George, George Theakston. Does that name ring any bells with you?"

At the mention of his name Mel froze, unable to get her thoughts straight. "Can you ask Sarah to phone me the instant she gets back, please? I need to speak to her. I can't have her driving around the countryside alone, with strange men."

"Mel, don't worry and don't overreact. What on earth's got into you? They've only gone out for a drive. I'm sure there's nothing going on between them. After all, he's old enough to be her father," James replied calmly, in an attempt to reassure his sister, who for some inexplicable reason had become quite panicked by their conversation.

Taking a deep breath, and deciding to break the promise she had made to herself nearly twenty years previously, to never mention his name to anyone, Mel spoke as calmly as she could muster. "James, I can assure you I'm not overreacting. If he's the same George Theakston you used to knock around with, then he's not just old enough to be her father, I hate to admit it, he is her father. And although I don't ever want to talk about it, I would never forgive myself if anything happened between them! So, please ask her to phone me as soon as possible," before hanging up the phone, her hands visibly shaking.

Chapter 14

The Present

Two weeks to go before the end of term, and for Jenny the countdown towards the holiday of a lifetime had begun. Having finally agreed to join Heather and Mel at the luxury villa Mel had chosen in Santorini in the Greek Islands, her feelings had vacillated on more than one occasion. One moment she was excited at the prospect of jetting off for three weeks of pure pleasure and relaxation. The next she was considering giving backword. She was scared it was too long to leave Harry and Emily with Jason and his girlfriend. She did not particularly like her, and knew the kids struggled with her too. What would they do without their mum, or more to the point, what would she do without them for that length of time?

When she had first toyed with the idea of going away to celebrate her fortieth birthday, she had tested the water with her mum, who in no uncertain terms told her to go. "Jennifer just go, have a good time and enjoy yourself. The kids will be fine, and we'll keep our eye on them too." Her parents had even offered to have their grandchildren stay with them if Jason was unable to deal with it, thereby ensuring she had no excuse whatsoever, at least as far as leaving the children were concerned. They even gave her money for her birthday, smiling as they told her to spend it 'unwisely' when she was over there.

Jason had been, unsurprisingly, less accommodating. He stated the obvious, that as her birthday was technically in May, then what was the point of going away in August to celebrate? After all, he had turned forty some years earlier, and had not felt a need to make a big song and dance about that. So, what was so special about her birthday?

Jenny had taken a deep breath, counted to ten and not reacted before responding. She was aware she was looking for a favour from him, so what was the point of antagonising him further? "I just need a break. It's years since we last went on holiday, and I could do with some sunshine to cheer me up. It's not that easy working full time, as well as bringing up the kids virtually alone, you know." It was a small attempt to touch a nerve and make him feel a little guilty. "Anyway, it's only three weeks, so it's half the summer holidays – and they'd be coming to you for that long, so what's your problem?"

"And can you afford it?" he questioned, attempting to find a new line of argument as he continued to put obstacles in her way. "You're always moaning on about not having any money, so how come you can suddenly afford a three-week holiday, in a luxury Greek villa?"

"That's really none of your business, is it? But rest assured, I've not been out selling my body to earn the extra cash!" she replied, almost snarling. She was affronted and annoyed that he was making it so difficult for her. "Will you have them or not, simple answer? I just need to know before I confirm the arrangements with Mel and Heather."

He grunted, "I suppose I can manage it."

Having eventually agreed to it, and with a huge sigh of relief, Jenny let Mel and Heather know to count her in.

Why did everything with Jason feel like a battle these days, Jenny wondered to herself as she stood in her bedroom the day of departure? She was nervously repacking her suitcase for the third time, checking she had everything she needed, whilst at the same time ensuring she did not exceed her luggage allowance, or put liquids or hair straighteners into the wrong bag. The taxi to the airport would be arriving in just over an hour's time, so no turning back now. That thought filled her with an excitement that until now she had managed to keep in check.

Over the last few weeks, sorting out her holiday wardrobe had proved more challenging that she would ever have imagined. All her summer clothes from previous years now hung off her, making her look both drab and dated. She had tried on her favourite go-to sundresses, and failed to make herself feel good in any of them. As a size 14, veering towards a size 16, she knew she had been slightly overweight for years. She had gradually added the pounds after the children had been born, due to a combination of diet, limited exercise and 'contentment', she believed. Plus, her inability to shake the post maternity flab, that no matter what she tried would not shift.

Now, staring into the full-length mirror, a piece of furniture that for so long had gone unnoticed in the corner of the bedroom, she saw herself differently. Jenny suddenly realised how much weight she had lost since she and Jason had split. On closer inspection, after examining her waistline and calves, she noticed how much her body appeared to have toned up. Gone were some of those extra pounds, the little 'love handles' Jason had referred to in happier days, as he had cuddled up to her on the settee, or made love to her at night in their bed. Okay, she may still not be model physique; she was no longer Miss Piggy either.

With a smile on her face, Jenny allowed herself a moment to appreciate the previously unquantified benefits of their split. The cumulative effect of rushing around after the children, cutting back on what she had been eating, mainly due to affordability, or not eating because of all the stress she was under, had taken pounds off her. It left her surprisingly pleased with her new look. "Not bad, if I say so myself," she thought, as she twirled in front of the mirror. "Every cloud..." she added, now laughing at her own reflection.

A trip to the shops was needed to get new shorts, t-shirts and dresses, all sizes 10 or 12, rather than size 14 or 16 she had worn for more years than she cared to remember. She also bought that new bikini Mel had almost insisted on, with the matching sarong Jenny could not resist. An appointment with the hairdresser was next, to get those early grey hairs and split ends dealt with. Sitting in the chair in the salon, admiring her new edgy hairstyle, that was apparently completely "on-trend madam," the hairdresser assured her, Jenny smiled back at herself.

As she handed over her credit card on the way out of the salon, whilst her confidence certainly felt bolstered by her recent purchases and her new look, sadly the same could not be said for her bank balance.

Jason had collected Harry and Emily the previous evening, giving Jenny an interesting look as he took onboard her new haircut, as well as the stylish jeans and shirt she was wearing, both of which emphasised her figure, and were new, as far as he could tell. Jenny noticed his admiring glance, but gave nothing away, simply smiled knowingly in response.

She stood and watched him from the hallway, as he prepared to take her children back to the house he shared with his young lover, a woman Jenny was not even prepared to give the courtesy of a name. He made several journeys to and from his car, laden with a multitude of things they insisted they needed for the duration of their stay. It had felt like a military operation, getting them organised for what was simply an extended stay with their dad. Neither child had made it easy for her in the days leading up to her departure; adding that extra level of guilt, both possibly sensing her weak point. They knew that if they begged, she would cancel the holiday and stay at home with them.

Jenny had not weakened, just chivvied them along, assuring them that as they had door keys, if they had forgotten anything, they could simply return home. Or, if things got too difficult living with their father, they could always go and stay at their grandma's house. It was not the end of the world, she assured them, just three weeks. And once she was home, she would spend the rest of their summer holidays making it up to them. However, the thought of Jason wandering around her house whilst she was away was something she was not happy with. What alternative did she have though?

Waving them off, Jenny thought how funny it was, and how so much had changed in such a short period of time. Only two years ago, everything she had was shared with him; her complete trust, her respect. And now, here she was worried about him entering her house when she was not there. There had been no secrets – well, not on her part anyway. All that trust and respect had just dissipated, gone up in a puff of smoke; almost as if it had never been real in the first place. How sad, to see the life and family they had built over so many happy years lost. Simply because her erstwhile husband's head had been turned with the thought that the grass was greener and fresher elsewhere.

To think, how many nights she had cried herself to sleep over losing him. Losing their relationship, their friendship, their lifestyle and everything that stood for. To say nothing of the impact it had had on their children, as they struggled to understand why their dad was no longer at home. Or, why he was living with another woman, tucking her child into bed, and not them anymore. How many nights had she waited for him to return, to admit he had made a mistake, and how eagerly she would have accepted him back with open arms. She would have forgiven him and moved on for the children's sake, if not her own.

Well, that was then and Jenny no longer felt that way. Over the last eighteen months she had seen her husband in his true colours. She had wised up to what he was truly like; flaky, easily influenced and above all someone ultimately that could no longer be trusted. How little she had really known him. No, they had been separated now for nearly two years, and although Jenny knew there had been difficult, and at times dark days, with no doubt more problems ahead, the time had come for her to move on. After all, she was only forty, too young to give up on life, or men come to that. She smiled at herself in the mirror, as she applied the finishing touches to her makeup before the taxi arrived.

A few weeks in the sun would give her some thinking time; time to process what she wanted next. A divorce, certainly – but on what terms? That was the sixty-four-thousand-dollar question she pondered, as the taxi beeped its horn to announce its arrival.

Chapter 15

The Present

When Heather had first seen the photos of the villa Mel had booked for their holiday, well, to say she was impressed was somewhat of an understatement. The concept itself, simply going away with her two best friends for a few weeks holiday, was more than she had ever imagined doing to celebrate her birthday. So, to actually see the place they would be staying was something else. Heather almost purred at the thought of relaxing around the pool, draped in one of those luxurious sun loungers, sipping a strangely named cocktail that Mel would have made; no doubt one Heather had never heard of, or tasted before.

Living in her cottage in a small village in the Scottish Highlands had many advantages, but easy access to sophistication, or the latest fashion trends were certainly not high on the list. Sure, she had as much fresh air and scenery as she would ever want, surrounded as she was by some of the most picturesque mountains and lochs in Scotland. The weather and changing seasons guaranteed a different perspective almost every day as she opened her front door, or peered out of the windows. She marvelled at the way the light changed from morning, to evening, to night, and by season. It never failed to create an awesome spectacle, remembering the occasions she had witnessed the northern lights, or the Mirrie Dancers as they were known locally. No, whilst it was certainly beautiful where she lived, on a popular-culture scale of one-to-ten, the village would struggle to score very highly.

The villa was ultra-modern with five bedrooms all ensuite, so much larger than the three of them would ever need. It also had its own swimming pool, and was fully-catered. A housekeeper and chef were thrown in as part of the package, to clean and provide all the meals. Mel had made it clear that none of them would be expected to lift a finger throughout their stay.

Heather had laughed when they had all been invited to complete a pre-holiday questionnaire. They were asked to confirm what foods they liked, disliked or any allergies they might have, to enable the meal plans to be drawn up. It also included questions on what wines or spirits they preferred, and any other points that needed noting, dietary or otherwise. It was certainly posher than any holiday Heather had ever been on before, although her experience was quite limited, she accepted. She had done very little overseas travel since her marriage to Bruce, less so since his death. Looking back now, she realised how staid she had become over the last two years, and how much she was looking forward to this holiday. If for no other reason, it would kick some life back into her otherwise drab existence.

According to Mel, the villa was located in a remote part of the island, in the hills, complete with stunning views of the Aegean Sea. It was about forty minutes' drive from the airport and the main town, where the larger shops and entertainment could be found. Locally, it was a short walk to the village, where a selection of smaller shops and bars could be found. It was also a ten-minute drive to the beach – all downhill through some winding roads, Mel had emphasised. The terrain could be quite rocky, she had added, emphasising the need to bring at least one pair of sensible shoes! The villa looked idyllic, so peaceful, leaving Heather with only one concern. "Might it be too quiet, too isolated? Just the three of us, rattling around all day?"

"Don't worry about that," Mel had reassured her. "We'll find plenty of things to do, I'm sure. Just bring a good book, or two, in case you get bored."

Heather sat in Santorini Airport's Arrivals Hall, a cup of coffee in hand, people-watching as she waited for Jenny to arrive. Bronzed bodies continually filed past her, wearing shorts and t-shirts, or summer dresses with open-toe sandals or flip flops on their feet.

Heather was feeling conspicuously hot under the collar, completely overdressed for the occasion, the occasional sideways glance of a passing holidaymaker adding to her anxiety. She contemplated whether to run into the Ladies to rummage through her case and change into something more appropriate, or bide her time until she arrived at the villa. The trousers, jumper and waterproof jacket, with the small ankle boots she had chosen for her early morning flight had seemed appropriate at the time. Especially given the amount of rain that had been pelting down throughout the previous evening and into the early hours of the morning, with no end forecast. Even the drive to Edinburgh Airport had felt chilly, the taxi driver offering to put the heater on when he collected her at six o'clock that morning.

Now, with the warmth of the midday sun blaring down on her and the air-conditioning in the airport offering little relief, she wondered how long she would cope with the heat. Had she been wrong to think three weeks in this weather would suit her?

Glancing up at the arrivals board, Heather was relieved to see Jenny's flight from Manchester was still on schedule, so fingers crossed it would be arriving within the next thirty minutes. That meant, provided there was no delay with collecting her luggage, within the next hour they would be in the taxi and on their way to the villa. She got herself comfy, retrieved her travel guidebook from her hand luggage and started to read about all the things they could get up to on the island. Her mind was instantly lost in the myriad of opportunities ahead of them.

Mel had flown in the previous afternoon, initially frustrated she was unable to co-ordinate her direct flight from Heathrow with the other two, but ultimately glad as it had given her the opportunity to check everything out before their arrival. Having devised the holiday plan, as well as spending so much money on the villa's rental, if anything, she felt the pressure of getting it 'just right' for her friends.

Any concerns Mel might have had were immediately blown away the moment she drove up the winding driveway and parked outside the villa. The sight of the sun setting over the horizon was an image she would never forget, with the views over the Aegean Sea and the villages below awesome. Instantly posting a couple of pictures onto Instagram to whet her friends' appetites, she smiled to herself. They had all questioned whether the villa would prove to live up to the blurb in the brochure. Mel, once she had toured it, and met with the housekeeper and chef, assured them that if anything it was better!

Roll on the next three weeks, thought Heather to herself, the sight of Jenny wheeling her case out of the customs area towards her instantly bringing her out of her daydream.

Chapter 16

The Past

The third and final year of university felt completely different for Amy, Heather and Jenny. They all missed Mel's calming presence in the house and her easy way of lightening the mood whenever any of them became stressed, which in that final year became an increasingly regular occurrence. They missed their ability to chat on a daily basis, sharing whatever news or gossip they had, or seeking her advice over a cold beer, or a glass of mediocre wine in the Student Union bar. Mel had always been the most worldly-wise of the four. She was the one they invariably turned to in times of need. Her absence had certainly forced them into becoming a lot more independent, more resilient, and if nothing else, more prepared for the world ahead.

Since the baby's christening they had hardly spoken, the occasional phone call once a week the most they could manage. They noticed after each call there seemed to be more distance between them, rather than it providing the sense of closeness they sought.

Mel was busy as a new mum to Sarah, bringing up her daughter virtually alone, starved of the full support of her parents. Neither Jenny nor Amy had any appreciation of what bringing up a baby, especially at their age, would involve, and the little experience Heather had as an aunt to her sister's baby seemed irrelevant. She only saw her niece infrequently, enjoying the cuddles and playtimes, but in reality had never really got her hands dirty with the baby, other than the occasional nappy change. No, Mel was learning the hard way. Her mother was at least supportive from a distance, whilst her father remained vehemently against it. He could never reconcile himself to the fact it had happened, regardless of his protestations. His granddaughter was there now, whether he liked it, or not.

So, whilst the weekly calls continued, with all four girls ensuring nothing was allowed to interfere or prevent them from speaking, Jenny, Heather and Amy had to be careful not to let Mel, or her worries distract them. They were heads-down, focussed on their final exams, the goalpost that graduation represented now firmly in their sights. Coupled with that was the challenge of looking for jobs, all of them knowing that without the trust fund Mel so happily relied on, they needed to work for a living.

Jenny was applying for whatever roles became available, her personal statement already well-honed and ready for firing off in support of anything in North West England that would allow her to complete her training and qualify to be a fully-fledged teacher. She had no desire to move further from home than was strictly necessary. Or to incur costs she could ill afford. She continually reminded herself of this fact each month as her bank statement dropped through the door. In Jenny's view, moving back in with her parents was the lesser of two evils. It would enable her to save a little money whilst she started on her chosen career ladder - even if that was at the cost of losing some of the independence she had enjoyed at university. Living under their roof again and complying with their rules would be a challenge, certainly, although what options did she have?

For Heather, her career path was less clear. The last three years had confirmed that art and design was truly where her heart lay. How she would ever earn enough money from it to support herself though remained a mystery. The course had been good fun and largely practical, meaning she had possibly had it much easier than the others. The number of assignments and reports they had sweated over, usually late into the night, or the number of hours they had locked themselves away in the library had not gone unnoticed. No, Heather's course had still involved a lot of work, and from the crates of samples she had created that lay strewn around her bedroom it was evident her style was nothing if not eclectic.

She had dabbled widely, with no particular field of design capturing her sole interest, other than something in the fashion industry was where she ultimately saw herself going. How she translated that into a job application though would take a lot of thinking about, raising the more worrying question of what call there might be for designers in Edinburgh. That was perhaps her biggest challenge, as like Jenny, Heather knew for certain she wanted to return home.

At the same time Amy was unsure how far her English degree would take her, assuming she got the first she had set her heart on. She had always aspired to be a journalist, but constantly worried what opportunities there would actually be once she graduated. She knew that moving to a city would be essential if she was to make it with one of the larger newspapers, something her heart was set on. Living at home with her parents in their small village would be the comfortable option, although the chances of ever getting a scoop that warranted an editor screaming 'hold the front page', would be non-existent. Nothing ever happened where she had been raised. Unless perhaps the local rag needed a gossip columnist, because she would never be short of material on that score. It was all she ever heard about when she rang home and spoke with her mother!

Whilst the three girls got on with their lives, Craig quietly got on with his own, after having jumped at the opportunity to move into the house with them. He fell easily in with their ways, proving to be a good housemate, if not a patch on his predecessor when it came to sharing gossip. He kept himself to himself, although the mere fact of having a man around the house proved useful, especially when the fuses blew. It was a problem they really needed to talk to the landlord about, given it was happening with increased regularity.

Craig also happily took on his share of the jobs, and made a mean curry when it was his night to cook dinner. Having been brought up just outside Bradford, doing casual work in one of the local Indian restaurants during his teenage years, he knew his way around a kitchen, and was never shy in showing off his skills.

Like Jenny, Craig was training to be a teacher, although to him teaching was not proving to be the passion, or the vocation everyone said it needed to be.

"Why don't you go into hospitality, or learn to become a chef?" Amy had asked one evening after Craig had made their dinner. "This is amazing, and it's clear that cooking is what you really love," she added, her mouth full of the lasagne he had cobbled together effortlessly that afternoon.

"You're right, Amy," he replied with a mournful look on his face. "I'd have loved to do that, but my parents were set on me not wasting my education. Dad was a headmaster before he died and Mum's a deputy head, so I suppose they just directed me down the same path as them. I'd have loved to open my own restaurant, serving customers with dishes of my own design. Instead, I'll be facing off to a bunch of spotty teenagers, no doubt stopping them from setting the chemistry lab on fire." Science and specifically chemistry was the subject he was aiming to teach, even though nothing in his demeanour suggested he had any love of it, other than the alchemy of putting ingredients together – a subject on which he clearly shone.

"Well, I think that's a real waste," Amy replied. "You're obviously not looking forward to teaching. And as far as I can see, you've made no effort to apply for any jobs. So why not reconsider your options? I'd love to see you in your own restaurant one day." As she spoke she smiled over at him lovingly.

Jenny and Heather sat back, quietly watching as the two of them debated the pros and cons of opening a restaurant; both aware of the feelings that were developing between Craig and Amy, even if neither of them chose to acknowledge it. Sensing it might be time to test her theory, and perhaps give the potential relationship an encouraging nudge, Jenny turned to Heather. "Heather, do you fancy popping over to the Horse and Hounds with me for a quick drink? We'll leave these two to finish up their chat over the washing up."

"Brilliant idea," replied Heather, for once not slow on the uptake.

"And don't expect us back before chucking-out time," Jenny added, visibly winking at Amy as they left the house. Their intentions could not have been more clearly communicated had they paid to have it splattered on the billboard outside the Student Union, in big bold capital letters.

Chapter 17

The Past

After the relatively slow start of 'dancing around their handbags', as Jenny impolitely referred to Amy and Craig's courtship, the relationship suddenly developed at a pace. Given the way they had tip-toed around each other for what seemed like an age, neither prepared to declare their hand too soon, Jenny and Heather had feared the two lovebirds would never get their act together.

However, with each passing day, Amy and Craig spent more time together as a couple; going to the pub, just the two of them, or meeting in the library to have some quiet time alone. Even grabbing lunch in the café, if their finances allowed. Amy, gradually drifting further away from Jenny and Heather, seemed to be the happiest anyone had seen her for quite some time. Neither Jenny nor Heather was particularly offended by it. They simply accepted it as a natural progression, although it was evident the halcyon days of their foursome, back in the days when Mel was around, were now long behind them. They were all having to grow up and move on and prepare themselves for the real world, as best they could. Life after university, and all that promised, would undoubtably bring a real change for them all.

By the end of May, with their final exams almost over, all four were starting to finalise their options and make decisions on where to go next. The house rental expired at the end of June; a fact that not only focussed their minds, but meant that whichever way they looked at it, there was no avoiding the need to move on.

"Craig and I have decided we're going to look for an apartment to rent together, somewhere near Leeds, we think," Amy announced one Sunday morning as they were all sitting around the kitchen table eating breakfast. It consisted of plenty of slices of toast to soak up the copious amount of alcohol from the previous night's drinking session, swilled down with gallons of orange juice to combat the dehydration.

"Nothing too expensive. Accessibility to the city is our only criteria," Craig added. "I need to be either on a bus route, or able to walk to school. I'd love to get a car eventually; for now even a bike's well outside our budget," he added, smiling over at Amy as he spoke.

Craig had eventually secured a teaching role at one of the high schools in Leeds, a role where he too would get the training he needed to complete his qualifications. Amy however was still looking for a proper job. She was starting to get a little nervous about how she would make ends meet. She still had her heart set on becoming a journalist and so far had sent her CV into several of the local newspapers, accompanied by a few articles to demonstrate what she was capable of. Although no firm job offers had been received so far, a couple of her articles had been published, earning her a small fee, with the offer of further freelance work, if she was interested. So, it looked promising. She just needed to bide her time, and provided she could earn enough to pay her share of the bills the rest would sort itself out. Amy was the eternal optimist and nothing was going to worry her, least of all not having a job. With Craig by her side, she felt confident they would weather any storm.

"That's brilliant news. I wish I had a plan." Heather's reply could do nothing to disguise the despair in her voice. "My only real option was going home to live with Dad. And now that's become my reality, if I'm being really honest I can't say it thrills or excites me. As much as I love him, being away from home and living with you guys for the last few years has been fun. Living on the outskirts of Edinburgh, back in my old bedroom, surrounded by my old Bay City Rollers posters, is not going to replace that in a hurry, is it?"

"Have you no other plans yet, in terms of work I mean?" Jenny could sense Heather was feeling more down than usual. She was usually a glass half full type of person, and today she appeared very much out of sorts. "I thought you said you'd applied to a couple of art galleries in the city?"

"Yes, I have. I'm just waiting to hear back from them. I'm sure the right job will come up, eventually," she replied, a wan smile on her face. "Especially if I cast my net wide enough," she thought to herself, regretting she had absolutely nothing to show for the dozen or so jobs she had already applied for. Try as she might, she was struggling to avoid becoming downhearted.

Heather knew she wanted to do something to do with the Arts, but had no real idea exactly what, or how she was going to make a living from whatever she eventually decided on. She loved creating things; jewellery, trinkets, pottery. In fact, she could turn her hand to almost anything, with her lecturers often commenting on her unique talent. Although she knew her eclectic style was not to everyone's taste, in her heart she felt that somewhere out there, there must be someone who would love her work enough to give her a chance. She just needed to keep going, praying that even if she could feel half the optimism Amy felt about her future, it would be enough to get her through.

"Well, thankfully there's no shortage of teaching roles," Jenny replied complacently, whilst trying to inject more positivity into their conversation. "I'm relieved I got offered that role I went for last month, and even happier it's within walking distance of home. No need to rent for me," she smiled, as she reached for another slice of toast. "It's not the best school, I know, or in the greatest area of Manchester, but it's a start. I can always look for something better in a year or so, can't I? Once I've got some experience, that is."

Jenny had avidly been searching the Guardian's teaching supplement for months, applying for whatever roles fell within the broad criteria she had set herself. She knew she could neither afford to be choosy nor demanding, given the complete lack of experience she had to offer. She just needed to get a job, anything that would get her on the career ladder and earning.

Her first few applications had fallen on stony ground, leaving her to scratch her head and question whether her personal statement was good enough; whether it had enough 'zing' about it to get her noticed. Perseverance, plus some subtle tweaking of her statement to include that extra 'je ne sais quoi' that would hopefully make her stand out from the crowd, meant she was eventually shortlisted for a couple of positions.

Her first interview had been an unmitigated disaster, leaving her kicking herself on the long train journey back, as she recalled some of the answers she had given to even the most basic of questions. Answers she had struggled to voice as her mouth dried up and her nerves got the better of her. Throughout the interview, the headteacher and the chair of governors had looked on her kindly, smiling as they patiently waited for answers to their questions. It soon became apparent from their body language that Jenny was not their preferred candidate. "So much for mock interviews," she thought to herself; the real world was proving to be much tougher than she had realised!

A great believer in fate, Jenny simply brushed herself down and told herself it was clearly not to be. Chalking it up to experience, she continued scouring the situations vacant adverts, her steely determination evident to everyone. Life was all about learning lessons, and if nothing else, that first interview had taught her a lot.

"Well, this time next month we'll be scattered to the four corners again, won't we?" Heather observed, despondently. "Once you two are settled in Leeds and Jenny, you're back home in Manchester, hopefully working and I'll be in Scotland. Not to mention Mel in London, busy with Sarah, how are we ever going to stay in touch?"

"I don't know, Heather," Amy replied, picking up on her friend's mournful mood. "I just know we will though. Best friends for ever is what we've committed to, so we'll find a way. There's always a way - so don't worry."

"I'll drink to that," Jenny added, raising her glass of orange juice. "Best friends for ever."

Chapter 18

The Present

It was nine o'clock in the evening and the sun was gently setting over the Aegean Sea as Mel, Heather and Jenny relaxed on the veranda, sipping their wine and staring out at the vista below them. They had just enjoyed another delicious dinner. Tonight's was freshly caught fish and salad, prepared by their personal chef, Carlos, on the small stove on the terrace. It was followed by the lightest of chocolate desserts. Now, the combination of the warm gentle breeze, the spectacular light show being created before their eyes by the setting sun and the copious amounts of wine they had consumed with their dinner, was proving almost hypnotic.

"That fish was amazing, and the pudding was to die for," Heather declared, bringing Jenny and Mel out of their daydreams. "Another couple of weeks of Carlos' cooking and I'm going to need to get a bigger dress size! I feel like I've put on a stone already and it's only week one." She laughed, in an attempt to keep herself and her friends from drifting off to sleep. The night was still young, but none of them looked like they had any intention of moving.

"Don't be daft," Jenny replied, smiling over at her friend. "I was only thinking earlier how well you're looking, and wondering if you've lost weight recently." Before adding quickly, "not that you needed to lose any, that is."

"I agree," Mel added. "You're looking really well too, Jenny. And Heather, I think the sunshine and the break is doing wonders for you. In fact, I think it's working its magic on us all. You wouldn't think we were forty, would you? We all look amazing, even if I do say so myself." Mel laughed, pleased that the holiday was having the desired effect on them all.

"Although I tend to agree about the food," added Jenny, patting her stomach. "I don't think I've stopped eating since we got here, and I hardly eat much when I'm at home. I'm not complaining though, and it's great to have some 'eye-candy' doing the cooking and the washing up for a change," she remarked mischievously, looking in the direction of their cook, who was busy tidying away the remnants of their meal. "I think, if I see another tin of baked beans or any more fishfingers when I get home, I'll probably flip!" Cooking was not something Jenny particularly enjoyed, especially when it involved doing it on a budget, saying nothing of the two pernickety, if hungry teenagers she had to feed.

"I know what you mean," Mel added. "When Sarah initially left home I'd go for days without eating regular meals. I also got out of the habit of eating healthily; too much take-away food, eaten alone in front of the television, late at night from a tray, not good! At least this is healthy food, although perhaps the alcohol is counteracting some of the benefits," she laughed, raising her glass of wine to the others.

The first few days of the holiday had largely been spent relaxing around the villa's plunge pool, reading a book or falling asleep on the comfy sun loungers. Or spent digesting the delicious food that Carlos provided; the endless plates of juicy fruits, or freshly baked pastries that he produced effortlessly and without prompting. The sunshine and fresh air had certainly worked marvels on their appetites, as they devoured everything he put in front of them, almost as if it was their last meal, or they had never eaten before.

Even though it was over twelve months since they had all last met up in person, they had easily fallen back into the comfortable banter they shared, like old friends invariably do. None of them felt a need to put on a show, or feign any pretence with the others. They could simply be themselves, and importantly not feel judged for it.

For the first couple of days, they had focussed on getting acclimatised after their journeys, each grateful that they were eventually able to switch off from the lives they had left behind. They had made a tacit agreement that their mobile phones would be switched off, unless it was an emergency, and that social media would be banned. No one wanted to be disturbed from the tranquillity of the villa by the minutiae of home, or tweets or Facebook posts from others. Problems that did not need to be faced for a few more weeks would be parked, for the time being at least.

Mel had soon got the hang of driving around the compact island, competently navigating the small FIAT they had rented up and down the winding roads, careful to avoid the many potholes along their way. Whenever they needed a distraction, they drove around the island, searching out small coves and beaches, or visiting the harbour for some people watching from one of the many bars. The previous day, they had even chartered a yacht for the afternoon. Their skipper, Lindsay, took them a mile or so off the coast, before encouraging them to jump in and swim around in the warm waters, once she had dropped anchor. Jenny had been amazed by the yacht – and even more so by the woman who confidently manoeuvred the boat, shouting orders to her young crew as she handled the vessel. She was perhaps their age, late thirties, early forties, Jenny imagined, although her sun-kissed skin, sun-bleached hair and toned figure made her appear much younger. She was stylishly dressed in a crisp polo shirt and fitted Bermuda shorts, no doubt all designer labels, Jenny suspected. She looked happy and full of vitality, leaving Jenny to simply dream about what her life must be like, compared to her own drab existence. A life at sea, fresh air and regular exercise versus a dingy classroom, cantankerous teenagers and school dinners – no contest!

Other days, they had simply wandered around the villages, checking out the quaint gift shops and exploring the narrow streets and alleyways for which Santorini was famous, before calling in at a taverna or bodega for some refreshment. The white painted buildings, with their blue roofs and tiled exteriors all shone in the reflected light of the bright summer sun. The views over the sea were spectacular, irrespective of where on the island they happened to be standing, or what time of day or night it was. It was pure heaven.

After another hour or so chatting, Heather started to yawn. "I think I'm heading up to bed now, if that's alright with you two?"

"I think I'll follow you," Jenny replied, as Mel indicated she was done in too. "This relaxing and doing nothing is tiring me out," she laughed.

"Does anyone have any plans for tomorrow?" Heather enquired, as she carried the wine glasses into the kitchen to put next to the sink for the housekeeper to sort in the morning. "It's just I was thinking of walking down into the village after breakfast. There's a little trinket shop I saw the other day that I fancy having a delve around. There were a few items I noticed in the window that I'm hoping might give me a little inspiration for some jewellery I'm thinking of making when I get home."

Heather, since Bruce's death, had thrown herself into making jewellery. They were mainly bespoke pieces, commissioned by customers who had either seen her display at the gallery where she'd worked, or on the website she had established. Although she would never make a fortune from it, she had managed to establish a good little business. It was something that kept her mind active and gave her a useful distraction. Above all, it stopped her from focussing on how alone she was becoming, living as remotely as she did, away from people and life in general. Loneliness was something she had never really experienced before. Now, over the last couple of years, losing both her husband and ostensibly her father, his memory failing more each passing day, it had crept up on her unannounced. And showing it the door was proving to be a real challenge.

"I'll come with you, if you'd like?" Jenny replied. "I need to pick up a couple of postcards for Mum and Dad. I think they're the only people I know who still like receiving them," she laughed, recalling how the technological age had all but bypassed her parents. Had Emily and Harry not constantly pleaded with them to upgrade their old television set to a smart TV, or to get a mobile phone so they could contact them after school, they would happily still be living in the last century.

"Oh, god. That reminds me. How on earth have I forgotten to tell you?" Mel said, almost panicking, believing she was losing her marbles. How could she have forgotten something so important? The wine or the sun must be getting to her! "I had a call earlier this evening, just before dinner, from Craig. He's asked if there's room at the villa for him to come and join us for a couple of days. Next week, I think he said. He's planning on flying over, and says there's a friend he'd like us all to meet, if we don't mind. JoJo, I think he called her, although he didn't give me any details. And for once, you'll be surprised to hear, I didn't pry."

"Oh, that sounds interesting!" Jenny replied. "I presume you said yes?"

"Yes, of course I did. It'll be lovely to catch up with him. And the villa's more than big enough for another couple, isn't it?" Mel replied. "I told him to just let me know when they'll be arriving, so that I can let the housekeeper and Carlos know. I'm sure it won't be a problem for them. I can easily sort that out."

The villa was spacious, with four double bedrooms, and one twin room, so could comfortably sleep eight people. For the month, in the height of summer, with the private chef and housekeeper thrown in, it was costing Mel an absolute fortune. But what was money for, if she could not spend it on some luxury, was her view?

"And is Poppy coming too?" Heather was excited at the prospect of seeing Amy and Craig's daughter again. "I feel guilty I haven't seen her for ages. She's growing up so fast and if we're not careful, she'll forget who her godmothers are."

"I know and I feel guilty, too." Like Heather, Mel had not seen Poppy or Craig for some time. "I did ask, but apparently Poppy's staying with her grandparents, Ron and Jean. I think it's easier. I get the impression, reading between the lines, that he's possibly bringing JoJo for our approval. I'm not certain though, so please don't quote me!" Mel added, a quizzical look on her face. "I think we'll just have to play it by ear when she and Craig arrive."

"Interesting," Jenny observed, for once almost lost for words. "Very interesting indeed."

Chapter 19

The Present

Over breakfast the following morning, their discussions proved to be more subdued than usual. They were nowhere near as upbeat as the previous mornings, when they had sat on the veranda, excitedly chattering about the day ahead; planning how they would while away the hours until they felt comfortable to declare cocktail hour had arrived. "After all, it's five o'clock somewhere," Mel was famous for saying whenever there was any suggestion of alcohol, or a drink being poured.

Not today. It was almost as if each of them had spent the night reflecting on the news of Craig's imminent arrival. They were all tired through lack of sleep, coupled with the strain of pondering what it might mean. If, in fact, JoJo was being brought for their approval, as they now all suspected.

"I'm not sure how I feel about Craig coming over," Heather started, openly sharing her reservations with her friends, unashamed to express the concerns she was feeling. "I was sure it would only be a matter of time before he found someone else. After all, he's a nice guy and doesn't deserve to be on his own, does he? I'd tried not to think about it before now though, or what it would mean to us, or more importantly to Poppy when it did eventually happen."

"I know what you're saying. And if I'm honest, I feel exactly the same way." Jenny absently stirred her coffee as she stared out to sea, unable to focus on the plate of fresh pastries Carlos had laid out in front of them only moments earlier. "I suppose he's entitled to move on, just like anyone else. After all, it's six years next month since she died," she added, almost unbelieving of where the time had gone. "I suppose all we can do is honour the promise we made to Amy. To look out for Poppy, and to be there for her as she grows up. It's not up to us to judge how he lives his life, or with whom, is it?" Jenny added sagely, silently hoping Craig had not traded Amy's memory in for a younger or shinier model, just as her estranged husband, Jason had done to her.

"Yes, you're right, Jenny," Mel added. "Let's not judge, or jump to any conclusions yet. It might all be very innocent, and I might have read more into it than I should have done." As she said it, she knew in her heart that was not the case. There had definitely been something in the way Craig mentioned JoJo's name that made it sound important. Someone he cared for, and not just a casual friendship, or a passing acquaintance.

Six years though, where had that time gone? Six years since they had seen the smiling face of their friend, or felt the warmth and kindness of her in their lives. Why was life cruel sometimes, and why was it always the good ones who died young?

Their lives had all moved on in their own various ways. Each had been forced to mourn the loss of their best friend in the only way they knew how.

Mel had Sarah to occupy her time. She was a stroppy teenager girl at the time of Amy's death, and was intent on making Mel's life a misery. Sarah was unable or unwilling to learn from her mother's mistakes, no matter how vociferously Mel voiced them. As a single parent, struggling to balance the challenges of parenting with those of running a business, Sarah's behaviour gave Mel no end of headaches. In an evening, it left her either pulling her hair out over something Sarah had said or done, or pouring over spreadsheets, a bottle of wine the only company she allowed herself. And that was a slippery slope, and one she struggled hard to avoid.

Men had come and gone, with none being encouraged to hang around for too long, or provide the male role model Sarah so desperately needed in her life. Mel had never had any contact with Sarah's father, the thought of that still made her shudder. And after her own father had virtually disowned her when she became pregnant, he too played little, if any, role in his granddaughter's upbringing.

No, she loved her independence too much, meaning nothing, or no one was going to take that from her, or have any say in the way she chose to raise her daughter. Now, having spent so many years coping by herself, fighting for what she believed in, how could there be any benefit in allowing someone else into their lives? Worse still, risk someone trying to take over what she had fought so hard to achieve.

Mel's business was still creating its own set of demands. In the early days, her challenges had been focussed on the risks of getting off the ground, establishing a brand and a customer base she could rely on. Around the same time Amy died, there was an explosion in the café culture, with shops springing up on every high street. Coupled with her earlier success, Mel suddenly saw limitless opportunities presented for '*Just Brewed*'. Her advisors began talking of expansion, suggesting she open more stores, develop more varied menus, and in so doing appeal to a broader customer base. Although Mel had no aspirations to rival the larger chains, the Costas or Starbucks of this world, she was confident her service ethos could not be beaten by the corporate giants, so embarked on a programme of expansion that continued to absorb her days.

Looking back now, she realised how bad a friend she had been to Amy in those last few years. Only now appreciating how much she could have done, if only she had been more available to her friend, less self-absorbed by her business. But also, how absent a godmother she had been to Poppy, who surely needed people around her. Why had she allowed herself to lose focus on what was important in her life, and was it too late now to make amends to both Craig and Poppy? Whatever she did would never bring Amy back, however there may be other ways she could help. She pondered, as she stirred her coffee, gazing out on the expanse ahead of her.

Jenny, always the pragmatic one, had Emily and Harry, as well as her marriage to Jason to fall back on for her support when Amy died. She also had her busy teaching career, which involved her working every hour God sent. It left her little time to worry about anything, other than keeping her head above water, the bills paid and her children fed.

Joking aside, and as much as she moaned about the workload, Jenny had really taken to teaching, and found she was quite good at it. She got a real buzz when a student, who had been struggling, suddenly had that Eureka moment. When all the pieces fell neatly into place. Or when a student, who had previously not seen any relevance of maths in their life made the connection. The sudden realisation that by understanding percentages was a benefit to them, especially when it related to the amount of money they could save in the sales, looking for those new trainers, or the latest must have outfit. Suddenly 20% or 50% meant something.

The year Amy died Jenny had been working towards a promotion as Head of Maths. With other, much more qualified teachers in the running she knew she had to keep focussed. Above all, she could not allow her personal life to get in the way or cloud her judgement. As devastated as she was at losing Amy, life had to go on. Wallowing in grief was simply not an option or something that was in her psyche.

Looking back, she realised how self-absorbed she had become. How she had bottled her feelings up and never really dealt with her grief properly. Amy was the first person she had lost who she had been close to. And for her to have died, at so young an age, made it difficult for Jenny to comprehend, let alone know how to act, or how to feel.

Rather than turn to Jason for support, she had almost shunned him, believing herself strong enough to cope on her own. There was no need to cry on his shoulder, was her mentality. He had his own worries, his own challenges, and as kind as he was, he did not need saddling with hers too.

Jason had known Amy and got on reasonably okay with Craig, but in truth Jenny recognised the two men had never really had that much in common, or hit it off. When it came to socialising as a foursome or as a wider group, at times it could get a little awkward. There was never any atmosphere; simply a politeness, with a feeling of forced conversation between the two men.

Try as he might, Jason could never replicate the natural bonhomie his wife had with her university friends. Whilst their five years age difference should not have been a huge obstacle, it was obvious Jason felt it; often joking that he felt like he was from a different generation when they all got together and reminisced about their university days.

Was Amy's death the point at which their marriage had started to unravel, Jenny now questioned herself? If she had turned towards, rather than away from her husband, would he have needed to look elsewhere for his happiness? If she had allowed him to support and care for her, which with hindsight she now realised he had tried, would that have made any difference to their relationship? How much were her actions responsible for propelling him towards another woman's arms? She shuddered at the thought. She had previously been unprepared to shoulder any blame for their current state of affairs. Now watching the sun rise over the horizon, she suspected she was perhaps not completely without fault.

Heather, with Bruce at her side as her stabilising influence, had quietly muddled through. As the calmest and most unassuming member of the group, she had never been one for big shows of emotion, or flights of fancy when it came to discussing her feelings. She remained the strong one – like so often before, the crutch for the others to lean on.

She recalled how Bruce had sat and held her as her body shook when the call had finally come through to say she had gone. Craig had phoned, not needing words to convey his feelings, his quiet cries on the other end of the phone told Heather all she needed to know. To think, she had dealt with the loss of Bruce himself, a matter of only four years later. How had she found the strength to do that, and to go on, not once, but twice? Knowing two of the people she loved most in the world had been taken from her.

Looking back now, Heather's biggest fear had been the impact Amy's death would have on Poppy, that beautiful baby Amy had barely had chance to know. She prayed her journey through childhood and into adolescence, and then onto adulthood, would be without incident. The thought of Poppy being raised without a mother was heart-breaking for Heather, knowing how much she herself had relied on her own mother growing up, and how she had felt when she had lost her at the tender age of fourteen.

Most mothers and daughters have fractious relationships at that stage, she knew Mel and Sarah certainly did. Heather had never had the chance to experience that for herself, her mother's loss forcing her to grow up much sooner than she would have liked. She had turned to Ellen, her older sister, her de facto parental adviser on any subject her dad would have been uncomfortable to talk about. Who would Poppy turn to when she needed to have those discussions, and was that where JoJo entered the equation?

Never having had children of her own, Heather lived out her maternal instincts vicariously through her nieces and godchildren. She recalled how every maternal bone in her body had ached, as she watched Craig carry his baby daughter to the altar for her christening, without his wife by his side, Amy's distraught parents his only support. It had to be one of the saddest days of Heather's life, as she, Mel and Jenny awaited their arrival at the cold church, wrapped up in their winter coats against the bitter wind outside. No words between them. She had never felt more frightened. They were about to take on the responsibility of being Poppy's godmothers, Amy's dying wish. How would Craig cope, and whatever could they do to help him get through his ordeal?

Six years on, Heather shuddered at what little she had actually done. The occasional visit, the Christmas and birthday presents, but nothing of any real substance. Life, as well as her own grief when Bruce died, had absorbed her and got in the way of all the good intentions she'd had. Perhaps now was the time to put that right, she mused to herself, staring out to sea for the inspiration she needed to deal with this.

Sitting there now, Craig's imminent arrival suddenly felt like the catalyst for the next phase of their lives; introducing an ominous, foreboding feeling into their otherwise happy group.

Chapter 20

As Craig had cradled his new baby daughter, the perfect image of his wife, in his strong arms, like Heather, he wondered how he would get through life without Amy by his side. He knew her parents, Ron and Jean were on hand to help with all the practical stuff, and that Amy's friends would be there to help as much as they could, but day-to-day how could he be both mother and father to this precious bundle? How would he ever replace a mother's love? A love that had been so strong Amy had been prepared to sacrifice her own life, for the sake of their unborn child.

The news of Amy's pregnancy had been such a joyous occasion, coming completely out of the blue. However any joy they had felt had been short lived. A series of blood tests carried out during the second trimester of the pregnancy led to the detection of ovarian cancer. The doctor advised that sadly it had already progressed quite significantly, informing them any treatment plan would need to protect her life, as well as that of her unborn child.

As Amy and Craig sat in the surgery, listening to the doctor outlining his concerns about her condition, try as she might to concentrate on what he was saying, Craig knew the words were simply washing over her head. It was almost as if he could see the cogs of her mind whirling round, the doctor's voice just background noise.

On the journey home, he remembered her ranting on. She was furious she had missed the early warning signs, casually putting any symptoms the doctor had outlined down to their hectic lifestyle. Working long and unsociable hours, irregular eating, all the lifestyle choices they had made to make their dreams of running their own restaurant come true were suddenly to blame. How many nights had she shaken off her tiredness, even the weight loss, never considering the ominous undertones of either? Why had she never thought to mention it to anyone; her mum, Craig, or any one of her best friends, who would surely have been there for her? She knew how tired she and Craig were feeling, to say nothing of how much pressure they were putting themselves under, so moaning about her health would have felt indulgent.

It was bad enough that the pregnancy itself had come as a shock, having decided to wait a year or so whilst the restaurant became established, or at least until after they were married before starting their family. Neither wanted to risk its success by getting bogged down by dirty nappies or night time feeds, a fact they had agreed on over a drunken night five months ago now! Apart from which, money was still tight, and the loans they had taken out to start the business needed to be repaid.

However, the best laid plans were often the ones that fell apart soonest, Craig soon found to his cost. The resilience he had needed to deal with the thought of an impending new arrival, in the midst of a business that was still very much a start-up, was nothing compared with the concept of losing Amy. Listening to the doctor's prognosis had not spurred him with optimism, especially

Angela Hartley

given she had categorically declared her intent to not embark on any surgery or chemotherapy treatment that would harm her unborn child, regardless of any personal risk to her own health.

After many a night trying to argue her round, Craig had to reluctantly accept that his words were falling on deaf ears. He knew Amy was well aware of the risks she was putting her body through, and of the potential consequences it would have, however no argument to the contrary would persuade her otherwise. It left him no option, other than to respect her decision and support her in the only way he knew how; by loving her and the new life she was carrying. He would also honour the promise he had made on her death bed to look after Poppy. He would put her first and foremost in his life, no matter what.

As Craig sat in his bedroom, his suitcase now packed and ready for his flight to Santorini to meet up with his friends the following day, he pondered what Amy would think of JoJo, or of the life he had made for himself and Poppy. Most importantly, he pondered whether she would approve of some of the life choices he had made since her death, that last question generating a small shudder down his spine, as he imagined her response.

Chapter 21

The Past

After university, Craig and Amy rented a small apartment on the outskirts of Leeds, above a Chinese take away. It was as close to the high school, where Craig's teaching position was, as they could afford. Life was tough for them in those initial years, as they struggled to pay bills and keep their heads above water. Craig's was the main salary, and as a newly qualified teacher that did not say much. Amy brought in the occasional wage whenever an article was published, or she managed to cover an event where she got paid on a freelance basis for the hours she worked. She knew it was neither the career she had dreamed of, nor the right use of her education, but she struggled on. She was ever the optimist, assuming the right role would come up for her eventually. Money had never been a key driver for her. Provided they were happy, that was worth more than riches, she would regularly say to herself, echoing the thoughts of her grandmother. These were values that had been instilled in her from as far back as she could remember.

After a couple of years of teaching, it became obvious Craig was not happy. Their discussions around the old chipped kitchen table on an evening demonstrated that perhaps teaching was not the vocation he had thought it would be. Spending all day with unresponsive teenagers, trying to get them interested in the Periodic Table, or how chemicals reacted under certain circumstances was simply not doing it for him. The curriculum was boring him as much as it appeared to bore his pupils, if some of the looks on their faces, or the responses they gave to questions he asked, was anything to go by. As the final bell rang, signalling the end of another day, it was difficult to see who was the most relieved, them or him?

Craig found himself rushing home as soon as it was possible. He was forever thankful science was not one of those subjects that required him to stay around, or worse still, manage after-school activities. He was a nice enough looking guy, with his dark curly hair and blue eyes that seemed to smile all the time. Although at only five feet, nine inches tall, and quite heavily set, he had never been the sportiest, or most agile of men. He often watched the PE teachers, with their honed, athletic bodies and envied them their physique and stamina, as they led the team sports events, their whistles casually hung on lanyards around their necks. He had never been tempted to join them, or even volunteer to run the line. No, sports were certainly not his bag. For that he was mightily relieved, particularly at this time of day when all he wanted to do was get home to Amy and plan what they would have for their dinner.

Amy had long since left the cooking to Craig. From the moment Mel left their student house and Craig had moved in, he had demonstrated a real flair and passion for cooking. He encouraged Jenny, Heather and herself to step back, while he effortlessly took over. He would then concoct the most appetising meals out of the basic, cheap ingredients they had around the kitchen. His innate knack for flavours, instinctively knowing what spices and herbs to add to make the ordinary taste extraordinary, meant mealtimes became events they would all look forward to. Although with the number of pots and pans he used in the process, none of them was too enamoured by the washing up afterwards.

Early one Monday morning, nearing the last week of the Easter term, Craig was struggling to summon up the energy to leave the house in order to walk the short distance to school. They had entertained Jenny and her new boyfriend, Jason, over the weekend. They had all enjoyed a good catch up, and Craig and Amy had got to know Jason a little better. He too was a teacher, working at a local primary school in Manchester, not far from where Jenny still lived with her parents. It was a small school, with only two hundred children on the roll, so everything felt very personal and intimate. Jason was able to develop close relationships with the parents and children alike, unlike Craig and Jenny's secondary schools. Those were big and impersonal, with the chances of meeting parents remote, unless of course an issue arose and they needed to be called in. With well over a thousand adolescents to deal with, most of whom struggled to pass the time of day with you, let alone develop a relationship, the challenges were somewhat different.

Craig sensed Jason was bright and ambitious, and having already been appointed to his first deputy head role, perhaps a little too smug with his achievements. Listening to him talk about the younger children, and the challenges he faced, seemed a world away from what faced him, and no doubt Jenny each day.

Craig had nevertheless pulled out all the stops and cooked his signature Sunday lunch; a roast chicken, with homemade stuffing and all the trimmings, including his Yorkshire Puddings. It was followed by a delicious rhubarb crumble and homemade custard. The aromas and tastes instantly reminded Jenny of the food they had enjoyed in the house together, and sitting in Amy and Craig's pokey apartment, an odd assortment of mismatched furniture around her, it transported her back to their student days. It evoked memories and stories that they laughed over as they ate their meal.

As Craig packed up his lunch box, using some of the cold chicken from the previous day, he suddenly turned to Amy. She was sitting slouched at the table, nursing her cup of tea and mumbling something about wondering what the day would bring. She had no plans and no work lined up. He noticed she was wearing her old quilted dressing gown over her clothes, no doubt to ward off the cold of the morning, unwilling to put the heating on and generate unwelcome gas bills.

Out of the blue, he declared in a serious voice, "Amy, I'm not happy teaching anymore." Seeing the startled look on her face as she raised her head, he continued, in a less serious voice. "Do you think you could write me a sick note, or phone the school to let Mrs Briggs, the headteacher know I can't come in today? I'm not bothered what excuse you give her. Any will do the way I'm feeling this morning."

"Hold on, where's this come from?" Amy enquired, his comment jolting her out of her own thoughts. When Craig did not reply, and guessing that although there had been an element of jocularity about what he had said, from the look on his face he was not joking, Amy added, "I get the feeling you're serious?"

Amy had sensed for some time Craig was simply going through the motions with his job, naively assuming it was part of his 'settling-in process', rather than the career crisis it clearly was.   There would be hiccups with any new job, Amy presumed, having still not secured a role for herself. So, she had not paid too much heed to his moods when he came home. The off-hand comments he occasionally made about staff, pupils, the school, or the fact he had no time to himself during the day, she just chalked up to him settling in.

Recalling now yesterday's lunch, and specifically some off-the-cuff comments he had made when speaking to Jason, she questioned whether that had been the catalyst for how he was now feeling. At the time she had shrugged it off, as once their guests left and the conversation moved on to 'non-school' topics, he was back to his usual self. Perhaps she had been too eager to dismiss it, she wondered now, as he looked forlornly at her.

"I am serious. And the more I think about it, the more I realise teaching's not for me," Craig sighed. "This weekend was the first time in ages I've really relaxed and enjoyed myself. I know I spent most of my time in the kitchen cooking, but I love entertaining people with my food, and I just don't get that buzz with teaching."

"Your food is amazing, and you make a great host. Although, unless you're thinking of training to become a chef, or planning on opening up your own restaurant, well, having friends around for the occasional dinner isn't going to pay the bills, is it?" Amy replied, unsure exactly where the conversation was going. At the same time, she sensed it was a conversation they needed to have.

"Well, as always, my dear, you've hit the nail on the head. That's exactly what I'm thinking of doing. And when I do open my restaurant, I'm going to name it after you. I'll even ask you to write a review for it, for the papers!" With that he picked up his lunch box and his bag containing the stack of books he had been marking over the weekend and headed towards the door, with more of a spring in his step than he had thought possible only a few minutes earlier.

Giving a stunned Amy a quick kiss on the cheek as he left he added, "let's talk more when I get home tonight. One thing's for sure though, by this time next year, if I have my way, I'll no longer be marking homework!"

Chapter 22

The Present

The taxi pulled up around five o'clock in the morning outside 9 Leader Close. It was a neat three-bedroom, modern semi-detached house, located on a quiet street in the middle of a residential area on the outskirts of Leeds. It had been Craig and Amy's first real home, bought just over ten years ago when they had finally decided it was time to put down proper roots. How grown-up they had felt the day they moved out of the small apartment above their restaurant, and into a real house. It was theirs to do up as much, or as little as they chose, without having to answer to a landlord. They had reached their thirties, *Amelia's* was doing well, earning them both a decent living, so it was finally time to grasp the nettle and take on the responsibility of a mortgage.

Their plans to renovate the house, including sprucing up the kitchen and the bathroom, even creating an office in the spare room, were all put on hold as they balanced the demands of owning a house with running a business. They found in those initial years they had neither spare cash, nor free time to contemplate getting any tradesmen in, and with barely a DIY bone between them, they had simply parked it for another day. Money was tight, so what did it matter if the wallpaper was peeling off a little, or the paintwork was chipped? It would all get sorted one day, was Amy's view. The restaurant had been their priority.

As Craig pulled the front door securely and quietly behind him given the time of day, he thought how upbeat Amy had been about everything. She allowed nothing about the house, the business or their general financial insecurity to bother her. "Tomorrow is another day, so why stress over the little things when they'll still be here tomorrow? As long as we have our health and we're happy, what else matters?" had been her attitude to most things.

"Hi, is everything okay?" asked JoJo, smiling over at Craig as he got into the back seat. "You looked very pensive as you were walking down the drive. Not having second thoughts about the trip are you?"

"Yes, I'm fine thanks, and no, I'm not having second thoughts." As Craig replied, he squeezed JoJo's hand in an attempt to demonstrate a level of reassurance that his face had obviously failed to portray. "It's just this is my first holiday since Amy died, and it's brought back more memories than I'd expected," he admitted, smiling over at JoJo. "I suppose it hit me when I got the suitcase down from the loft yesterday. It still had the baggage tag on from when we went to Benidorm the year before we moved into the house, which is over ten years ago! That was probably our first and last real holiday abroad, a few days in the sun. I remember Amy lounging by the pool, happy to switch off. Whereas I could never truly relax, or sit still for more than five minutes. I was always worried the chef I'd left in charge would burn the restaurant down, or drive the customers away before I returned."

"Well, I don't think you'll have that problem this time." JoJo laughed. "I get the impression Marco is more than competent to run the restaurant for a few days. And with the reviews you've been getting recently, I don't think the customers will desert you this time either."   The Leeds Gazette had produced a dining out supplement in its weekend paper the previous Saturday, and *Amelia's* had received a very complimentary review.

"No, I'm sure you're right," Craig replied. "It's just got me thinking, that's all, about what I'm doing."

JoJo noticed Craig's smile still did not reach his eyes. "Look, it's not too late to cancel if you're worried. I'm more than happy to postpone until the time feels right. We can always book another time, or go somewhere different if introducing me to your friends is what's really worrying you," JoJo offered, sensing that was perhaps what was causing Craig's real concern. "It's a big step you're taking after all, and if you're not ready, then let's wait a while."

"No, let's do it. After all, if Poppy likes you, and as far as I'm aware her grandparents haven't reported you to social services yet, then my friends will be a walk in the park," Craig added, with more conviction than he really felt.

"Manchester Airport, Terminal 1 please," JoJo said as the taxi driver looked in his mirror to check whether they were coming or going before he set off.

Craig had first met JoJo three years ago, at the time when his restaurant, *Amelia's,* was having a much-needed refit. He had finally realised that he could not wallow in his grief indefinitely. He had relied on those around him to shoulder the majority of the day-to-day running of the restaurant, whilst he 'played' at managing it, without ever moving it forward, or bringing new ideas to the table. The menus were becoming tired, and unless he did something about it, the business he and Amy had worked so hard to create would be lost. Competitors were forever biting at his heels. New restaurants and take-aways were opening up all the time, as the desire to eat out really took hold. No, he needed to seriously start investing both his time and his money back into the business, in order to create the type of restaurant he and Amy had dreamed of, and something of which in time Poppy would be proud.

Having initially worked in other bars and restaurants for four years, working towards his qualifications and honing his creative skills, Craig at twenty-seven had eventually felt sufficiently confident to embark on his own venture, assured Amy would be there to support him. They had looked for suitable premises, landing lucky when they bought the restaurant as a going concern, from an elderly lady whose husband had recently passed away. He had left her the sole benefactor of his estate, but she had no desire to run a restaurant. She had even less interest in employing someone to do it for her. All she wanted was to sell up and move to sunnier climes, the sooner the better. She agreed a fair price for Craig and Amy to buy it lock, stock and barrel, and as the premises also came with a small apartment on the first floor, it allowed them to finally move out of their rental too.

They secured a bank loan, the repayments for which, along with the other bills meant in those early days there was little spare cash around for the niceties. So, rather than a fancy restaurant to attract their customers, they had to rely on the quality of their food to keep people coming back. Thanks to Craig's skills that strategy had paid off.

But the competition had become much more fierce. Now, several years on, with the financial security that sadly had come from the life assurance pay-out he had received following Amy's death, Craig knew there was no longer anything stopping him from making their dreams come true – even if Amy was no longer there to share them with him.

The property was in a good area of the city; however, it had become dated and was in need of more than basic maintenance. A lick of paint and a sticking plaster would no longer suffice. It needed a complete make-over, and Craig had to bite the bullet when it came to the cost.

With the help of an architect, plans were drawn up to overhaul the front of house, creating a relaxed, contemporary décor as well as some outdoor dining space to attract passing trade. He also drew up plans to extend the kitchens, installing state-of-the-art appliances and creating enough space to employ an additional chef and kitchen staff. The restaurant was popular, and more space would allow more customers; with Craig needing to employ more staff to service them, if he was to avoid turning people away.

"So, what do you think of the plans I've drawn up? Now you've had chance to go through everything, that is?" the architect asked Craig one afternoon after they had finished talking through all the details over a coffee before the evening service started. "Have I captured the essence of what you're looking for, and would you be happy moving forward with them, along with the costings I've prepared?"

"I think the plans are perfect, and in terms of the budget, it's in the right ballpark." Craig had replied, a little apprehensive given the size of the investment he was being asked to consider. "Subject to finalising a couple of points, I think Mr Wright, we have a deal."

"That's, brilliant," the architect replied, standing to shake Craig's hand. "And if we're going to be working together over the next few months, please call me JoJo," a broad smile on his face.

Chapter 23

The Present

Having arrived at Santorini's airport around twenty minutes early, Mel was waiting for Craig's late morning flight to arrive, peacefully sitting in one of the small cafés. She had a double espresso in hand, the extra caffeine shot coming in useful to keep her awake. People-watching was one of her favourite pastimes, and something she found paid dividends in terms of her business. Her knack of weighing people up, even second guessing what they were thinking was a skill she had honed over the years, with her instincts generally proving correct.

She waved as she saw Craig approaching, dragging his suitcase behind him, his rucksack casually flung over his left shoulder. He appeared to be by himself, with Mel assuming JoJo had perhaps popped into the Ladies to freshen up before the short drive to the villa. It should only take them around thirty minutes.

Walking alongside Craig was a striking looking man, perhaps in his early forties, tall with blonde short cropped hair, who she would best describe as a David Beckham lookalike. He and Craig appeared to be chatting, as men do, striking up conversations with the most unlikely of people. They looked like an odd couple, one tall and blonde with superstar looks, the other short and dark, and although not bad looking, by comparison quite ordinary. Mel assumed they had met on the flight, or perhaps had passed the time of day waiting for their luggage at the carousel, and presumed the guy would peel off towards his own taxi or car, to go wherever he was going. Although, having now given him a good looking over, she would not be too disappointed if he wanted to join them. He was a very attractive man, and her bed had been short of them for far too long! She might have a fight on her hands though with Heather and Jenny, she presumed laughing to herself. Although she felt confident she could stand her corner, if push came to shove.

"Hi, Mel." Craig moved effortlessly into Mel's outstretched arms and kissed her on her cheek. "Lovely to see you again, and thanks for offering to pick us up, and for letting us stay. I'm looking forward to catching up with you all again, it's been so long!"

"No problem. It's lovely to see you again too. You're right, we shouldn't have left it this long." As she replied she was conscious the good-looking man was still standing alongside Craig. He had not made his way to the taxi rank, as she had presumed he would.

"Mel, let me introduce my friend, Jonathon Joseph Wright, to you," Craig continued, turning towards the man standing at his side. "Or simply JoJo. JoJo, meet Mel, one of Amy's oldest friends. And as you're already aware, one of Poppy's three amazing godmothers."

"Lovely to meet you, Mel, and it's JoJo. Only my mother calls me Jonathon these days," JoJo replied, his hand outstretched to shake Mel's, with the broadest of smiles on his already tanned face. "I've heard so much about you. And thank you for inviting us both to stay for a few days. I know how much Craig appreciates it. I can't wait to meet you all."

"Nice to meet you too, JoJo." As Mel took his hand, she noticing how smooth his skin was. For once, she felt completely lost for words and at a distinct disadvantage. She knew nothing whatsoever about this man, or his relationship with Craig. Her erstwhile skills of reading people had obviously forsaken her this time, but at least she knew she was no longer waiting for someone, who she had presumed would be Craig's girlfriend, to emerge from the Ladies!

After Mel had shown Craig and JoJo to the two remaining guest rooms at the back of the villa, joined by a shared Jack-and-Jill style bathroom, she left them to unpack and freshen up. She'd suggested they might want to grab a cold beer, or some food from the fridge, before joining the others outside when they were ready.

"Dinner won't be for another few hours, but there's plenty to nibble on, if you're hungry or fancy some lunch that is," she had said as she left them alone, conscious of the unintended double-entendre, before returning downstairs to join Heather and Jenny on the veranda where they were finishing off their salads.

They were waiting, a glass of chilled wine in hand, unsure exactly what to think after having seen Craig and his friend arrive earlier. They were both equally surprised when no girlfriend appeared to be in tow and were keen to hear what Mel's view was. Having driven them over from the airport, surely their conversation had given some clues as to why Craig was here, or how he knew JoJo. Evidently not to seek their approval, as they had previously assumed.

"Well, I'm not sure where JoJo's hailed from, or even if he's from this planet," Jenny whispered as Mel approached. "He's gorgeous, and those muscles are divine. Did you see them?" Jenny appeared to be in more of a daze than Heather or Mel had ever seen her before. "I don't think I've ever heard Craig mention him, but I'll fight you for him Mel, unless Heather beats us both to him," she joked. "So much for 'soon to be ex-husbands'. Give me a bit of that, every day!" Any thought of Jason, with his comparatively wiry physique and milk-bottle complexion was suddenly far from Jenny's mind.

"I know what you mean. His eyes are dreamy – and what impeccable manners! The way he kissed my hand after he shook it has left me all in a dither; my imagination is running wild, almost like a Mills and Boon novel." Heather sighed as she allowed her mind to wander, envisaging all manner of situations she and JoJo could lose themselves in, as he whisked her off into the sunset for a midnight swim, or simply massaged sun cream into her skin. The mere thought of him was making her blush.

Mel laughed, unsure whether her friends had had too much sun over the last few days, or whether the strong cocktails had done the damage. Jenny was certainly more distracted than usual, her behaviour not at all typical. And Heather, it was almost as if she was in a world of her own, saying the oddest of things on occasion.

"Get a grip of yourselves, will you. You sound like two sex-starved hussies!" Mel whispered, as she giggled at her friends' reactions to the handsome newcomer, unsurprised to realise their thoughts mirrored her own. "And keep your voices down please. I'm not sure how sound travels in the villa, and we don't want to embarrass him, or ourselves before we've all been properly introduced, do we? Apart from which, there might be an equally attractive supermodel keeping his bed warm at home that we just haven't heard about yet. So don't get your hopes up too soon." She felt a need to manage all of their expectations.

"Oh well, we can always dream!" Heather continued smiling and wistfully staring out to sea, as Jenny and Mel exchanged a strange look, somewhat concerned about their friend.

"Hello ladies." JoJo confidently strode onto the veranda, now wearing a perfectly fitted pair of shorts and a smart polo shirt, both of which emphasised his toned physique; a point that did not go unnoticed by any of the women. He walked over to where they were sitting, noticing their glasses were half empty and a bottle of wine sat cooling in the chiller.

"Do you mind if I join you, and could I top any of you up?" he enquired. "Craig's just gone to get us a beer from the fridge, and something to eat as he's apparently starving. I don't think he's the best of travellers. He hasn't eaten at all since we left Manchester," he added, with a lightness to his voice.

"Thank you, yes, you can top me up, please." Heather immediately offered him her glass, whilst the other two smiled and nodded, unable to form the words; Jenny's mouth remaining proverbially wide open.

"This villa is amazing by the way. Wherever did you find it, Mel?" he asked, once he had topped up all the glasses, draining the bottle in the process. "The design is stunning, both inside and out, and the architect has made such great use of the space and the natural light. The views from every aspect are incredible. I hope you don't mind, I had to explore. Force of habit, I suppose."

"I just looked online for rentals, I'm afraid. Nothing too clever. It seemed to tick all the boxes for us, and was available for the weeks we wanted," Mel replied, smiling over at her friends. "I was looking for somewhere quiet, with a touch of luxury, so we could celebrate our birthdays in style."

"Well, it's certainly got style," he nodded. "Craig mentioned it was all your fortieths coming up this year, and that you all met at university and have been friends ever since. That's quite an achievement. I don't think I've managed to keep in touch with anyone from my university days."

"So, how did you and Craig meet then?" Jenny as always was straight to the point in her usual direct manner. "Have you been friends for long? It's just that I don't recall him ever mentioning your name before. Did you know his wife, Amy?"

"Sadly, no I never met Amy. I feel like I knew her though." JoJo was careful how he responded. "In fact, I only met Craig a couple of years ago, when he had *Amelia's* refurbished. My company 'WrightDesign' was who he employed to design and oversee the project. And as it's named after Amy, he spoke quite a lot about her during the process. He wanted the essence of her to be in the structure of the new restaurant, so hence quite a lot of talking about what she liked, didn't like – you know that kind of stuff."

They all nodded, touched that Craig had been so thoughtful. "I'm an architect by trade," JoJo continued. "And we just seemed to hit it off as we worked through the plans and designs together. His vision and mine seemed compatible, and we've been friends ever since."

"Well, you did an amazing job – that's for sure," Heather remarked. "I remember the last time I went to *Amelia's*; come to think of it, it probably was the re-opening night. The place was truly transformed, and in a really sensitive way. I'm quite arty myself, but I have to admit what you did was stunning. I'm sure Amy would have approved."

"Yes, I agree. It's very impressive and I'm certain Amy would have been delighted by the result," echoed Jenny. "It's just a shame she wasn't around to enjoy it," she added, without wanting to sound too melancholy.

"I recall now, Craig once mentioned your name to me." Mel suddenly made the connection. "I was looking for an architect around the same time as he did the restaurant, to remodel my cafés. He suggested I speak to you. For whatever reason, I didn't get in touch. I ended up finding someone local to manage it. He didn't do too bad a job in fairness, although had I known you were such good friends, I'd have tried harder to contact you. It's good to support friends where you can, isn't it?"

"And will your wife be joining you while you're here?" Heather enquired, her question as direct and to the point as Jenny's had been. "Santorini is such a romantic island, I find."

"I agree. It is a beautiful island, and one I know well from a couple of previous visits. But no, I'm not married, and there's no Mrs Wright in the picture." As JoJo answered Heather's seemingly innocuous question, he realised, and not for the first time that day, how difficult the discussion about Craig and him was going to be with his friends. It was certainly going to be much more of a challenge than either of them had ever imagined, and he was concerned how Craig would cope with that.

Chapter 24

The Present

After a late dinner, they all took their drinks on to the terrace to enjoy the balmy evening, and relax watching the sun setting over the Aegean Sea. The bright sunlight was gradually melting away into the sea, disappearing over the horizon. It was a view none of them would tire of, although as they sat, Heather struggled to stifle a yawn.

"I think I might call it a day and head up to bed, if no one has any issue with that?" she began. "It's just that I'm feeling a wee bit tired after my walk into the village earlier, and could do with a good soak in the bath before I turn in."

Heather and Jenny had headed to the village after lunch to mooch around the shops, leaving Mel to crash by the pool for a couple of hours to concentrate on her suntan. Having done the airport run earlier that morning, she felt she deserved a little down time, with no desire to walk into the village, to poke around the small selection of gift shops, again!

"No problem," Mel replied. "I'll probably not be too far behind you. I've promised to FaceTime Sarah tonight. She's looking at booking her return flights in the next day or so, and has mooted the idea of a stopover here, on her way home. She fancies a holiday and a chance to join us for our gala birthday dinner."

"It would be lovely to see her, although that's a major detour isn't it?" Jenny asked, surprised by what Mel had suggested. "To say nothing of the extra cost! I presume she's looking for you to fund that too, is she Mel?" She laughed as she watched Mel's knowing look. As much as Jenny loved her goddaughter, she knew how easily Sarah found it to wind her mum around her little finger. And how readily Mel gave in, always eager to see her daughter happy and avoid unnecessary conflict.

Over the years, Mel had paid for everything Sarah had ever asked for, partly by way of compensation for the fact she was not always around, and partly because she simply did not know how to say no to her daughter, once she laid on the charm. Building up the business had taken a lot of Mel's attention, particularly in those early years, and Sarah had on occasion had to play second fiddle, which had come at a cost. Over the years a habit had been formed, that now neither of them had ever tried to get out of.

"I know, and I presume so. I'm going to try to dissuade her, particularly now that Craig and JoJo are here, as we no longer have the room. All five bedrooms are taken, so there's no room at the inn, so to speak. And she's not bunking down with me, because she snores like a trooper. I need my beauty sleep these days!"

JoJo and Craig exchanged a glance; one that did not go unnoticed by the rest of them.

"Well, if you're both going up, I think I'll join you." Jenny suddenly felt a little uncomfortable at the prospect of being left alone with the men.

"I presume it's okay if we leave you boys down here to lock up and switch the lights off when you've finished?" Mel enquired. "I imagine after your early start it won't be too long before you're turning in either?"

"Yes, that's fine." Craig stood ready to give his friends a goodnight kiss. "And in the morning, when we're all fresh, we can have a proper catch up."

"Yes, and Mel don't be too hasty about Sarah and her flights," JoJo said, looking over at Craig again. "If you want your daughter to join you for your party, then it won't be a problem. I'm sure we can find a way to make that work."

As the three women reached the top of the stairs, none of them had said a word as they ascended. Their minds were working ten to the dozen about the implications of what they might have just heard.

"Come into my room for a minute, will you? I don't know about you, but I think we need a quick powwow. And in private, before the morning," Mel whispered to Jenny and Heather.

"Well, if you're thinking what I'm thinking……," Jenny added, in an even quieter voice, unsure she was even contemplating what she was, "I'm right behind you."

"You can't both be thinking what I think you're thinking, can you? That's impossible." Heather was afraid to even let her mind go to where Jenny and Mel's had obviously already gone. All she wanted was to have a long soak, read her book and dream about all manner of things, not be forced to consider the almost unthinkable about her friend. No, it can't be right. It's just a simple misunderstanding.

As Mel closed the door, the three of them simply looked at each other, none of them prepared to utter the first word. Eventually, Jenny said, "I get the distinct impression that JoJo might be gay, which I personally don't have any issue with. For the life of me though, I can't see what he's doing with Craig."

"Neither can I," added Heather. "I thought JoJo was too good to be true, and I had my suspicions that something wasn't right, the way he said there was no MRS Wright, with heavy emphasis on the MRS. But Craig's not gay, is he, so are they just friends?"

"I'm not so sure," added Mel, her suspicions on full alert. "One thing is for sure though, we need to find out tomorrow. We have a responsibly for Poppy's welfare, above all else, and something to me just doesn't add up at the moment. Craig's come over for a reason, and we need to find out what that reason is. And importantly, what that means for Poppy."

"Yes, you're right. Let's sleep on it tonight, and think about how we should best approach it. Then see how tomorrow goes." Jenny's suggestion clearly reflected she too had her doubts.

"Okay," Heather added, a little reluctantly. She had finally accepted that the peaceful soak in the bath she'd had planned, was not to be. Instead of lying back and allowing the pleasurable thoughts of Santorini to wash over her, whilst she reflected on all the joy this place was bringing to her previously quiet and sheltered life, her thoughts would now be replaced by more darker thoughts. Thoughts of Craig, and the particular nature of his relationship with the mysterious David Beckham lookalike.

Chapter 25

The following morning, the sun was already streaming through the bedroom window as Mel opened the pretty white shutters to see Craig sitting all alone at the breakfast table on the veranda. Looking at her watch, she realised it was already after nine o'clock, and unusually late for her to be getting up. Other than Craig, there appeared to no one else around.

She took in a deep breath of the clean fresh air, as she surveyed the spectacular views around her and stretched in an attempt to get her body in gear, before hurrying into the shower. It was the first morning of the holiday that she had not woken early, refreshed after a good night's sleep. Instead, she had restlessly tossed and turned until the early hours, thoughts of Craig and JoJo invading her mind; dozing, on and off throughout the night.

"Good morning," she said to Craig ten minutes later as she joined him downstairs. "Where is everyone? The house is so quiet, and I didn't see anyone indoors when I came through."

"JoJo's gone for his morning run, about fifteen minutes ago." Craig instinctively looking at his watch to check the time. "He obviously missed it yesterday with travelling, so was keen to make an early start. He likes to run at least five kilometres each day, as well as going to the gym, if he has the time," he replied. "I've not seen

Heather or Jenny though. I just presumed you all liked a lie in, so didn't think anything about it. I've helped myself to coffee and pastries, by the way - hope that was okay?"

"Yes, no problem. You're to make yourself at home whilst you're here. Carlos, the chef, will prepare you whatever you need if you ask him. I presume JoJo has no allergies, or there's anything you can't eat, but if there is, just let Carlos know." Mel smiled over at him, helping herself to some coffee at the same time.

"Thanks. It's a fantastic set up here, Mel. Such a beautiful location and an amazing property. JoJo couldn't stop going on about it all yesterday evening. He recently bought a plot of land, just on the outskirts of the Yorkshire Moors and is designing his own property. I think the villa's given him some inspiration. I don't think the views of the moors though will be anywhere near as spectacular as what you've got here, or the weather!" Mel noticed the way his face lit up at the mention of JoJo's name.

"Yes, he mentioned he was an architect, so I presume that's his dream – to design his own home. What's he thinking of building?"

Before Craig had time to answer, Heather joined them, smartly dressed in a pretty blue sundress that accentuated her curves, and wearing a wide brimmed straw hat. "Good morning, Mel, Craig," her voice indicating she was full of the joys of spring and had not struggled to sleep, in the same way Mel had. "I'm planning on walking into the village again this morning, does anyone want to join me? I'll probably get a coffee and some breakfast there for a change."

"I thought you walked in yesterday morning, with Jenny?" Mel was a little puzzled by her friend's obvious excitement and desire to get off so early in the morning. "Did you forget something, because there's nothing much else there to interest you two days running, is there?"

Before Heather had time to answer, Jenny joined them.

"Sorry guys. I think I must have overslept." She had clearly come straight from her bed as she was still wearing her pyjamas, her hair ruffled, with traces of yesterday's makeup around her eyes.

"Don't worry, I think we're all guilty of that this morning – apart from JoJo who's apparently put us all to shame and gone on a long run!" Mel replied. "Heather was just about to tell us what's so fascinating about the village, because she's heading off there again – even before she's had her coffee, or Carlos' pastries."

"Well, before you go Heather, I'd like to have a chat with you all, together if that's okay?" Craig voice a little faltering and displaying more nerves than he knew how to deal with.

"Fire away." Mel exchanged a knowing look with her friends.

"I'm all ears," Jenny added, already onto her second croissant.

"No problem." Heather pulled a chair up and poured herself a coffee, now resigned to delaying her visit to the village for another hour, at least.

Craig and JoJo had talked into the early hours of the morning, snuggled up together on top of the large king-size bed in one of the two bedrooms they had been allocated, conscious of the growing need to speak to the women. Sooner rather than later they realised, if they were to do what they needed to do and enjoy their holiday.

After JoJo's talk with Mel, Jenny and Heather earlier that afternoon, and their questioning of him, particularly about a potential wife, he correctly presumed they had no idea about his sexuality, or for that matter Craig's. He had actually sensed they had all perhaps been flirting with him, making him more than a little uncomfortable under the circumstances. To a large extent, women's behaviour towards him was something he was used to, and generally he employed quick and effective methods for dealing with it, to avoid anyone's embarrassment. However, on this occasion he had not wanted to react too quickly, or say or do anything that aroused their suspicions. And certainly not until Craig was ready. The consequences were too high, for all of them.

Then having spoken more, both during and after dinner, even sharing stories of Poppy and how she was growing up into a beautiful, if not mischievous little girl, it was obvious the ladies were curious about him. Particularly where he fitted into Craig and their goddaughter's lives. There was no hiding the fact that Craig and JoJo were close and spent a lot of time together, but tales of JoJo dropping her off at the school gates, or collecting her from swimming was time that could not be explained away as simply two lads enjoying a beer together after work.

No, it was not something they could put off any longer, and certainly not something Craig would be happy for his friends to simply deduce for themselves; something that would be inevitable over a short period of time if they acted normally around each other. The dilemma though of 'how to break it to them' left them both scratching their heads.

"I think, given they're your and Amy's friends, Craig," JoJo had said carefully after they had gone round the buoy several times trying to find the best approach, "it might be easier if I wasn't there when you told them." Realising he needed to explain his rationale, JoJo added, "and that's not me trying to get out of it by simply dumping it on you. If you don't agree with me, then I'll be there to hold your hand. I just think it'll be more uncomfortable if I'm there, for all of you."

Craig went quiet for a moment, thinking over what JoJo had just said. JoJo, unsure whether he had misread the situation, continued reassuringly. "They're going to be shocked – that's for sure if today's discussions are anything to go by. And I presume some choice words will be used, some of which might turn personal. But, if they're the type of friends you've told me about, then I imagine they'll understand, eventually. Especially when they realise how happy we are together, and more importantly that Poppy's cared for. I sense she'll be their real concern in all this, don't you?"

Eventually, Craig agreed. "Yes, you're probably right," nestling in closer to JoJo, as he spoke. The comforting warmth of his body and the tone of his voice assured him they were doing the right thing. It made him realise this was the happiest he had felt for some time. "Why don't I try to tell them in the morning, while you're out on your run? And if, for whatever reason I fail, or I can't get them all together, we'll try again later on."

"Sounds like a plan. And if all that fails, I'll book us both on the next flight home, and we'll be done with the lot of them," he laughed, trying to release some of the tension Craig was obviously feeling. "Now, I'd best make my way back to the other room, before anyone mistakenly scuppers our plans, and outs us before the morning." He laughed as he got off Craig's bed and walked back through their shared bathroom to his own twin room, blowing a kiss behind him.

Chapter 26

"So, take me through that again, because I'm not sure I get it. One minute you're heterosexual, married to our best friend, father to our goddaughter, and the next you're telling us you're gay, and in a relationship with David Beckham. How does that work?" Jenny exclaimed, completely non-plussed by what Craig had just told them. "Is this for real, or just a wind up, or what?" she asked, looking over at the others for support. "I grant I had my suspicious about JoJo, especially after last night's discussion over dinner, but I'd never have thought that of you, Craig. Please tell me it's not true!"

"Jenny, calm down will you, let Craig speak." Mel was nowhere near as surprised as Jenny. Craig's admission had effectively confirmed some of the suspicions she had harboured the previous evening, as she had observed their body language as they relaxed over dinner. Now, sitting across from Craig, she felt his discomfort as she watched him try to explain. Trying to justify something that none of them, in truth, really had a right to expect of him. It was his life to lead, and who were they to question how he chose to do that?

Heather had not spoken a word. Shock had been her most powerful emotion, that and the realisation that her trip into the village was now going to be put off for another day.

"Thanks, Mel." Craig suspected at least she had understood what he had struggled to articulate. "I know this has come as a surprise to you all, and I'm sorry for that – but I can assure you it came as much as a surprise to me, too."

"So how long has it been going on? And is it perhaps just a phase you're going through? Or, are you really serious about this?" Jenny continued to probe, bombarding him with questions. She was still not buying the fact Craig and JoJo were a couple. They looked the least like a couple than she could imagine. Mr Menzies, who taught art in lower school, was gay, as was Mr Brent who taught drama, and on the rare occasions she had met both their partners at various school functions, there was no doubting they were couples. But JoJo and Craig? JoJo was gorgeous, wealthy and obviously successful professionally, with more style and charisma than most. And as fond of Craig as Jenny was, loving him as a friend, she would never have described him as a 'looker', or even in JoJo's league. So, what on earth had attracted him to Craig, a grieving widower, someone who had just lost his beautiful wife, saying nothing of having a newborn baby to bring up? Jenny was bemused to say the least.

"We've been together for a little over two years now, as a couple that is." Craig looked around the table to judge their reactions, and found from their expressions it was difficult to read. "I'd wanted to tell you all sooner; it's just the right opportunity never came up. To be honest I didn't know exactly what to say, or how you'd react. And I suppose, I didn't want to say anything, until there was actually something to say." At this point he looked directly at Jenny. "Because as you rightly said, Jenny, I had to be sure myself this was real. Not just a phase, as you called it."

"Well, I think he's charming." Heather tried to lighten the mood. "And he has lovely manners, as well as beautiful skin." Being part of the arts and literary world, Heather and Bruce over the years had socialised with several gay men, and women for that matter. Some were clients of Bruce's, others people who had frequented the gallery where she worked, with their dress sense or mannerisms never leaving their sexuality in question. Edinburgh was well known for being one of the most gay-friendly cities around, and people embraced the freedom they felt there, comfortable to talk, dress or act just the way they chose. JoJo had certainly fooled them all, and by the looks of it, so had Craig, Heather now realised, recalling embarrassingly how each of them had almost fawned over him the previous day.

"So, how did you actually get together?" Mel enquired, attempting to steer the conversation into safer waters. "JoJo told us yesterday you'd employed him as your architect when you remodelled *Amelia's*. So, how did it go from a professional relationship to where you are now, if that's not too personal a question?"

"No, and I've often asked myself that," laughed Craig, a little self-deprecatingly. "I suppose it all started one morning when I was poring over the final designs for the restaurant – all those little touches Amy had inspired. I was sitting alone in the office behind the kitchen, before the lunch service started, when JoJo walked in unexpectedly. He saw my eyes, tears were streaming from them, and although I tried to quickly wipe them away, he'd noticed. He's so caring and sensitive to people's feelings. At first, he presumed his designs had upset me, so asked what he could do to rectify them. I had to explain that it was nothing to do with the designs, they were perfect. It was just that they had brought back so many memories of Amy, my best friend."

"What do you mean, your best friend?" Heather was slightly confused. "Did he not know she was your wife?"

"Well of course he knew, but above all, she was my best friend. We'd gone through so much - we worked together, we laughed together and we loved each other. We shared everything about our lives. And when she died, I missed her so much. Although if I'm honest, we were not particularly active, sexually I mean, as a couple. Sorry if that embarrasses you. Sex was never what attracted us, or held us together. We were above all friends, who occasionally had sex, and both of us were happy with that arrangement. I suppose we never considering any alternative."

"That's quite sad, Craig." Mel placed her hand over his, careful how she continued. "I presume you never considered that you might have been gay, I mean before you married Amy, or met JoJo?"

"No, not really. I suppose I never let myself think that. I just focussed on the business of getting by, you know, paying the bills. When Amy got pregnant, it was as much a surprise to me as it was to her, with the decision to get married more a reaction to her cancer, and her prognosis, than anything else. Poppy was her principal concern, and she wanted to ensure the baby would be safe and looked after, if and when anything happened to her. I went along with it, because above all, I wanted to make Amy happy. She was my life. My best friend and I'd have done anything for her."

"So how did it progress with JoJo?" Jenny asked, still bewildered. "It still seems a huge leap to me. I mean, to go from where you were, a grieving widower with a young toddler, to this?"

"Well, nothing happened for a while," Craig continued. "I didn't really know JoJo, other than professionally. And as you've all worked out for yourselves, he's not openly gay, so there were never any hints. We just kind of bonded when we worked together on the restaurant. He probably took a more personal, or perhaps closer involvement in my project than some of his other clients. At the time I didn't realise that. When the restaurant closed for the renovations to begin, some nights we'd work late into the evening at home, finessing details over an occasional bottle of wine, or a take-away. He was sympathetic to my feelings, and I found him so easy to talk to, and over time I opened up to him.

One weekend, Poppy was staying over at her grandparents' house for the night, and I'd started to cry about something. I can't even remember what it was now. JoJo just took me into his arms and hugged me, telling me everything would be okay. Nothing more than that, but it felt right." He looked round and saw tears had started to form in Heather's eyes and smiled over at her, grateful for her support and understanding at least.

"From there it progressed slowly. I suppose I started to develop feelings for him. At first I didn't know how to express them, and if I'm honest I was a little scared. At the same time, it was obvious he was developing feelings for me too. Although looking at me I've no idea why," he laughed to himself, knowing JoJo could have had his choice of partner. "And as they say, one thing eventually led to another and our relationship has grown from there. I'd never slept with a man before, so although that was weird initially, with JoJo it felt right."

"And I suppose the question now is, do you love him?" Mel asked, understanding perhaps this was what Craig had come to tell them, what was behind his request to join their holiday.

"Yes, Mel, I do. And what's equally, if not more important, is Poppy does too. She thinks the world of him – even Ron and Jean are as comfortable with it as they can be, under the circumstances," referring to Amy's parents, who had been surprisingly stoic when they learnt their son-in-law now had a gay partner, and that their granddaughter was being brought up, effectively by two daddies.

"So, what's next?" Jenny was still slightly non-plussed by the whole tale, although at least she now had a little more understanding.

"Well, JoJo's asked me to marry him – and I've said yes. So, I was thinking of asking the three of you if you would do me the honour of giving me away!" As he spoke, he laughed, relieving some of the tension. "I know it's not traditional, but you are my oldest friends, and somehow it seems fitting. So, what do you think?"

Before any of them had a chance to respond, JoJo arrived back from his morning run, looking slightly sweaty from his exertions, and with an expectant look on his face as he tried to read the mood language. From the reaction of Craig's face though, the only thing JoJo was certain of was that he was going to need to employ a full charm offensive to win these women round.

Chapter 27

"I'm going down to the village for a mooch around when I've finished my coffee. Does anyone want to join me?" Heather enquired, shortly after JoJo re-joined the group. He had grabbed himself a large glass of the freshly squeezed orange juice Carlos had brought out earlier, before sitting down at the table next to Mel. Sensing from the way the conversation had gone quiet when he arrived, Craig had told them something, but he was struggling to understand exactly what had been said, or more importantly what their reaction to it had been.

"There're a couple of shops I noticed yesterday that I fancy looking around a bit more," continued Heather. "There's one that sells jewellery, similar to some of the pieces I make, and a gift shop, where I can pick up a couple of postcards to send to Ellen and Dad."

"Postcards?" remarked Jenny, dismissively. "Does anyone still send them these days? You'll be home back in Scotland before they arrive, so why bother? Why not just message them, or send them a photo from here? It will be so much easier, and cheaper." Her mood had not been lightened by Craig's earlier announcement, and for once Jenny was lost for words. In fact, since Craig had informed them he was getting married, saying nothing of his request to give him away, none of them had known exactly what to say, or how to respond, and other than a collective "Oh," had given nothing away.

"I think I'll come with you," Mel offered, her tone a little distracted. "The walk will do me good. I didn't get any exercise yesterday, so yes, count me in. I'll go and grab my bag, and perhaps we can have a drink when we get there."

"Well, I might as well come along, too," Jenny conceded eventually. "I could see if there's anything in the shop for Emily and Harry, or my parents. I promised them a present and Mum loves her fridge magnets, so I can always get her one of those, if there's nothing else."

"Will you two be okay if we leave you for an hour or so?" Mel questioned, looking over at Craig and JoJo. "You're more than welcome to join us, if you'd like a walk."

"No, I think we'll be fine here, thanks Mel. We'll see you when you get back, and then we can perhaps talk some more?" Craig smiled over at them, his eyes asking the question that still remained unanswered. He knew they needed time to digest his bombshell, and time to discuss it between them. They had all been as thick as thieves over the years, with the girls particularly seeming to possess a sixth sense, meaning they could usually read each other's minds. For once, Craig felt like an outsider to their group, and at a complete loss to what they were thinking.

As he watched them saunter off down the hill, unusually not arm-in-arm, and without the usual giggles or chatter that accompanied them, he just prayed that their walk would not only clear the air, but would return his friends to him. Their friendship was something he had always cherished, and as much as he loved JoJo, he did not want to risk anything that would jeopardise that.

Half an hour later and Mel, Jenny and Heather were sitting outside the small taverna in the village square, sheltered under a bright red parasol to avoid the heat of the midday sun. They had hardly spoken as they had walked to the village, each lost in their own thoughts, taking in what Craig had told them. The young Greek waiter had just placed a carafe of chilled white wine in front of them, with a meze of plump Kalamata olives, freshly baked breads and dips to tempt their appetite. The wine and the food remained untouched, with each wondering who was going to speak first.

Eventually Heather started, as Mel reached to pour the wine. "Well, that was a shock, wasn't it?" She left the question hanging, unsure what else to say.

"You can say that again," Jenny replied. "I certainly hadn't seen that coming. I think I'd worked out JoJo was gay, which is a great loss to womankind I might add. Although I had no clue about Craig. I wouldn't have even thought that was possible!"

"Oh, it's more common than you'd think." Mel was thoughtful as she spoke. Living and socialising in London, she had witnessed all manner of things over the years, with her often thinking there was little left to shock her. "I'm aware of several of my clients, as well as some of my friends who've done similar, both men and women who have 'come out', so to speak later in life. Some more surprising than others. I suppose tradition and convention drives people down a particular path growing up. Expectations to get married, have children etc.. And, I guess, over time you can't continue to live a lie, can you? Not if it's not what you truly want, or feel."

"I agree, Mel. Bruce had quite a few colourful characters among his clients, a lot of whom were gay. We just accepted it as the norm," Heather recalled, remembering some of the evenings they had shared dinners with Bruce's clients and the tales they used to tell over a bottle or two of wine. "Edinburgh, like London appears to be a magnet for gays. You see rainbows displayed everywhere these days, so I know what you mean."

"Yes, I suppose you're right," Jenny eventually conceded. "As you both say, nowadays the whole LGBT community is so vibrant and celebrated in all walks of life. There's certainly not the same stigma attached to being gay, as there was years ago. Even twenty years ago, when we were at university, I don't think I knew any gays at all, did you? If I think about it, some of the kids in our school are already questioning their sexuality. I suppose, they're testing the boundaries, and at fourteen, fifteen they're not even old enough to have really experienced sex properly. I'll be honest, I've not come across anyone who's changed from heterosexual to homosexual, or even bisexual before. I suppose I must live a much more sheltered life than you two," she admitted, a little embarrassed by her naivety.

"I wonder what Amy would have thought had Craig come out whilst she was alive?" Heather pondered. However, knowing how pragmatic a person her friend was she added, "I think she'd have probably said something like 'Oh well, c'est la vie!' and just got on with it."

"You're probably right, Heather. Amy was the most accepting and down to earth person I'd ever met. And whatever hers and Craig's relationship was, I'm sure she would want to see him happy, and living the way he was intended to live."

"Yes, I bet she's up there right now, looking down on us and laughing her socks off." Jenny giggled at the thought, feeling more relaxed with the way the conversation was going.

"And if Poppy's loved and cared for, then what does it matter if she has two daddies bringing her up?" Heather added, her goddaughter always front and central to her thoughts.

"Well, I suppose the only question left, before we head back and give Craig and JoJo our blessing," Mel pondered as the other two looked on quizzically, wondering where her thought process was going. "Is what on earth are we expected to wear to give him away? I, for one, intend to look absolutely glamourous for the occasion. You never know, David Beckham might be inviting some equally gorgeous friends to the wedding, who I might just want to impress. After all, they can't all be gay, can they?"

At that, she smiled over to the waiter and signalled for him to bring their bill, leaving Jenny and Heather to collapse into fits of laughter at their friend's audacity. The reality however was more sobering. Here they were, three good looking women in the prime of their lives, and the only man on the scene, between the lot of them, was gay. What did that say for them, or their chances of finding love?

Chapter 28

"Mum, I can't talk for long as we need to run for the connection. The flight's due to arrive tomorrow morning, sometime around elevenish." Sarah was unsure exactly what time she was due to land into Santorini. With all the time zones she had travelled through on her journey home, and the tiredness that was beginning to creep up on her, in truth was unsure what day it was, let alone the actual time of day. "Are you still okay to collect us from the airport, or should we get a taxi?"

"No, I'll be there darling. I wouldn't miss it for the world." Mel was excited Sarah had suggested she divert her flight home, as had been mooted earlier in the week - even if it was costing her a fortune for the pleasure of seeing her daughter. "I'm so looking forward to seeing you again and holding you. It seems ages since you went away."

Mel recalled how desolate she had felt, dropping her daughter off at Heathrow back in January, knowing it would be over six months before she would see her again. It had been the longest time they had ever been apart, and she had feared, particularly in those early weeks, if either of them would ever cope with the separation. As mother and daughter, they had a tight bond. Even though they had FaceTimed almost every other day, and messaged all the time, it was not the same as hugging her or holding her in her arms, or actually being in the same room together. Mel had missed her daughter desperately. Over time, she had adjusted to being alone, rattling around the big empty house, shopping and cooking for one. She had even resorted to talking to herself at her lonelier times. For some reason, it had felt like a part of her had been missing, a part of herself was not there.

Sarah, by comparison seemed to have thrived on the experience. Her Antipodean tales of life in Australia something Mel had looked forward to hearing, sensing the maturity in her daughter's voice as she explained what she had been up to, or the people she had met. It had not all been work and grape picking, as she had initially suggested it would be, when James, Mel's brother had originally proposed Sarah's visit. No, there had been countless BBQs on the beach, learning to surf in the gentle waves off Adelaide's coastline, even snorkelling in the warm waters off the Great Barrier Reef during a family trip up to Cairns with Aunt Connie and her two cousins. There had also been the trip James scheduled to Ayers Rock, or Uluru as Sarah rightly corrected her; an early treat for her twentieth birthday, he had insisted, when Mel offered to pay towards it.

Listening to each new adventure being recounted, Mel had dreaded Sarah was settling too well into the laidback lifestyle. She feared perhaps she'd even find a dishy Australian and fall in love, meaning she may never want to come back home. The sheer panic that thought had generated was something Mel tried hard to disguise. She suspected Sarah was not completely oblivious to her concerns, especially given most of the conversations they had were liberally peppered with the phrase 'when you get home', whenever Mel was updating her on news from London.

"Mum, promise me you're not going to embarrass me at the airport, will you?" Sarah begged. Public displays of affection were not her thing! "And you've not to embarrass me in front of Jake, either at the airport, or once we're back at the villa. At least promise me that!"

"I'll try, but I can't guarantee Aunty Heather or Aunty Jenny won't say anything, or Craig for that matter. As you know, they've all got plenty of material on you." Mel laughed as several stories immediately came to mind that Sarah would probably not want discussing in front of her new boyfriend. "And as you've sprung Jake on us all, and at such short notice I might add, we're all bound to have the odd question or two for him, I'm sure."

"You'll love him, Mum, just like I do. Please don't give him a hard time." Mel heard the smile in her daughter's voice as she spoke, whilst noting it was coupled with a level of anxiety. A feeling no doubt induced by the thought of bringing her first real boyfriend home to meet the parents. "Now, I've got to go. See you tomorrow," she said, blowing kisses down the phone as she hung up and ran for her flight.

When Mel had spoken to Sarah a few days earlier, confirming her flight details, until that point, there had been no mention of a friend flying back from Australia with her; a friend Sarah had hardly mentioned during the preceding months, other than in passing when she talked about the few friends she had made during her travels.

Mel had at least been glad she was now able to offer Sarah a bedroom, given Craig and JoJo were officially sharing one room.   Although the thought of accommodating another friend was not something she really wanted to consider, even if it would only be for a few days.   Not least of all, because selfishly she wanted her daughter all to herself. She did not want to be forced to share her.

"Why does your friend want to come via Santorini?" Mel had questioned. "Surely he'll want to make his way directly home to his parents? That would certainly be cheaper too, wouldn't it?" At which point, Sarah had informed her mum that Jake's family, although originating from Devon, where his grandparents still lived, were now settled in Australia, having taken citizenship over twenty years previously. Jake and his twin brother had been born and raised as Australian, albeit with very much a British heritage and strong ties back to their homeland. "He'll visit his grandparents and his extended family when we get back to England. But Mum, he's travelling home with me because he wants to spend his time with me, and to see what London has to offer now that he's graduated. We're serious about each other. So, don't worry about me, and don't worry about the fact there's only one bedroom left. We'll share. I can assure you, Mum, we wouldn't want it any other way!"

It was at this point Mel realised how much her daughter had matured over the previous six months. Whilst she may have put a young girl on the outbound flight back in January, it was clear it was a young woman she would be collecting from the airport. Sarah now had a mind of her own, and the confidence to speak it. Recalling how headstrong she herself had been at Sarah's age, and with the sure knowledge of where that had landed her when she'd faced up to her own parents, pregnant and effectively disowned, she decided there and then to go with the flow. If her daughter was serious about this young man, then who was she to say anything against it? She might never have been able to hold a relationship together, but that did not mean her daughter would similarly fail. She was coming home, that was the important thing.

Her job now was to ensure she stayed home, and was not enticed back to the land of opportunity by some hunky Australian!

Chapter 29

Over the remaining week or so, the household fell into a comfortable routine, with everyone finding their own way of amusing themselves and getting along together. The mornings would see Mel and Jenny spending their time lazing around the pool, a book in one hand, a drink in the other. They would occasionally swim if it got too hot, or they needed a distraction before lunch. JoJo continued his daily runs, returning after an hour's exercise looking almost as fresh as when he'd set off, glistening rather than displaying huge sweat marks. He would then join the ladies by the pool, intent on working on his tan, and chat, allowing them to get to know him, and finding a little more about each of them. After all, they were Craig's oldest and closest friends, so he had to make them his friends too. He had an easy going and engaging style, developed over many years of having to keep his customers happy. He always had a tale to tell, or an anecdote to share that would soon have Mel and Jenny laughing.

Sarah and Jake would normally be the last ones to surface, content with their own company, and so obviously not morning people, by the look of their body language when they eventually emerged into the sunshine, stretching and yawning. Sarah would head straight for the shade, a coffee in hand, whilst Jake would dive into the pool and do a few lengths to loosen up. Like

JoJo, he had a toned body, and an even tan, courtesy of living in the sun and enjoying a healthy outdoor lifestyle. He was a keen surfboarder and a strong swimmer, with sun-bleached blonde hair, and a smile to die for. Mel could easily see what her daughter had been attracted by, and having spent time in his company she would tend to agree.

Jake was laid back, but at the same time had an intellect, and was nobody's fool. At twenty-seven, he was a few years older than Sarah, which was no bad thing; with a maturity and a purpose in his life. He and JoJo had hit it off immediately, especially after they discovered they had a shared passion for architecture. Jake informed him he'd recently graduated in architecture, and completed a twelve-month work experience programme with a local design company in Adelaide. He would be looking for another placement as soon as he got home, one that would enable him to work towards his final qualifications.

Craig had never been a great sun lover, nor one to expose his body without cause. He had always carried a few extra pounds around his waistline – one of the occupational hazards of being a chef who enjoyed his food too much – and was always happier in a kitchen than anywhere else in the house. He spent his time chatting with Carlos and helping out with the meal preparations. The two of them were often found exchanging recipes and discussing food whenever they had an opportunity. Craig was being introduced to different foods and culinary techniques, absorbing both like a sponge, eager to take the ideas back to the restaurant and develop new dishes. And Carlos in turn, was learning all about the best of British cuisine.

Of the group, Heather was the least comfortable spending her time lazing around the villa or mingling with the others. She would often be the first up in a morning, and as soon as breakfast was finished, would bid them all goodbye and walk off in the general direction of the village, her beach bag in hand, stuffed with all manner of things. Some days she would not return until late in the afternoon; always in time for dinner, and the odd cocktail or two. She would then comfortably watch the sunset with the others, finally allowing herself to relax.

"What do you imagine she's doing, or where she's going all day?" Jenny had asked Mel on more than one occasion. "I didn't think there was that much to see on the island!" Having not wanted to venture much further than the village, Jenny was happy to just chill and de-stress. Her batteries were long overdue a re-charge, and after her recent troubles with Jason, she had no intention of traipsing around the dusty streets sightseeing. Not when she could just sit and be pampered. No, there would be enough stressing when she got home.

"I think it's probably just that she's so used to the solitary lifestyle, living remotely as she does in Scotland. Being around so many people probably makes her feel a little crowded," Mel had offered, thoughtfully. "She's probably just found a quiet area to sit and read, I guess. I don't think there's anything to worry about, or that anyone's upset her, do you?"

"No, not at all. When she returns she's always in a good mood. So, wherever she's going all day, or however she's spending her time is obviously making her happy," Jenny replied. "Perhaps we should follow her one day, and see what she's up to. What do you think?"

"No, that sounds like too much effort to me," Mel replied, rearranging herself on her sunbed and smiling over to her friend. "Live and let live is my motto. I'm sure if there's anything she wants us to know, she'll tell us – eventually. Now, shall we have a quick cool off in the water and work up an appetite, before lunch?"

Heather, rather than feeling unhappy with the villa, or more specifically Santorini, had actually fallen in love with it. She spent her time exploring as much of the island as she could. She would take the local buses to reach some of the more remote parts, if it was further than she wanted to walk. She jotted down in her notebook all the interesting things she was seeing, even doodled sketches of flowers and plants, or small insects and butterflies – basically anything that attracted her attention. Santorini was one of the smaller Greek islands, less than seven miles at its widest point and only ten miles long, so easily somewhere she felt comfortable to explore by herself. Even happier that she did not feel she would get lost.

She particularly loved the vibe of the small villages, the relaxed lifestyle of the locals and enjoyed learning a little about their culture, popping in to ask questions wherever she saw a tourist information point. She loved to mooch around the shops, or sit on the terraces of a café or a taverna, happy to watch people going about their daily lives. She was contented as she drank her coffee, or one of the local wines Santorini was famous for. Most of the locals appeared to have a smile on their faces, regardless of the fact their lifestyle was not particularly glamourous, or that they were being invaded by a seemingly endless influx of tourists during the holiday season. They appeared simply to be happy to live on such a beautiful island. An island that appeared to float effortlessly in the Aegean Sea.

The villa was stunning, with all the modern conveniences and luxurious touches tourists would want, well at least those who could afford to pay for them, thought Heather. She had no idea how much Mel had paid to rent the property, but knew it would not have come cheap. And as beautiful as the gardens and terraces were, relaxing around the pool was not a draw for her. Nor was losing herself in a book, or snoozing the afternoon away enjoying a siesta. She tired of that within the first few days and wanted to explore, finding a thirst for it that she had never previously experienced.

Once she was outside the villa's gates, and away from the areas that were designed to attract the hordes of tourists, the countryside soon became very rural. Small farms and cottages dotted the landscape, many of which appeared basic in structure, and in some cases, run down or derelict. There was a peculiar charm to it though that appealed to Heather; in a way not dissimilar to Bruce's cottage all those years ago. She recalled that first time he had taken her to see his home, nestled in the Scottish Highlands, before they had married. She remembered she had instantly fallen in love with it, the pull of the cottage almost as strong as the love she had for Bruce. And with each passing year of their marriage, that love had simply deepened. But without Bruce, was the cottage, and the lifestyle she had enjoyed there, still enough for her? Being in Santorini had certainly given her time to think, and plenty to think about.

Chapter 30

On the Thursday afternoon of their last week, two days before the end of the holiday, the scene was set for their gala dinner. It was the highlight of the holiday, and the celebration of their collective fortieth birthdays. Mel had arranged for extra staff to be brought in to support Carlos, both for the meal preparation and to wait on the tables; insisting tonight was one night Craig would not be allowed into the kitchen to help. Mel said it was as much his fortieth celebration as it was hers, Jenny's and Heather's, giving him strict instructions to let his hair down and be waited on, for once.

JoJo had echoed the sentiment. He was well aware Craig had a tendency to put himself in the background, forever shy if caught in the limelight, or draw attention to himself. Whilst his humility was one of the things he loved about him, JoJo also yearned for him to have more confidence and enjoy life, whilst he was still young enough to do so. Craig had undergone a lot of sadness, as well as being forced to work hard for everything he had achieved. Nothing had ever been handed to him, or Amy, on a silver platter; with him also knowing how easily everything could be taken away too. Consequently, he struggled to fully appreciate, or enjoy the fruits of his labours, fearful how long they would last. Life was tenuous, he understood that more than most. But he did need to let his hair down more and learn to relax. JoJo knew, for Craig this was a work in progress, a challenge he was more than up for supporting, once they were married.

"Mel's right, Craig," he said, nodding in Mel's direction. "You're not to leave my side tonight on the pretext of checking the food. And in terms of dancing, I intend to boogie the night away, as if there's no tomorrow. I'll show you some moves, ladies - George Michael will have nothing on me by the time the night is up!" He gave them a look that left them wondering what he had in store for their entertainment.

It was going to be a formal affair. Champagne would be flowing throughout the evening, and the 'best of the 80s music' would be streamed for everyone to get up and dance to, once the food was finished. Mel had warned them earlier that afternoon, "woe betide anyone who doesn't have a hangover in the morning, or cries off too early. Or worse still, doesn't hit that dance floor!" At the time, the terrace was being decked with balloons and strings of fairy lights; scented candles being dotted around to create a perfumed atmosphere, as well as a deterrent to keep the bugs at bay.

They had all contributed their ideas to the menu throughout the previous week, allowing Carlos to provision all their favourites, and ensure nothing went to waste. Although, looking at the final selection, for them to get through all the courses they had planned would be a feat in itself.

"Right, I'm off to get my shower and change into my party clothes," Mel announced to the group around five o'clock. "Cocktails at seven, with food from eight, is the plan. So, don't be late!"

Mel had gone to a lot of trouble, saying nothing of the expense involved, so tonight was going to be a night to remember.

Approaching midnight, and the group was not only starting to show signs of tiredness, but the copious amounts of alcohol consumed was resulting in tongues becoming lose, finding some of them opening up in a way that left a few surprised, if not shocked faces among them. The dancing had not long since finished, the table was littered with empty champagne and wine bottles, and most of the candles had burned out. The group was sitting around the terrace, relaxed and soaking up the final moments of the evening, before heading up to their respective rooms, to await their hangovers.

Their celebration party, whilst a happy occasion, had acted as a catalyst. It had not only marked the end of a wonderful three-week holiday, but the realisation that life was due to resume in a few short hours. They would all be returning to the real world, and everything that meant. Saturday morning would see Heather and Jenny heading to the airport, along with Craig and JoJo, who had managed to book seats on the same flight as Jenny, directly into Manchester. A taxi had been booked for eleven o'clock to collect the four of them with their luggage, allowing plenty of time to check in ahead of their mid-afternoon flights.

Mel, along with Sarah and Jake, were flying out early the following morning, directly into Heathrow. Whilst this gave them a few more hours' time around the villa, in reality it did not amount to much. Mel needed to drop the hire car off at the airport at seven o'clock on Sunday morning, resulting in a very early wake-up call for

Sarah and Jake – the idea of which neither of them found appealing.

As Mel stood up to start blowing out the remaining candles, Jenny grabbed her arm, pulling her back down into the chair. "Have I told you I don't want to leave here? I've had such a wonderful time, and I don't want to go home and face Jason, or that bloody woman he's been shacking up with." Her words slurred as she drained the last of the brandy JoJo had found in the house and brought out to them. "This will finish the evening off nicely," he had said, pouring them all double measures.

"Neither do I," Heather added, equally tipsy, her tone of voice quite maudlin. "At least you've got Emily and Harry waiting for you, Jenny. I've got no one. Just an empty house, with my dad in a nursing home – hardly remembering who I am these days, and a sister who's only got time for her own family. It's just me and a cat, who's frankly not bothered if I'm there or not. I'm just rattling around in a cottage, miles from anywhere."

"Have I told you, I've decided I'm going to divorce the bastard as soon as I get home?" Jenny continued; her question directed at no one in particular, and completely insensitive to Heather's observations or feelings. "Two years, watching him make an exhibition of himself, with a woman, almost young enough to be his daughter. And where's that left me? The laughing stock of the staffroom, no doubt. Anyway, enough is enough, I've decided. She's welcome to him. Men, who'd have them?" Whilst some people were happy drunks, Jenny was not one of them. And certainly not when she was on the subject of her errant and soon to be ex-husband, by the sounds of the way the discussion was going. The holiday had given her plenty of thinking time, and now that her mind was made up, she was determined to share it with her friends.

"They're not all bad," Heather replied thoughtfully. "Bruce was kind. I miss him."

"Yes, and where's that left you? Alone again, like me and Mel. Who'd have thought, at forty, not one of us would have a decent man among us! You're widowed, I'm soon to be divorced, and Mel here's a single mum, with neither sight nor sound of Sarah's father for the last twenty years." Looking around at her friends' shocked faces, she appeared on a roll. "Perhaps we should all be like Craig and just turn gay. We might have a bit more luck then, what do you think ladies?" she asked, insensitively.

"I'm not sure it works like that, Jenny," JoJo replied, calmly. It was an attempt to defend his partner and at the same time take some of the heat out of the discussion. Particularly noting Mel's face when the comments about Sarah's father were made, and the embarrassed look Sarah had given her mother. "You don't just decide to become gay overnight, Jenny. You must realise that? And also understand that Craig had not been living his true life before we met." JoJo had to be careful in terms of how much he could say, without mentioning Amy, or touch on Craig's feelings towards his wife before her death. Talking along those lines would only have provoked an even stronger response from her friends, and an argument was the last thing they needed after a few drinks. Tempers were already flared and emotions high. Removing their rose-tinted glasses about their friends' idyllic marriage would certainly not have helped calm things.

"Look, it's late. Let's not spoil the evening," Mel began, taking her lead from JoJo.

Before she could say anything else, Jenny continued. "Mel, why have you never told us anything about Sarah's father? In all these years, I don't recall you ever mentioning a single word about him, not even his name, or how you met him. What's the mystery? Is he still around, or did you just lose touch?"

"Yes, and there's a reason for that." Mel looked around at her friends, completely unprepared to be drawn on that subject. "I suggest we call it a night, and I'll see you all in the morning."

It was not quite the conclusion to the evening she had hoped for, but as far as Mel was concerned, it was certainly the end of the evening.

Chapter 31

As Mel lay in bed, restless and struggling to get to sleep after the highs of the party, she pondered the question Jenny had asked her, and more specifically her reaction to it. Had she been overly sensitive, even rude in the way she had responded? And importantly, why had she never confided in her closest friends, or anyone other than her brother about the events of that evening? It was over twenty years ago now and she still had not been able to process it, or move on.   The look Sarah had given her was also etched on her mind – that same look she had seen on numerous occasions, whenever the question of her paternity was raised. It was a sorrowful look that she could not explain, and in reality still did not know how to deal with.

With the passage of time, why should this still have such an effect on her feelings, or the sensitivity of what had happened? Or was she perhaps guilty of overthinking the issue? Was it time to come clean, tell Sarah the truth and deal with the consequences? After all, she had raised it with James a couple of months previously when Sarah was in Australia, and the sky hadn't come crashing down yet, had it?

Going downstairs to get a drink of water, her mind went back to the fateful evening of the Millennium party, New Year's Eve, 1999. She had been nineteen, basically the same age as Sarah was now. She was home from university for the Christmas holidays, feeling grown-up and looking for some fun, after months of studying law and politics.

She remembered the few days leading up to Christmas Day, and even now could only describe them as 'weird', with the days between then and New Year becoming even less normal. Everyone around the house appeared to be playing a part, not themselves. At the time Mel could not work out the reason for that. Her parents, who normally had a fractious relationship, were for once acting all loved-up, leaving her and James confused and unsettled by their behaviour.

It later transpired that it had all been an act, for the sake of appearances, a situation of which neither Mel nor James had been aware.

Their father's latest affair had apparently ended a few weeks earlier. Lawrence Barker MP had been caught with his pants well and truly down, with none other than the Speaker's wife in his House of Commons office. It was late one evening, when everyone should have long since vacated the building. A security guard had walked in on them after noticing the lights on, reportedly hearing strange animal sounds coming from behind the doors. The scandal, had it ever been allowed to come out, would certainly have ended Lawrence's parliamentary career, to say nothing of his marriage, which, at best, at that stage could only have been described as superficial.

Mindful of the embarrassment it would have caused Mel's mother, Julia Milton-Barker, the story had been quashed - at great personal and financial expense to Lawrence's father-in-law. Geoffrey Milton had managed to call in a few favours at his club, "for the sake of the family's reputation," he had told his wife, when she saw how much hush money he had been forced to part with. The Milton name was well respected in London, old money, and the humiliation his son-in-law's behaviour would have caused had to be avoided, at all costs.

In exchange for the cover up, and the avoidance of a scandal, Geoffrey extracted a promise from Lawrence that he would mend his ways; otherwise, there would be untold consequences, he had warned him. Geoffrey had never believed Lawrence was right for his only daughter, always suspecting he had used Julia as a stepping stone into the world and lifestyle he craved. He traded on the family's money and connections to enhance his own political agenda, and in so doing move himself into the upper echelons of society, mixing with the right sort of people.

There was no doubting Lawrence was good looking, well educated and exuded charm and charisma, with his working-class background making him stand out from the usual public-school boys Julia was accustomed to socialising with. And there was an edge about him. A determination that displayed a darker side. He was different and played on the differences to his advantage, soon succeeding in making Julia fall for his charms, if not her parents. Tolerance of their daughter's choice was the best they could offer.

That Christmas, Lawrence was being extra solicitous to Julia in an attempt to make amends. All Mel remembered of that time was how creepy, contrived and uncomfortable it had felt to be around them when they were together. It was as if a picture of happy families was being played out, for anyone who cared to show an interest.

Having been away at university, and hence shielded from the worst of it, Mel had been oblivious to the real reason for their behaviour, with everything only becoming clear a couple of years later, when his promise to be faithful had once again been broken. This led her mum to finally reach her senses. Julia had had enough, and she was no longer embarrassed to tell anyone the real reasons for her demands for a divorce from the lying, cheating, bully of a husband.

Mel's estrangement from her father resulted in her siding wholeheartedly with her mother, the rose-tinted glasses a daughter wears long since having been removed. Although by this time Sarah was nearly three years old, Mel was still raw from the way her father had treated her following her pregnancy. His reaction, when she refused to have the abortion he'd demanded, resulted in their relationship never fully recovering. She listened patiently to the long list of woes and venom Julia spouted against her erstwhile husband, feeling a real empathy for her mother. For the first time she realised the full extent of what her mother had been forced to endure.

Mel also recalled the millennium party she had attended, hosted by one of James' Hooray Henry friends from Eton, at his parents' country house in Surrey. They were away in the Caribbean for the holidays, leaving their son to fend for himself, a cellar full of fine wine at his disposal. James, along with a group of friends, had been invited to attend and stay over for the night, with the assurance there would be enough food, drink and drugs on offer to ensure the New Year went with a bang.

James initially had been reluctant to include Mel in his plans, but equally sensing the toxic atmosphere at home, was loathe to leave her desolate and alone whilst he partied. Most of the guys that were going to the party he knew, and generally speaking they were decent types. And as far as the others were concerned, Mel was sensible enough to give them a wide berth, he presumed. Eventually, agreeing to her tagging along, they had both packed a small bag, thrown it into the back of his Mini Cooper and hit the road.

It had taken James an hour to drive down to Surrey, Mel recalling how cold she had felt in her flimsy party dress by the time they eventually pulled into the secluded, sweeping gravel driveway of the restored country manor house. It was miles from anywhere, and at one stage they had considered turning back, believing themselves to be lost. However, the sight of the house that met them was truly amazing, leaving Mel particularly awestruck. The house was beautiful, and even without the vibrant spring flowers or summer colours, the gardens looked stunning. It was obviously well maintained, regardless of the season or time of year.

Abandoning the car, they made their way towards the front door, which despite the weather had been left wide open. There were loud noises reverberating from somewhere at the back of the building, with people hanging around in the grounds, bottles in hand and clearly already in the party mood.

Once inside, James soon became distracted by a group of friends, leaving Mel to wander around by herself – taking in the relaxed style of the property against the traditional furnishings, whilst noting how exquisitely everything had been arranged. It felt homely and comfortable, and after the charade of her parents' house over recent days, she immediately felt some of the pent-up stress leave her body, as she relaxed into the party mood.

"Can I get you a drink?" She turned, and saw a good-looking man standing behind her, his fringe flopping over his eyes; the brightest blue eyes she had ever seen staring back at her. "I'm George, George Theakston by the way. I don't think we've met before." He was tall, with broad shoulders, and the most delicious smile, his top lip lifting slightly at the corner when he smiled, producing a cheeky grin.

"Err…. thank you, yes please," she replied, falteringly. She noticed the way his eyes were boring into her, almost as if he was assessing a priceless work of art. "I'm Melissa, by the way. My friends call me Mel and no, I don't believe we have met. I've come with James. I'm his sister." Mel still recalled how confused it had made her feel, that first and what turned out to be her last meeting with George.

"Right, James' sister, follow me," he said, taking her hand and continuing to smile back at her confidently. "And we'll work on becoming better acquainted, shall we?" Mel had simply followed, in awe of this handsome stranger, who had appeared from nowhere to claim her.

After several more drinks, the origin or content of which she was unsure, as well as some dubious drugs that seemed to be being handed around freely, like sweeties at a kid's party, Mel was completely relaxed, albeit feeling slightly woozy. The music had been toned down, and the tempo of the night had changed. They had all been outside to let fireworks off to welcome in the new millennium, and on returning back inside, rather than the night air waking her up, it had created the opposite effect. She suddenly felt very drowsy.

Although no one had specifically allocated her a room in which to sleep, or even noticed she was there, she was at the stage where she needed to sleep. So, she casually mentioned to George that she wanted to go to bed. Some people had already left the party, mainly couples who'd had the sense to pre-order taxis. Whereas others, largely groups of lads, were still drinking. They were acting raucously, showing no obvious intention of stopping. Some had even crashed out on the staircase, or the sofas in some cases, with glasses or cans still in their hands. Other bodies sprawled out on the rugs, surrounded by expensive cushions and throws that had been pulled from the furniture and flung to the ground.

"Follow me, I know where we can lie down," he had replied, confidently taking her arm and leading her upstairs to the first floor. He opened a series of doors until he eventually found a bedroom that no one had already claimed.

"Oh look, it's got a double bed – big enough for two," George had exclaimed smiling. He swiftly pushed the door shut behind them, before falling onto the bed and pulling Mel down with him, the two of them laughing as they fell into the soft mattress. As the laughing subsided, they started to kiss, and before long he moved on top of her with ease. Sensing no resistance, he immediately started to fondle her small breasts through her flimsy party dress.

Mel didn't have the energy, or the inclination to fight his advances. As the kissing intensified, it was not long before George deftly removed her underwear, at the same time slipping out of his own trousers with practised ease.

Any protests Mel may have tried to put up would have been dismissed in the heat of the moment as he entered her.

Over the years, Mel often wondered whether she had been raped, or not. Her memories of that night were unclear at the best of times. She was certainly drunk, she was definitely high, but was she compliant in terms of wanting to have sex? Or, had George taken advantage of her and the situation? That was the question she often asked herself, and in the darker moments she felt she had been raped. At other times she was not so sure. Her memories could not be relied on.

He was an extremely good-looking man, someone she had been attracted to, with the attention he had paid her throughout the evening flattering. He made her feel special, at a time when she most needed to feel loved. Although in the cold hard light of the morning, as she woke to find herself alone and naked in a stranger's bed, she could not help thinking she had been used. That feeling only intensified when she learned George had hightailed it back to London at first light, in order to celebrate New Year's Day with his fiancée's family! Mel was livid.

Either way, it was not her proudest moment, and definitely not a story she wanted to blab to the world, least of all to Sarah. What would it do for her to know she had been conceived as a result of a drunken moment, with a man engaged to be married to another woman? What's more, Sarah had recently, if unknowingly, come face to face with her father, so how would that make her feel? Especially as she had got on so well with him, according to James.

Whilst keeping the incident to herself had created some issues in those early years, she had successfully managed to avoid telling her friends, or her parents, who the father of her unborn child was, or the circumstances that had led up to her becoming pregnant. Until now, and other than James, the only moment Mel had been sorely tested had come many years later, when Sarah was almost ten years old.

Mel and her mum had unwittingly got onto the subject of Mel's father's behaviour, prior to their divorce. It was over a rather nice Sauvignon Blanc and a late luncheon in a swanky restaurant in the West End. They'd had a girly shopping trip and were rewarding themselves. Julia, by this stage was well and truly over her marriage, happily divorced and able to recount some of her ex-husband's indiscretions without fear of reprisal, or concern about what others might think. It was water under the bridge, with her even finding humour in some of the anecdotes she shared.

By this stage, Lawrence had remarried, so was well and truly out of her life; unable to influence her, or her behaviour any more. "Good riddance," she often said, especially after she had decided to move on and seek out other lovers to warm her bed. After all, she was an independently wealthy woman, in the prime of her life. Someone who was no longer shackled to an egotistical bully.

"To think, he was once caught with his pants down, humping Sylvia Theakston, no better than a wild dog; you know, the mother of that nice boy who went to Eton at the same time as James. I'm sure you've met him, haven't you? Anyway, her husband at the time was the Speaker of the House of Commons, and quite a catch. He was a very handsome man, bit of a silver fox, if I recall correctly. He'd once toyed with becoming a vicar, I believe, before turning to politics. Quite bizarre really. Thankfully Daddy managed to hush it all up at the time. Not sure what she was doing messing around with your father, though!" she had said, recalling the incident with some glee.

Although Julia was laughing, Mel went almost cold. Having never heard the details surrounding this particular story before, as much as she had wanted to confide in her mother, she assessed that now was certainly not the right time. The knowledge that she and Sylvia shared the same grandchild would undoubtedly knock the smile off her mother's face and after a couple of glasses of fine wine, Julia's reaction, or language, could not be relied upon.

No, that particular little pearl of wisdom would have to wait for another day. Leaving Mel questioning, not for the first time, if that day would ever come!

Chapter 32

September arrived, and for Jenny it was the start of a new school year and the time to enact the plans she had devised whilst staying at the villa. The holiday was almost a distant, if not pleasurable memory. What those three weeks away had given her though was the space and time to contemplate what she wanted from life, what her future needed to look like. No longer was she prepared to put up and shut up, standing by whilst Jason played his little game.

Emily and Harry had been pleased to welcome her home and thankfully were not at all traumatised by the time spent with their father, that woman and her young son, the name of whom Jenny could not be bothered to recall either. Jason had by all accounts made an effort with the children when she had been away, even taking them up to Scotland for a few days camping, as well as allowing them to have friends to stay over. They had gone out for pizzas and burgers, or prepared BBQs in the garden, so intent was Jason on keeping his children happy. He had definitely splashed the cash, thought Jenny to herself, when Emily told her what they had been doing. No doubt to assuage his guilty conscience, she believed, as she listened to her daughter happily telling her how they had spent their holidays. Whilst Jenny was glad her children were happy, it did irk her that he could make the effort when he wanted. Just not for her, it would appear.

On the flight home, whilst Craig and JoJo had snoozed in their seats across the aisle from her, Jenny had quietly mulled over the pros and cons of a divorce – from every imaginable angle. It dawned on her that perhaps she had been too hasty declaring her intention to her friends the evening of the party. After a few drinks, when her tongue was a little loose and without giving the concept its full consideration, or even mentioning it to Jason, was she being fair? Now though, with the holidays over, and the drudge of normal life returning, she knew she was right to draw a line under her marriage.

"What do you think, Mum?" Jenny had asked her mother a few days later. She had called in after school one Friday evening, finally remembering to bring with her the fridge magnets she had bought from the gift shop in Santorini; a ceramic one of a little donkey and one with a stunning photo of the sunset. The photo had been captured over the rooftops of the hilltop town of Oia, one of the most picturesque places Jenny had ever visited.

The kids were both out and she had a couple of hours to herself.

"Do you think I'll be able to cope with two teenagers, by myself, or am I being too rash?" Panic had started to settle in, with Jenny fearing sixteen years of marriage was perhaps a lot to be throwing away.

"Oh, love," her mum had replied, unable to disguise the gentle sigh in her voice. "I can't tell you what to do, other than to say you've got to be happy. And if being married to Jason isn't making you happy anymore, then perhaps it is time to do something about it. Marriage isn't always easy, and we all have our ups and downs to deal with. Only you two know if you can survive this, or whether you even want to try. What does Jason say, does he want a divorce?"

"I've still not specifically mentioned a divorce yet." Jenny had tried to discuss it the previous weekend when he had called around. They were interrupted when his mobile rang, and the moment was lost. "I guess at some stage he'll want to draw a line under whatever it is we have at the moment. He knows I'm not happy, but every time I try to start the conversation, something happens, or it doesn't feel like the right moment. Our relationship is neither one thing nor the other. We're married but separated. He's half moved out, but some of his clothes are still hanging in the wardrobe. And his tools are still all over the shed, and I'm not sorting them out!" Jenny took a slug of the wine her mum had poured. "I feel like my life has been paused, put on-hold in case he feels like coming back when this midlife crisis, or whatever it is, has passed. He's moved on, it's just with all his stuff still around, and him popping home whenever he needs a screwdriver, how can I move on? Can you imagine me bringing a friend, or another man back, with all his junk littered around? I'm not sure how that would go down, are you?" The frustration was obvious in her voice.

"Well, you really need to speak to him, love," Pat replied, conscious this was the first time her daughter had mentioned another man, or even the concept of moving on in any serious way. Until this point, Pat had sensed her daughter harboured a desire to get back with her husband, and was playing the long game. If there was a new man on the scene, well, perhaps that was no longer the case.

"This last couple of times we've spoken about it, you seem to have become more determined, as if you've made your mind up. So, perhaps the time's right," Pat observed sagely. "Do you want me to have the kids to sleep over at the weekend, so you can talk without being interrupted?" she offered. "Or if you just want the house to yourself to entertain a friend perhaps, then they're welcome to stay here anytime," she probed, wondering whether her daughter would offer any more information about this mystery man.

"Yes, you're right. I've got to grasp the nettle and not keep putting it off, because it's not going away, is it?" she said, smiling at her mum. Although reading her expression like a book, she felt the need to clarify. "And Mum, before you start wondering, there's no one else on the scene. So don't go getting any ideas on that score. I think I've had more than my fill of men for the time being at least, don't you? I won't be making that mistake again. Not for a very long time!"

Chapter 33

As Heather's taxi from the airport approached her Highland cottage, she was surprised to see that it looked strangely bleak and drab. For the first time in living memory, the sight of it had failed to work its usual magic on her, or uplift her spirits in the way it had from that day she had first seen it. Although it was only August and still the height of summer, the clouds were heavy, with rain looking imminent. The usual bright sunlight was hidden from sight, creating a grey tinge to the landscape.

"Bet you're glad to be home?" suggested the taxi driver in a kindly tone, as Heather paid him the fare, plus a generous tip for carrying her suitcase to the door. He had chattered most of the journey, giving Heather little time to relax, or even get a word in edgeways by way of having a discussion. "No doubt, time to put the kettle on," he'd laughed as he ambled back to his cab, his radio already screeching details of his next fare.

"Yes, it's always time for tea. Thank you," she replied lethargically, forcing a smile onto her face, whilst slowly putting the key in the door. There was no obvious hurry to get inside.

Switching the lights on and removing her coat, Heather shivered. The cottage felt unusually cold and damp for late August. The warmth of a fire was not something she would normally need at this time of year, but as she struggled to get warm her body seemed to be missing the heat of the Greek sunshine on her back. The sight of the cat curled up on the window seat made her smile, although the fact he neither miaowed nor mewed on seeing her did little to raise her spirits.

"I see I've not been missed, Misty." Heather made a vain attempt to at least get the cat to acknowledge her presence. "Mrs McNally's obviously been looking after you too well," she said, rubbing the cat's ear when it became clear that Misty had no intention of moving off her cushion. Heather's elderly neighbour had offered to pop in every couple of days to put fresh food and water down and change the litter tray. Otherwise, Misty was an independent, if not particularly affectionate cat, and certainly not an animal that needed people to pander to her.

"Right, let's get that kettle on and I'll start unpacking." Heather continued talking to herself, as she moved the suitcase to the bottom of the stairs and flicked the radio onto its usual channel. Since Bruce's death she had developed a tendency of talking to herself, without even realising she was doing it, even on occasion answering herself when the mood took her. The silence in the house could be deafening; the background noise of the radio making it just that bit more tolerable.

By dinner time, Heather had unpacked her suitcase, put the first load of washing into the machine and checked on her house plants, pleasantly surprised to see they were all still alive, some even coming into bloom in her absence. "Thank you, Mrs McNally," she said with a sigh, grateful her neighbour had taken it upon herself to water these when she had come in to feed Misty. By six o'clock the house had warmed up a little, and the promised rain had held off. As Heather sat on the settee ready to watch the evening news, a defrosted ready meal for one on her lap, still in its aluminium tray, she felt desolate. After three weeks of fresh air and sunshine, good company and laughter, delicious food and wine, to now come home to a cold, empty house, well, it felt completely deflating. The highs of the holiday had fizzled out almost faster than it had taken the kettle to boil, leaving her to wonder whether it had all been worth it.

As the news played out in the background, flicking between coverage of stories that did nothing to capture her imagination, Heather found her mind wandering back to the beautiful island of Santorini, and the luxury of the villa. One moment, she was walking down the roads recalling the shops and bars, the farms and the buildings she had walked past on her almost daily travels. She recalled conversations with the locals, even the occasions in the bodega or the taverna when she had taken her phrase book out of her beach bag in an attempt to order a glass of wine, or a bottle of water, in Greek. Then ended up laughing at herself when she saw their reactions. Greek was a difficult language to master on a good day, but when she attempted to speak it in her broad Scottish accent, what chance did the locals have of understanding her?

The next moment, she was staring out at the water, marvelling at the vistas, the sunlight playing games as it danced on the clear blue Aegean Sea beyond her. Whether it had been the early morning sunrise, the glare of the midday sun or even the gentle sunset, it had simply been magical. And the moonlight was something else, with the countless stars and constellations clearly visible in the clear night skies. JoJo had impressed everyone with his knowledge of the stars and planets, confidently pointing out the Milky Way, along with some of the other wonders in the night sky. Those evenings, when they had all just sat and talked after dinner, taking in the majesty of what was around them, had been so precious. Such special times.

"Yes, on balance it was certainly worth it," Heather concluded to herself as she retired to her bedroom later that evening. "It's just time to get back to reality now," she admitted reluctantly, switching off her bedside light as she laid down and tried to sleep.

By the last week of September Heather's restlessness at being home had still not settled. The summer was well and truly over, with the darker nights now drawing in. It was creating a sense of loneliness in her that appeared to be getting deeper by the day.

Heather was not one that tended towards moods or despair, but she knew she needed to do something to bring herself out of the current slump she was feeling. She tried to re-establish her routines, in an attempt to bring back her sense of order and ward off the depressive feeling being home was producing.

In the mornings, she would busy herself doing whatever housework needed to be done, or drive to the supermarket in the neighbouring town to pick up any essentials. Once or twice each week, she would visit her father or sister for a distraction. She would time her journey into Edinburgh for after the morning rush; avoiding people heading to work or school and avoiding adding to the growing traffic chaos around the city. In the afternoons, she would head to her workshop in the back garden and throw herself into her jewellery making. She was never sure whether it was a hobby or a business;

the little income it produced, thankfully not something she was forced to rely on.

There were a couple of commissioned designs that needed finishing and shipping out that were her priority. Other pieces that she had started working on before her holiday needed final touches adding, before being photographed ready to put on her Instagram page. There was also a selection of sketches she had drawn, for which she needed to source materials, as well as some designs that needed finessing before they would be at the stage where she could start to produce them. Normally by this time of year, she would be organised, with a selection of items already in stock and available for the Christmas market.

This year, whether it was the holiday to blame, or something more fundamental, Heather had struggled to conjure up her usual level of motivation. Her designs lacked something, and her heart was not in it. Every time she went back to the drawing board, or sifted through the designs she was working on, she found her mind was elsewhere. The inspiration she sought in all her usual places remained somewhat illusive.

"Come on – get yourself focussed, Heather," she chided herself, as another scrap of paper was screwed into a ball and thrown towards the now overflowing wastepaper bin. "What's wrong with you?" For days, every piece she had worked on had simply not worked out. She felt like Goldilocks, declaring each piece too big, too small, too clunky, not the right colour. Nothing seemed just right.

Staring out of the window at the mountains and fields that normally provided her the inspiration she sought, she sighed. She reached for the now cold cup of coffee that sat on the edge of her desk. Out of the corner of her eye she saw her tattered old notebook, sitting on top of a pile of brochures still in their cellophane wrappers, delivered whilst she had been away. The brochures were largely junk mail, but before they were confined to the recycle bin Heather normally sifted through them, occasionally finding ideas to inspire her designs. As she reached for them, her notebook fell off and lay open on the floor. The notebook was one of her most treasured possessions and travelled everywhere with her. It was full of all manner of things that had inspired her over the years, and if nothing else could be relied upon to bring a smile to her face.

"Oh, that's exactly what I need to do!" Heather almost shrieked when the page of doodles she had made on holiday caught her eye. Reaching for the book, she turned a few of the more recent pages. "Why on earth didn't I think about that before?" she exclaimed, suddenly pleased with herself.

Almost as if she's had a Eureka moment, she ran back into the house to make some phone calls. As far as she was concerned, she did not have a moment to waste.

Chapter 34

"So, what are your plans today?" Mel asked Sarah as she was getting ready to go to her café- cum-office. It was not quite eight o'clock in the morning, but it was already promising to be a beautiful day, almost an Indian summer. Mel was considering walking to the office. The exercise would do her good, and the fresh air would hopefully help with the mild hangover she was feeling after the night on the town the previous evening. Since she had returned home from Santorini there had been a lot of catching up to be done, both socially with friends and at the café. Odette, her office manager, had handled everything admirably in her absence, although now she was back there were things that needed her attention. Her priorities were specifically related to the expansion and the franchising proposals, with people she needed to see, and decisions that needed to be taken.

They had been back for just over three weeks, falling easily into a routine that suited them; Mel finally happy the house no longer felt so empty. When Sarah had initially gone away it had taken several months for her to adjust to the cold empty rooms, the solitude, the quietness. Although now she was home, it was creating a further period of adjustment, with a whole new dynamic around the house. Their new routine was nothing like the one that had existed before she had left for Australia, over seven months ago now. For one, that routine had not involved Jake!

"I'm not sure yet," she replied, yawning as she fed a small silver capsule into her coffee machine and pressed the on switch. "I think we're planning to head back down to Devon this weekend, to see Jake's grandparents again. They are so lovely. So, we'll probably need to get that sorted as soon as he surfaces. I've found a nice inn online, a few miles from their cottage. So, I just need to check it out and see if we could book a couple of nights there."

Jake's grandparents still lived independently in a small two-bedroom cottage, just outside Dartmouth, in a pretty little village not far from the sea. Both now in their eighties, they were remarkably sprightly and doing everything they could to avoid the 'extra help' the family was insistent on calling in for them. "We've lived in this village for over forty years, and we've got friends and neighbours who'd happily help with the odd job or two, if asked," his grandad had argued when Jake had enquired how they were coping, and whether they were getting out and about. "Your grandad's not doddery yet, and neither am I!" his grandma had added when he had gently probed if there was anything he could do, or sort out for them whilst he was in the UK. "Just come and visit us as often as you can. It's lovely to see you in person, and with such a pretty girl in tow, well, that's a bonus," his grandma had said with a twinkle in her eye, her comment making Sarah blush.

"So, what other plans have you two got?" Mel continued. The weekend was one thing, but her focus was more on the longer term. Mel was interested to understand where her daughter's mind was, to say nothing of what Jake intended doing whilst he was in the UK. As a house guest for the last few weeks, Mel had got to know him and his ways reasonably well; his exercise routines, his late mornings, his eating habits, his tastes in music. She had even noted the increasing number of personal items of his that were scattered around the house. His belongings were no longer confined to the bedroom he was sharing with Sarah. He was certainly making himself at home, and although Mel had grown fond of him in a strange sort of way, even enjoying having a man around the house again, him living indefinitely under her roof was not a concept she relished.

However, pushing him into making a decision too soon could drive Sarah out. Even back to Australia - and that was certainly not her intention. No, Mel needed to choose her words carefully whenever the subject of 'what's next' came up. Particularly as it was clear Sarah's option for starting university in September had now come and gone; the place she had deferred from the previous year effectively shelved. Mel knew her daughter's heart had never been in studying. She was not the least bit academic and had no interest in following the herd, simply because that was what others did, or what was expected of her. However, if that was no longer an option, what was?

"Well, actually Mum, we're thinking of heading up north to stay with Craig and JoJo for a few days," Sarah replied, now making the second cup of coffee, no doubt to take back upstairs for Jake, in an attempt to get him moving.

"Oh, that'll be nice," Mel replied, struggling to hide the surprise from her voice. "I didn't realise you'd spoken to Craig since we got back, or that you were planning a visit. Is everything going well with their wedding plans?"

"I'm not sure, as I've not really spoken to Craig. JoJo and Jake have been talking quite a bit though. It seems JoJo might be interested in Jake working for him, even helping him to finish off his qualifications whilst he's living over here; you know give him some real work experience. He also mentioned possibly sponsoring him if he needed to go back to college, or apply for a work visa, or whatever. I'm not sure exactly what it all involves, to be honest. When we go up, they can have a chat and work it out, can't they?" Sarah smiled at her mother as she spoke, the excitement evident in her face. "I've been thinking, I might even ask Craig if he wants any help in the restaurant whilst I'm at it, or perhaps some support with Poppy - because if Jake's working up there, I might as well be too. I don't want to sit around an empty apartment all day, waiting for him to come home, do I?"

"No, I don't suppose you do," Mel replied, a little taken aback that all this had been going on in the background without her knowledge. "It seems you've got it all worked out. So, I'm just wondering when you were planning on telling me?"

Mel was glad she had asked the question, although at a loss to understand if she had not done, would she have come down one morning to an empty house, a note saying 'See you soon Mum, love Sarah xx' propped up against the toaster?

"Oh, don't worry Mum!" Sarah went over to give her a hug, correctly sensing she was feeling a little put out by her revelations. "It's all happened very quickly. We only really decided last night, whilst you were out gallivanting, I might add! So, we were planning on telling you when you got home this evening. Jake's really excited, in fact we both are."

And on that note, she picked up the two cups of coffee and headed back upstairs, leaving Mel to contemplate what had just happened, her headache suddenly feeling much worse than she had originally thought.

Chapter 35

"Hi. I'm back, and you'll be pleased to hear the meetings all went well," JoJo announced excitedly as he walked into the kitchen at *Amelia's* around four o'clock in the afternoon. He had been driving for over four hours, and rather than feeling tired after the journey was buoyed up. "I think I'm finally happy with the latest plans for our house. I've just been speaking to Jim in the car," he added smiling over at Craig.

Craig was up to his eyes in preparation for that evening's service, his chef's whites smattered with bolognaise sauce and other substances JoJo failed to identify. "I'd come over and show you how happy I am, if you weren't covered in flour, or whatever else it is that's all down your apron," he laughed suggestively at Craig, noticing his hands busy kneading what looked like dough.

"Yes. The builders are finally on board, the drawings are complete and Jim says the planning application will be with the council by the close of next week. Then, as soon as we get the approval we'll be good to go!"

"That's brilliant news," Craig replied flatly, more than a little distracted. "Sorry, I'm really excited for you, it's just I'm busy at the moment, so can't really stop to chat. Why don't you grab yourself a drink, or something to eat?" Moving the bowl to one side, and picking up a second one that had been standing next to it, he continued to work as JoJo outlined some of the finer points he had discussed with the builders.

Craig was not really listening. Time was against him today. He was a man down in the kitchen after one of his sous chefs had phoned in sick, and problems at home had delayed his start. Preparations were taking longer than usual, with nothing seeming to go to plan. The clock was ticking, the restaurant would be open for business in less than two hours, and he was starting to feel the pressure.

"Craig, is everything okay? You look stressed. Can I do anything to help?" JoJo asked, sensitive to the fact that something must be wrong, although at a loss to understand what it was, or more importantly how he could help. He could tell Craig was not listening to him, nor appeared to be at all happy to see him.

JoJo had been away in London for a few days, staying in his old apartment and meeting up with clients and such, so had not been home for a while. Having now committed to Craig and their relationship, and to a full-time relocation to Yorkshire, he was having to balance his southern commitments as best he could. He was forever grateful that the internet allowed him to do so much online, and that he had someone in London to manage his other properties when he was not there. The property portfolio was relatively easy to deal with remotely, whereas some of his corporate clients were less so. They required regular face to face sessions, especially when there were issues that required his attention, or plans that needed to be adapted. His manner was both confident and reassuring, qualities they needed to steady the ship, and that could not be handled from a distance. After all, that was a huge part of the expertise they were paying handsomely for. He had learnt early on in his career that drawing the plans was the easy part of the architect's job.   Hand holding the client through the development phase was by far the hardest part of the premier service he offered.

He and Craig had spoken each evening whilst they were apart, and regularly messaged throughout the day – and at no stage had he sensed anything was wrong. Everything, even this morning when they had spoken before breakfast, had appeared to be in order, so what was bothering him now?   Granted, the house development was his project, and it was he that was finalising all the details, even footing the bill, but it was to be their home; the place where they would live once they were married. So, for Craig not to be excited was unusual, especially as they were now so close to the finish line. JoJo had been keen to ensure Craig was involved every step of the way, with all the plans and decisions to date being taken jointly. They had even had input from Poppy on how big her bedroom should be, the colour of her wardrobes and where her toy cupboard and dolls house would be built – two things JoJo had personally committed to construct once they were finally settled. So, him having the final meetings without Craig by his side wasn't the issue, surely?

They were now all living in the small house Craig had lived with Amy, the three-bedroom semi, with a shared bathroom, limited privacy and space at a premium. It was early days, and although there were awkward moments with Amy's things still evident around the house, her pictures and personal possessions scattered everywhere he went, they were making it work. It was certainly not ideal, but for the time being there was little alternative if they wanted to live together and commit to a proper relationship.

Following their holiday, they had taken the decision for JoJo to move in. Craig was comfortable that they, as a couple, had received tacit acceptance from Mel, Jenny and Heather. JoJo had been sceptical beforehand as to why this was so important to Craig, although remained reluctant to push the issue before their holiday, or create a scene once he was there. He did recognise however that it was a big issue for someone like Craig. A widowed man with a young child, to suddenly come out and define himself as homosexual, when the world until then had identified him as heterosexual. To JoJo the 'godmothers', as Craig repeated referred to them as a collective, had been an enigma; a problem he had never fully understood, but knew was important to Craig. Having now met them, and thankfully having won them over, it was a hurdle overcome, one less issue to worry about. This left Craig more relaxed to invite JoJo to move in with him, as well as to come out to his wider friend set - including the staff at the restaurant, completely oblivious to the fact it had been an open secret between most of them for some time anyway.

JoJo helped himself to a drink, plus a small snack from the fridge, realising he had missed lunch, and sat back patiently waiting, believing Craig would open up as soon as he had attended to the bread he was making. Eventually, realising that was not going to happen he forced the issue. "Come on Craig, just tell me what's the matter, please. I can sense something's wrong, and you're starting to worry me. You've not said a word since I've been sitting here. Put that bowl down for a minute and just tell me, please," JoJo pleaded after another ten minutes had passed, and other than shout at one of the staff who had walked past about something trivial, there had not been a single word uttered.

Craig looked up. Noticing there were tears in his eyes, JoJo walked over and put his arm around him. "Hey, what's the matter, mate?" he asked quietly, before turning to one of the other sous chefs. "Can you please take over while Craig has a few minutes?" JoJo steered Craig out of the kitchen and into his office at the rear of the building, closing the door quietly behind them.

Once the door was shut, Craig simply turned towards JoJo and almost whimpered. "It's Poppy, she's sick. JoJo, I can't lose her too, not like I lost Amy," before breaking down, sobbing.

Chapter 36

Mel was sitting quietly in the sitting room, her feet tucked beneath her on the settee, a mindless quiz show playing out on the television. She was wearing a sloppy jumper and exercise pants, her feet wrapped in the fluffy socks she loved to wear around the house. She had just eaten a late lunch off a tray on her knees, comfort eating, the dirty plates still languishing beside her. She was seriously contemplating closing her eyes and having an afternoon nap. The rain had been pelting down outside all day, with no indication it would be stopping any time soon, and it was forecast to get worse as the night progressed. It was a miserable Thursday; the end of September, with autumn definitely on its way. Summer now long gone, a distant memory.

Mel really should have gone into the office to catch up before the month's end, but having woken late had opted to phone in and say she would be staying at home. One of the joys of being her own boss. She was desperately in need of some 'me time' she realised, as she fed her trusty assistant, Odette, a line about needing to stay at home to do some essential tasks. The story failed to convince anyone, but who cared? She had no one to answer to. Sarah and Jake had left the previous morning, travelling up to Yorkshire to meet with Craig and JoJo, and as it was a day her housekeeper did not come in, the house was empty. The perfect time for her to relax and clear her mind.

"Why has life suddenly become so complicated?" Mel thought forlornly to herself. At forty she should have her life mapped out by now, surely? She was rich, successful and not bad-looking, even if she did say so herself. She had a daughter she adored, a mother and brother she loved and a father, who although she did not talk to, she recognised was still around if she ever got really desperate. So, why did she feel so out of sorts, and of all people, what did she have to complain about? Mel knew she needed to pull herself together sharpish, before this state of depression hardened, because that was somewhere she was not prepared to go again.

The holiday had been amazing. It had just not provided the lasting boost she had hoped for. Life had simply gone back into its comfortable rut. Whilst her business was booming, it was neither taxing her nor providing the excitement she craved anymore. There were no great challenges left, just more of the same. It had started to feel a little like she was on a hamster wheel, leaving her to wonder at what stage she should be jumping off. Everyone else seemed to be getting on with their lives. Craig was moving on with JoJo, Sarah would be leaving home soon, Jenny had taken a big leap forward in terms of sorting out her life and relationship. Even Heather appeared to have a spring in her step, so why couldn't she? What was holding her back?

Hearing the doorbell ring, Mel considered ignoring it. After all, she was not expecting anyone and really could not be bothered getting herself up. Looking like she did, without makeup, in her scruffs and in desperate need of a hair brush, whoever was at the door

Angela Hartley

would only run a mile seeing her, anyway. The ringing persisted.

Mel, eventually making her way into the hallway shouted, "okay, hang on a minute. I'm coming." Not at all pleased to have been disturbed, she became further annoyed when she finally opened the door to see the back of a man, as he retreated down the steps and away from her. He appeared to be carrying a small parcel in his left hand. The large black umbrella he was carrying disguised him, leaving Mel unaware who he was, or what his business might be.

"Hello, hang on a minute..." she shouted above the noise of the cars as they sped past the door. "Hello," she repeated, this time a little louder, standing on the wet step, anxious to attract his attention.

The man turned and looked directly at her. "Oh hello. Sorry to disturb you. I'm looking for Sarah, Sarah Milton-Barker. Is this the right house by any chance?" he enquired, politely.

"Yes, I'm her mother. Can I help you?" Mel replied, almost catching her breath as she returned his stare. It might have been twenty years since she had last seen him, but she would not forget those piercing blue eyes anywhere.

"Yes. I've got a package for Sarah. Is she at home perhaps?" he queried. "I've brought it back from Australia with me. Her uncle asked me to drop it off when I was in the area."

"No, she's not at home. You can leave it with me, if you'd like," Mel began, just as a flash of lightening lit up the skies and the rain became heavier. Feeling guilty that she was leaving him standing out in the storm, Mel suggested, "do you want to shelter inside for a few minutes, just while the storm passes?"

"Thank you, that would be very kind," he replied, his manners almost polished as he smiled back at Mel. It was a smile she had never forgotten, no matter how hard she had tried. The way his top lip curled up at the corner, lighting up his whole face. "I'm George Theakston by the way, I'm an old friend of James'." He entered the hallway, careful to shake the worst of the rain from his umbrella outside, before closing the door behind them.

"Hello. I'm Melissa, James' sister." It was obvious from the way he responded George had absolutely no recollection of her, or of the fact they had met. Had she really changed that much over twenty years? Or were there simply so many women he had slept with over the years that he could not be bothered to recall all their names or faces?

Handing over the parcel he had been carrying, George smiled. "Sorry if this is a little damp, and I sincerely hope I've not damaged it in any way. Apparently, Sarah left it in her bedroom. Your brother thought she would be missing it." He smiled, that smile again. "I was visiting, then called back, to see him again before I returned home. He gave me the address and asked me if I'd carry it home for her," he said, by way of an explanation.

"That's very kind, thank you. I hope it's not inconvenienced you," Mel added, more formally than she intended.

"Oh, that's no problem and it was no inconvenience, whatsoever. I only live a few miles away," George assured Mel. "I've no idea what it is, so I thought I'd better bring it around straight away. I only arrived home on Tuesday. Yesterday was a complete wash out. Jetlag doesn't get easier as you get older, does it?"

"No, I'm sure it doesn't." Mel, now curious to know what it was, opened the parcel. Smiling, she saw it was the small silver photo frame Sarah kept next to her bed, and had packed to take with her when she had left all those months ago. Mel had given it to her as a present for her thirteenth birthday, complete with a photo of the two of them blowing out the candles on her cake. Over the years Sarah had never changed the photo.

"Oh, I wondered where this had gone," Mel exclaimed, carelessly holding the frame up so that George could see what he had carried, before realising she needed to be careful what she said and did next.

"What a lovely frame, and what a beautiful photo," he commented. "Is that Sarah when she was younger?" he enquired. "And I presume that's you with her? I only met her briefly in Australia, so I can't say I know her too well. She seemed a lovely young lady, who spoke of you often. May I?" he asked, taking the frame carefully from Mel.

As Mel handed the frame cautiously to George, she never took her eyes away from his, watching the expression on his face as he studied the photo, a little too closely for her comfort.

"Sarah has a distinct look of my daughter, Ruby," he observed, after what appeared like an eternity to Mel. "She's just turned fourteen, and looking at the two of them you'd think they were sisters. It's uncanny, isn't it?" He gently laughed as he spoke.

"Yes, it is." Mel, feeling more than a little uncomfortable, took the frame back before George could comment further. She placed it face down on the hall table, making it clear from her actions that it was perhaps time for him to leave. The rain had ceased.

"Mel, do you mind me asking before I go, have we met somewhere before? It's just looking at that photo has given me a real déjà vu moment, and it's left me with the strangest feeling that we might have. The problem is, I'm struggling to think when, or where."

Today's storm might have passed, but as Mel looked at George she was unsure how to answer his direct question. She could lie, she could be vague, or she could tell the truth. It was her decision. Whichever way she went though, she feared the next storm was not too far off the horizon.

Chapter 37

"Hi Mum, just thought I'd ring you to let you know we're here safely." Mel noticed her daughter's voice was a little hesitant when she picked up the phone later that evening. It was only eight o'clock, it just seemed much later. And after the day Mel had had, a long hot bubbly soak in the bath was in order, with perhaps a glass of chilled wine to help her relax. She was then planning to nestle into bed with a good book, before hopefully getting a good night's sleep.

"Glad to hear that, darling. I was just heading for an early bath. Is everything okay? You sound a little worried." Mel was used to the nuance of her daughter's voice and tonight it had none of its usual upbeat tone. And certainly, it demonstrated none of the excitement she would have expected after listening to the pair talking through their plans before they had set off the previous day.

"Well, no, not really. That's why I thought I'd best call you. I'm a bit worried. I think something's wrong with Poppy, but neither Craig nor JoJo have said anything, so I'm not sure," Sarah began, hesitant how to continue. "We called at *Amelia's* for dinner when we arrived, as planned. Craig wasn't there. The staff said he'd gone home earlier that afternoon because his daughter wasn't well. They didn't know anything, or when he'd be back at work. When Jake and I drove around to the house to check everything was okay, JoJo suggested we call back tomorrow. He said now wasn't a good time. I'm phoning from the Travelodge; I just didn't want to go to bed without letting you know."

"Oh, that sounds odd. Thanks for letting me know, darling," Mel replied. "I'm sure it's nothing to worry about though. Why don't you and Jake have a good evening and I'll ring Craig in the morning. I'll let you know what he says, shall I?"

After hanging up Mel sat on her bed, contemplating whether to ring Craig or leave it until the morning, as she had told Sarah she would. Something niggled at her though. For Craig not to be at the restaurant, or for JoJo not to mention anything or even invite Sarah into the house, suggested all was not well. She wracked her brain to think of possible scenarios, at a complete loss as to what the issue might be.

Deciding to take the middle ground, Mel messaged Craig. That way he would at least know she was thinking about him and could reach out if he wanted to.

"Just spoken to Sarah. She sounded a little worried. I'm here all evening if you need to speak, just ring. Mel xx"

Five minutes later Mel's mobile rang, prompting mixed feelings when she realised it was Craig calling her straight back.

"Hi Craig. Is everything okay?" she answered quickly, none of the usual small talk.

"Hi Mel, it's JoJo. Craig's not feeling up to speaking at the moment. He suggested I ring you, to let you know what's going on."

"Okay, you're worrying me now, JoJo. What's happened – is Poppy alright? Sarah said the staff at *Amelia's* told her there was a problem with Poppy."

For the next ten minutes or so, JoJo outlined what the problem appeared to be, keeping the conversation as factual as possible, at the same time trying not to worry her more than was necessary.

Poppy had apparently been lethargic, according to her grandparents, when she had stayed with them when he and Craig had been on holiday in Santorini. She had been off her food, tired and generally out of sorts. Not her normal self at all. Ron and Jean had not been especially worried initially, presuming Poppy was simply missing her dad. Possibly even playing up or looking for attention, as kids do. After a couple of weeks when it had not settled, they suggested to Craig that he should probably make a doctor's appointment now that he was home, which he had done.

The doctor undertook a series of blood tests and examinations, the results of which had come back earlier that day. The doctor had phoned Craig at the restaurant to discuss the findings. A rare blood disorder had been detected, with a referral for further tests with a specialist being made as a matter of urgency. The doctor was not specific in terms of what the issue was, preferring not to speculate, or worry Craig unnecessarily. Her appointment should be expected in the next few days.

Craig was effectively left on tenterhooks in the meantime, simply waiting and worrying. Memories of Amy replayed in his mind, memories of the blood tests she'd had, tests that had detected her cancer. Logically, Craig knew blood disorders were a byword for all kinds of ailments, some more innocuous than others, but none of that stopped his mind going straight to the worst-case scenario. He had been there before and did not want to go there again.

As Mel sat and listened, she found herself unable to say anything. Earlier that day, she had been bemoaning her lot, worrying about the trivia that was going on in her life, whilst Craig had this to deal with. It was not fair, was it? Amy, having died from cancer was traumatic enough, but for Poppy, beautiful little Poppy at only six years old to be at risk too, was simply heart breaking. Words simply escaped her.

"What do you need me to do, JoJo? Just name it and I'll be there." It was all Mel could offer, knowing even that would never be enough.

"Thanks, I appreciate that. We'll be in touch. In the meantime, Craig's asked if you can let Heather and Jenny know, just in case. I don't think he's up to talking to anyone at the moment."

Assuring him she would do that, Mel hung up and sat back on the bed. Any plans she'd had to soak away the problems her chance meeting with George earlier that day had created, were suddenly pushed to the back of her mind. Her focus now was on Poppy and Craig, and the nightmare he must be going through.

Chapter 38

"What do you mean, you're packing up and going back to Santorini. Are you mad?" yawned Jenny, surprised as she listened to Heather early the following morning. She was discussing her plans for the following month, her face alight with excitement. "You've only been home a few weeks, so you surely don't need another holiday so soon, do you?" They were waiting on the group video chat for Mel to join. Regardless of the hour, Heather could not contain her joy, as she told Jenny she had spent the previous evening looking online at both flights and accommodation options for her forthcoming trip.

"No, I don't need another holiday, but I do need a change of scenery." Heather sighed, realising her friend did not appear to share her enthusiasm. "I recognised as soon as I got back home that something wasn't right, nothing felt the same. I felt depressed being around the cottage; everything just felt so small, so restricted. All the magic seems to have gone and I can't seem to focus on my designs; nothing's working, or inspiring me at the moment."

"But why on earth Santorini?" interrupted Jenny, taking a sip of her coffee as she continued waiting. She only had half an hour to spare before she needed to leave the house and head to school. She was starting to get impatient, and it was evident in her tone. "There wasn't that much to do there, other than lie around the pool and relax, was there? It was nice enough for a holiday. It wasn't that inspiring though. Can't you go somewhere else, closer to home perhaps, for your inspiration? Even go on one of those retreats, or whatever it is you artistic types do?" Jenny was tired and already feeling in a depressed state of mind, so, listening to her friend taking positive steps to improve her wellbeing was the last thing she needed at this hour of the morning.

Jenny was almost a month back into the autumn term. Her new class was decidedly more edgy than the previous year's, taking longer to settle down to their studies, and it was really trying her patience. It was more of the same in terms of pressure, without any noticeable reward for all her drudgery. The headteacher himself had even indicated to some of the senior staff that he was also feeling the pressure. He was anticipating Ofsted knocking on his door any day soon, with fears the school might be put into special measures, if things did not improve. Frankly, Jenny was at the stage where she'd had enough, professionally as well as personally. She was well and truly in a rut, with no obvious or easy options available to her.

Jenny had told Jason the previous Sunday that she wanted a divorce. She had mulled it over, finally deciding she had reached the end of her tether, as far as their sham marriage was concerned. She was forty and needed to move on, to start thinking about her own wellbeing. She did not want to remain chained to an arrangement that only appeared to be working for him. She knew it would be difficult initially, and could even get messy as they split their lives and home apart. The legal and financial arrangements would become tricky, with pensions and their lack of savings likely to be brought into sharp focus. It all left Jenny worried how she would survive in the long term, especially if he became difficult with her. "Money's not a sufficient excuse to stay married though, is it Mum?" she had replied when Jean had questioned her on how she would cope.

So, when Jason had returned Emily and Harry home around eight o'clock that Sunday evening, laughing and joking about their fun camping trip to the Lake District, how the tent had almost collapsed as they attempted to secure the guy ropes, whilst dumping bags of wet, dirty clothes and muddy walking shoes on the doorstep for her to deal with, it proved to be the final straw.

To say the conversation had not gone as planned was an understatement. Any attempts Jenny made to make Jason realise she was serious were laughed off. He chose to presume she was simply reacting to having to clear up after him and the kids once again, failing to see the funny side of their adventures. Further, rather than him accepting that the time was right to formalise their arrangement, he had thrown her a curveball, informing her that he was seriously considering moving back home. Spending time with Emily and Harry over the summer, and increasingly over the weekends, had made him realise he was missing out on them growing up. He even hinted living with his fling was not all it was cracked up to be. "Perhaps it's time to come home," he had suggested.

There was no mention of him missing her, or feelings for Jenny expressed in any terms. Just an arrogant assumption she would welcome him back with open arms, and on his terms. There was not even an attempt at an apology. Until then, she had taken no steps to change the locks on the doors, but as she watched him swagger back to his car, laughing off any suggestion of a divorce, it seemed that now might be the right time to call in the locksmith. That man was the limit, and she was left seething!

Before Heather had time to say any more about her plans, or Jenny had time to counter with her own feelings, Mel joined the call. Her flustered image appeared on the screen in front of them.

"Hi Jenny, Heather, sorry I'm late. I've just got off the phone to Sarah." She was a little out of breath and looking dishevelled.

"Mel, Is everything okay? You look awful, as if you've not slept all night!" For Jenny, tact had never been one of her strong points.

"Thanks, Jenny. To be honest, I haven't slept much at all. I've been up most of the night worrying about Poppy – hence why I messaged you both earlier to suggest we have a chat."

"Poppy?" questioned Heather. "Why, what's wrong with Poppy?" Heather had not spoken to Craig since they had all said good bye at the airport. Once again, she felt guilty for not being in touch, allowing herself to get reabsorbed by her own troubles.

"Yes Mel, what's the problem? Something must be seriously wrong for you to summon us for a video call at this hour of the morning. I've got to get to school, so it had better be quick."

"Well, I'm not really sure what the problem is – or more importantly what we, or anyone can do about it. I just thought I needed to share what I know."

After replaying the conversations she'd had with JoJo and Sarah the previous day, Mel could hear and see

Heather's gentle sobs on the other end of the line. Heather had always been the most sensitive, caring member of their group; always concerned about other people's welfare before her own. Never having had children, over the years she had channelled whatever maternal instincts she had into her godchildren. Sarah, Emily, Harry and Poppy had never been short of love, but of them all, it was no secret Poppy was her favourite.

"Why's this happening again? Hasn't he gone through enough, already?" she sobbed. "Surely Craig's wrong, or perhaps he's jumping the gun."

"Yes, we need to wait for the doctor to advise in a few weeks, after Poppy's seen the consultant and the results are back," Jenny agreed, her earlier irritations now parked. "In my experience, those symptoms are quite apparent in countless childhood related illnesses. I see a lot of fatigue and listlessness in our students, and more often than not it's a combination of growing pains, or bad diet, or something else that's relatively innocuous. So, perhaps we shouldn't worry." Jenny was no expert, however working with children and being responsible for safeguarding many a troubled teenager over the years had certainly taught her a lot. Even so, whilst trying to put a positive spin into the conversation, she remained concerned. Childhood cancers were certainly on the rise, and sadly the symptoms Poppy was displaying were clear indicators of these more sinister conditions, with the maternal links and similarities to Amy's condition not boding well, at all.

"Sarah and Jake are booked into a hotel up there for another few nights, so they're both on hand to help, should they be needed. And if I hear anything else, I'll let you know."

The Godmothers

As the three women hung up, all were left with a sense of foreboding. Each fought to dispel the memory of a similar phone call, six years earlier; the night Craig had contacted them to let them know Amy was unwell. "Lightning can't strike twice in the same place, surely?" they each silently prayed.

Chapter 39

Throughout October Heather felt powerless to do anything useful, placing whatever plans she may have had about going to Santorini indefinitely on the back burner, at least until there was news about Poppy's condition. She tried to remain positive, never allowing her mind to contemplate the alternative; operating virtually on autopilot, as she wandered around the cottage trying to occupy her mind and failing miserably to achieve anything of value.

She had phoned JoJo directly after the videocall with Mel and Jenny had ended, principally to let them know she was thinking of them all. Also, as Mel had done, she offered to do anything she could to help. As the one without any real commitments she could easily be on a direct train down to Sheffield and be with them within a few hours, if required.

"Thanks Heather, I'll let Craig know as soon as he gets home. He's just popped over to *Amelia's.* I think he wanted to at least open up, as well as let the staff know what's happening. They were obviously concerned when he'd left so suddenly the other day and have been great keeping things ticking over. I've stayed home with Poppy. We're just watching Frozen for the second time this morning, and between us have eaten a family packet of cheesy Wotsits for breakfast. I think Poppy thinks she's Elsa, and I'm Olaf, although my singing's not up to scratch, apparently," he laughed. Heather could hear Poppy giggling in the background.

JoJo had limited knowledge of children in any shape or form. What they liked to do, to eat, games they liked to play, or how to entertain them remained a complete mystery to him. So, spending time with Poppy and living under the same roof, morning, noon and night was proving to be a whole new learning experience. Each day presented its own set of challenges and pressures, with routines that he had never contemplated ever being involved in. The last few months had certainly opened his eyes to the concept of being a parent. What it involved, both the good and the bad!

Being an only child, JoJo had never had siblings around the house, or nieces or nephews to concern himself with as he grew up. He had only had himself and his wants to consider, living a relatively solitary and increasingly independent existence. He had grown up, selfishly never having to factor anyone else into the equation. Materially, he had wanted for nothing as a child, with parents that provided for his needs, sending him to public schools, enrolling him in the best clubs and ensuring he got introduced to the right people. However, there never seemed to be much love or emotion around the house. Hugs or cuddles were not things he associated with his parents. They both appeared aloof or detached whenever he was around, displaying a polite coolness with others. His parents were busy, professional people who really had not been cut out for parenting. So, as far as parental role models went, they had little, if anything, to offer their son by way of positive example as he grew into adulthood.

After leaving university JoJo moved far away from home, putting emotional as well as physical distance between him and his parents. He bought his first apartment with money his grandparents had left in trust for him; a smart, low maintenance bachelor pad in a modern purpose built complex. After a few years of working with a reputable, if niche firm of architects, he decided to branch out on his own, establishing a company that aimed primarily at redesigning business premises in and around London and the South East. All his concentration was ploughed into building up his client base and a name for himself, a reputation he could trade on. Life had been busy ever since, with work absorbing the majority of his energies. Family life or socialising were never his first priorities, with the few close friends he did have mainly male. And of them, none with children.

So, when he met Craig, and realised there was a mutual attraction, to learn there was a child in the picture, to say nothing of a dead wife, a mother and a clutch of sisters, it initially knocked him for six. In addition, Craig was only just coming to terms with his sexuality and had baggage, leaving every bone in JoJo's body telling him to simply walk away, not to get involved. JoJo, having had several short-term gay relationships before, was experienced enough to realise Craig had no understanding what he would be embarking on, if and when he decided to come out. However, there was a vulnerability in Craig that JoJo simply could not ignore. There was a sensitivity that touched a side of him that he'd never been exposed to, and he was captivated by it.

Although he knew he would be taking a huge risk, JoJo in hindsight had never fully assessed the true extent of that risk, or assumed it would ever develop into anything serious. A brief fling, some fun, even an opportunity to feel good about himself as he eased Craig through his transition was his only motivation. Children was not something he had ever baked into his life plan. He had certainly never seen them as being material to him, or any future relationship he might have. No, developing feelings for Craig was one thing, but a child, well, that was another matter entirely. Until now, JoJo had certainly not had any intentions of adapting his lifestyle to accommodate children. His patience had definitely never been tested to this level before. Somehow though, he was revelling in it!

"Elsa's one of my favourites too," Heather laughed in return. "I'm more than happy to come down and spend a few days watching Disney movies, if that would help. I presume you've got work to do, clients to see?" She was eager to suggest any way of relieving some of the pressure Craig and JoJo must be feeling, whilst at the same time wanted to make herself useful. "After all, I've nothing else to do," she thought to herself, without wanting to voice that. It would only make her sound completely sad, as well as desperate.

"Thanks. I'll certainly let Craig know. We're probably okay for now, though. Sarah's staying around for a few days and she's said she'd be happy to sit with Poppy if we both need to go out. And Jake's here too. I'm talking to him later today about possibly helping out with my business, which might ease some of the strain. I think he's keen to remain in the UK for the foreseeable, so he's looking for any help I can offer with that..."

"Well, you know where I am if you need me." As Heather hung up the phone she felt even more desolate than before at not being called upon to help.

As she stared out of the window, listening to the rain as it beat a steady rhythm against the panes of glass, she sighed. Greece would have to wait. She resigned herself to remaining in the wings, and waiting, at least until there was news she could act upon.

Chapter 40

"Mum, I know. Please don't worry. I promise I'll phone you, as soon as I hear anything." Sarah was becoming exasperated as she listened to her mum asking question after question, for what seemed the umpteenth time that day. "There's nothing you, or Heather or Jenny for that matter, can do – other than wait, like the rest of us. Phoning on the hour is not going to help, is it? The specialists know what they're doing." Sarah felt like an overworked telephonist, constantly fielding calls from everyone, churning out the same answers to family and friends alike. "Yes, everyone's fine." "No, there's no news yet." "Yes, we'll let you know as soon as there's any update." At least, she consoled herself, by doing so, they were leaving Craig alone. He was emotionally drained and had nothing else to offer, walking around the house like a zombie, waiting for the phone to ring, his mobile perpetually in his hand. Poppy's blood test results were expected any day now, so all that was left was for them to be patient.

Sarah had got into a routine of coming around to the house most days, to sit with Poppy and keep her company, or amuse her whilst Craig and JoJo got on with whatever they needed to do. Jake occasionally joined her, regularly making Poppy smile with his funny Australian accent and jokes about kangaroos. More often, he spent his time talking with JoJo. They had now had several exploratory discussions about how Jake could support JoJo's business, what work he could get engaged in and how it might help with his overall goal of getting sufficient hands-on experience to finally gain his qualifications. It sounded promising.

Poppy continued to be lethargic and off her food. Other than that, there were no obvious signs of her condition, whatever that was, worsening. The consultant had suggested she remain off school until they had a clear diagnosis, after which he would make a judgement call on the right course of action. Craig had initially wanted to simply sit by her side and wait, unprepared to leave her for any moment, or run the risk of something serious happening to her when he was not around. He fetched and carried whatever she asked for, treating her like the princess she was. Bed time became the only time when she was left alone, and even then he had installed a monitor in her bedroom, just in case she woke in the night, or called out for him. He was looking for any signs of deterioration. Forever hoping for the best, always expecting the worst. No amount of discussion would stop him drawing parallels with Amy.

After a while, JoJo decided enough was enough. He was a patient man, but it was not healthy for Craig to be acting like this, or for Poppy to be under constant scrutiny. Her every move watched, her every action analysed, her every whim acted upon.

"Why don't you leave Poppy with me, or Sarah for a few hours? Go and have a lie down, or take a walk in the park to get some fresh air. Better still, why not go and check on the restaurant? Marco rang last night and you've not rung him back yet, have you?" questioned JoJo. "Whatever you do, just do something, because all you're doing is wandering around, fretting, making us all feel nervous. You need a break."

JoJo was worried about Craig. He had hardly slept or eaten in the last few weeks, napping on the sofa when he failed to keep his eyes open in front of the television, or tossing and turning when they eventually made it upstairs to bed. He was also nibbling on food; his normal healthy appetite had deserted him.

JoJo attempted to cook for all of them, although he was not the best of cooks, nor very good at planning family meals. He was used to city living, which involved eating out, or late-night takeaways, even microwaving meals for one if he was alone in his apartment. He'd rarely entertained, or had cause to invite people over, preferring to keep himself to himself.

Living with Craig and Poppy had changed all that, and under normal circumstances, his attempts at making dinner would have made them all laugh. There would be pots and pans discarded all over the kitchen, burnt and often indescribable offerings setting the smoke alarm off, with whatever food eventually making its way to the plate being presented in a less than appetising way. At the moment though, no one seemed bothered what he put in front of them, or what it looked or tasted like. Consequently, the weight had dropped off Craig, leaving him looking gaunt and exhausted, the worry making him appear much older than his years would suggest. Poppy was getting away with snacking on foods that were not good for her. No one dared say no, when she asked for another biscuit, another packet of crisps, another chocolate bar. No one wanted to annoy her, or make her more anxious. She already looked like the life was draining out of her, her complexion pale and pasty.

Eventually he replied, "I might," in an attempt to placate JoJo, although his heart was clearly not in it.

"Well, I'll put the kettle on. We can have a cup of tea whilst you think about it….." JoJo began, just as Craig's mobile phone started to ring. He seized it from the table, recognised the number instantly and pressed the accept button.

"Yes Doctor, it's Craig here. Yes, now's fine to talk ………" he said anxiously, quietly closing the kitchen door to prevent Sarah and Poppy overhearing them talking from the lounge. They were both busy watching television, the music clearly audible. He sat down at the kitchen table, bracing himself to receive the news he had been praying for, but dreading at the same time.

For the next five minutes, JoJo watched the expressions on Craig's face as he listened to the doctor speaking, his partner barely offering a word in response to what he was being told. From Craig's body language, it was difficult to judge whether it was good or bad news. He sat, almost statue like, the concentration on his face obvious, giving no signs either way.

"Thank you Doctor, for your time and for going through that with me. It's good to know," Craig said after what seemed like an age. Now smiling over at JoJo, he added, "I'll make an appointment, as you've suggested, and bring Poppy into the surgery to see you. First thing tomorrow morning. Thank you once again, you can't imagine what that means to me. It's certainly a massive weight off my mind."

Immediately, after hanging up the phone, he turned to JoJo and broke down, unable to contain his emotions any longer, emotions that had been bottled up for so long. Emotions he would have struggled to articulate, even if he had wanted to. Taking him in his arms, JoJo looked directly into his eyes. Still unable to read exactly what they were saying.

"So, what did he say?"

"It's not cancer." Craig sobbed; the relief he was feeling obvious as he slumped into JoJo's embrace. "I suppose that's the main thing. I'm not sure I took in much more after that. He says Poppy is very anaemic, and that's highly likely what's causing the symptoms she's feeling. Especially the tiredness and the loss of appetite, and the fact she looks so pale. He said something about her iron levels being low and her diet needs looking at. He wants to run a couple more tests, then have a longer chat with me to decide what to do, moving forward that is. But the bottom line is, it's treatable and not uncommon in children Poppy's age. Above all, it's nothing I should be getting overly worried about. JoJo, the important thing is my daughter is not going to die."

"Our daughter," JoJo added, with a reassuring smile on his face, physically allowing himself to relax for the first time in weeks too. The love he felt for both Craig and Poppy had never really been tested before, but as he stood in the kitchen, cradling Craig in his arms, JoJo knew deep in his heart he was certainly in this relationship for the long run. Whatever the future might hold for any of them they were a family now. His family.

Chapter 41

"That is certainly good news!" Jenny exclaimed, as she, Mel and Heather spoke later that evening. Sarah had phoned Mel earlier to let her know what the doctor had said. "Mum, Craig will no doubt phone you himself later and let you know the details. I just wanted to give you a heads-up - to stop you worrying, if nothing else." She was glad she was finally able to put her mum and her godmothers out of their misery. Craig had asked her to phone while he phoned the rest of his family and Amy's parents directly, knowing they too had been awaiting news. A feeling of relief finally settling on the household.

"Yes," Heather echoed. "That is excellent news. I imagine Craig is relieved tonight. To think, he could have lost Poppy, just as he did Amy, was unthinkable."

"You're right. It doesn't bear thinking about, does it? Children, we never stop worrying about them, do we? From the moment they're born, no matter what age they are." Jenny was feeling quite philosophical, thinking about her own two, Emily and Harry. How would she feel if either of them became ill, or if anything bad happened to them? They were both reasonably well-adjusted children, relatively independent for teenagers. Nevertheless, that desire to protect them, to wrap them up in cotton wool never went away. No one knew what was around the corner, that was for certain. And if the worst happened, how would she cope, alone?

She had been giving this serious thought over the last few weeks, ever since that odd discussion with Jason.

The one where she had asked for a divorce, and he'd countered with a suggestion that he move back home. It had been so bizarre she could still not get her mind around it, and if she could not make sense of it, then how could she expect her children to deal with it? Recently they were getting on well with their dad, enjoying the time he was finally lavishing on them; for once feeling part of his life, albeit as an adjunct to what he had with his new family.

The sheer disbelief they had felt when he'd originally left home had been greatly toned down, with them now adjusted to their new family dynamic. They had found their own niche in the family their dad had established with Louisa, surprisingly feeling unthreatened by the existence of her son. Jason had worked hard to convince them he had not walked out on their lives; he was just not living at home with their mum. Given the choice, they would probably support his suggestion to move back home. They would undoubtedly welcome him with open arms, should that option ever be presented to them. From their perspective, Jenny felt that would be preferable to watching their parents go through a divorce. Regardless of whether it was amicable or messy, it would still be traumatic for all concerned. "Is that reason enough to agree to his suggestion," she'd thought to herself? Or, was she just taking the easy route and setting herself up for the next disaster. The next chapter of his midlife crisis, whatever, or whoever, that turned out to be?

As Jenny was mulling over her particular parenting dilemma, Mel was equally worrying about her own daughter, and more specifically the conundrum she now faced. How should she deal with the looming presence of Sarah's father in her life? Since George had turned up unannounced on her doorstep the previous month to return the photo frame Sarah had left in Australia, Mel had been left in a real quandary. Her feelings for him had been reawakened in a way she had never imagined. George had asked her the direct question of whether they had met before. As much as Mel wanted to deny it, she had been unable to. It was not in her nature to lie, and try as she might she could not devise a better story on the hoof.

"Yes, I believe we may have done. Many years ago, I imagine. I'm not too sure," she had replied, keeping her answer as vague as possible, without directly telling an untruth. His eyes had locked onto hers, giving her the strangest feeling that he was almost searching deep into her soul for the answer, knowing it was in there somewhere.

"I'm sure it will come to me in time," he'd said smiling, before thanking her for letting him shelter from the storm. Making his way back out onto the wet streets, he pulled his overcoat around his neck, turning one last time to glance and smile in her direction. The rain may have stopped but the gloom of the day was still there, the nip in the air reminding them winter was on its way.

Since then, Mel had lived in dread of him turning up again on her doorstep, declaring to all concerned he had remembered. The night now firmly etched in his mind, the memories of their brief relationship playing out in glorious technicolour in front of him. Although, saying that, the chances of him admitting to a one-night stand with his mate's teenage sister, were so remote, if non-existent, it was laughable. Particularly, if he felt any shame or guilt whatsoever about his behaviour that night, he would surely stay as far away as possible. No, on balance she was safe, she was reasonably confident of that.

Heather also had her own thoughts to contend with. Whilst she had no children to worry about, or for that matter another half to consider, she had still been badly affected by everything that had been happening since the news of Poppy's condition, and the events leading up to it, when Craig had told them about him and JoJo. People had rallied around Craig and Poppy, anxious to help in whatever way they could. Who would rally around her, should she ever need it? Her dad was now in such a state he hardly recognised her, so he would be no help. And in terms of her sister Ellen, well, probably not much help there either. Although they were geographically close, their lives and lifestyles nowadays were too far apart. Ellen, in her late forties was already a grandma, happily married, with a growing family to occupy her time. She had her own worries, her own challenges and as much as Heather hated to admit it, they had drifted apart. Heather's role as the doting aunt had long since dried up. And whilst her sister's life had moved on, Heather felt hers had fallen deeper into the doldrums, especially these last few years since Bruce's death.

She needed some excitement, something for her, and the more she thought about it, the more her plans for Santorini came back into focus. "Time to take them off the back burner," she thought to herself, deciding it was time to share her thoughts with her friends.

"I've been thinking, now that Poppy appears to be on the mend, I might go back to Santorini," she began, nervously.

"Not Santorini again? You mentioned that a few weeks ago. I'd have thought you'd moved on by now," Jenny remarked, remaining as negative about the island as previously.

"Have I missed something?" enquired Mel. "What are you two talking about?"

Heather brought Mel up to date, realising that when she had started to tell Jenny some weeks earlier, Mel had not been party to the conversation, and since then their lives had been derailed by the news of Poppy's illness so the subject had never been brought up. She had not even got into detail with Jenny, having fallen at the first hurdle, with Jenny ridiculing the idea, saying the island had nothing to offer.

Now, feeling more buoyed up, she told Mel her plans. It was quite simple, really. Move over there for a few months, find an apartment or a small cottage to rent, and then rediscover her artistic side. She would allow the beauty of the island to work its magic on her.

"Sounds amazing." Mel was a little taken aback by how much thought Heather had already put into her plans. "I never appreciated you'd spent so much time discovering the place when we were there. I just thought you'd wandered off into the village to get some peace and quiet occasionally. I hadn't realised you'd been exploring the island too."

"Well, I think you're absolutely barking!" Jenny declared. "You'll be home within the month, I'll bet. Your paint brushes, or whatever else you use, stuffed into your bag, and your tail between your legs. Who do you think you are? Shirley Valentine, or something?"

"Perhaps not quite the endorsement I was looking for," thought Heather to herself. However,

Jenny's comments were not going to deter her. Nothing ventured, nothing gained, was her view. And, after all, what did she have to lose? The cottage and her old life would still be there when she came home, so what was the risk?

Chapter 42

By the end of November life was starting to settle back to normal after all the upset and worry of the previous months. Well, for some of the friends at least!

It was a cold, wet and windy autumnal morning and Mel was sitting in her office, finalising the December promotions they would run in the cafés. Odette, her super-efficient office manager was sitting alongside her, her laptop open and spreadsheets at the ready, as they fed in the figures and stock distributions for the various *Just Brewed* shops, based on their expected demands. The run-up to Christmas was always busy, and in truth they were behind in some of their preparations. Today was key to getting back on track. The franchise plans were still being worked in the background by Mel's legal teams, so for now at least she only had to concentrate on the existing cafés.

"Right, I'll go and sort all that," Odette offered once they had finished their discussions, closing her laptop and walking swiftly to the door. "Do you want me to bring you a coffee through and a sandwich, or something? You haven't eaten all morning."

"Thanks. I think I'll wander through myself. I could do with a stretch and some fresh air. It'll be nice to sit and have a chat with some of the regulars too. It's been a while since I've been able to do that, with one thing or another." Mel loved to keep herself grounded and remember why she had started the business in the first place. Today it was all about finance and margins, whereas twenty years ago, when she had first started out it had been completely different. She never wanted to lose sight of that. Standing up and stretching she smiled, "I don't think I've moved for the last couple of hours. You're a hard task master when you get started," she laughed as Odette retreated out of her office.

Odette, now in her late fifties, had been with Mel from almost the first day of the café's opening. In fact, she had been one of Mel's first customers, arriving early one morning for a coffee after dropping her youngest daughter off at school. If she was honest, she was more interested in having a nosy around to see what all the fuss had been about. Living in the next street, she had often walked past the café and was curious to see what the renovation would look like now that it was finished. It had been an old greengrocery store cum minimarket beforehand, somewhere you could buy almost anything, if you had the patience to rummage around the shelves. The old premises though had been tired, and in Odette's view would need considerable investment if it was to be turned into something fashionable and trendy. She was intrigued.

The café had been busy, and as she walked in Odette witnessed the new young proprietor behind the counter getting flustered. The till appeared not to be working and the lady was clearly struggling to serve and take money at the same time. Odette approached the counter. "Do you want a hand, Chère?" she said in her gentle French accent, before taking off her coat, walking behind the counter and starting to serve the waiting customers. She had a proprietorial air about her and enough confidence to never consider the answer might be no. Mel had been grateful for her support then, and every day since. Over the last twenty years she had remained thankful for the day the petite French woman walked into her life, always considering it a good omen. Odette, in turn, treated Mel like one of her own daughters, never afraid to speak her mind if she had any misgivings about what Mel was considering. She had always had her back, feeling she had a stake in the success of the business too.

After grabbing a sandwich, a latte and a slice of her favourite lemon drizzle cake, Mel wandered around the café looking for a friendly face and somewhere to park herself for a few moments while she enjoyed her break. She smiled at a few regulars, but there was no one she immediately recognised, or appeared willing to engage with her. That is, until she turned the corner and that smile disarmed her. He was looking up from his mobile, just as she walked alongside his table. She was unable to do anything other than acknowledge him.

"Oh hello. It's George, isn't it?" Her voice struggled to hide the surprise.

"Hello again. It's Mel, isn't it?" he replied, equally surprised. "Would you care to join me? It looks busy today, and you might struggle to get a table otherwise." He stood to pull a chair out for Mel to sit on, whilst effortlessly relieving her of the tray she was carrying. "I'm a regular - I come in quite often on my way to the office. Although not usually at lunch times. I'm normally a lot earlier, and it's generally not this busy."

Once they were seated, George smiled over. "I know this sounds corny, but do you come here often? I must admit, it's one of my favourite coffee shops in the area. I much prefer it to the larger, less personal ones. The staff are so friendly and polite, so welcoming, I find."

Mel returned his smile, unsure what else to do, or more importantly what to say to George's direct question.

"Actually, I come in most days too. I'm surprised I've never seen you before. And yes, I agree the staff are very friendly. It's also one of the things I like most about the place."

After a couple of minutes of small talk, mainly directed at the state of the weather and preparations for Christmas, allowing Mel a chance to eat her sandwich and drink her coffee, George glanced at his watch. He looked like he was getting ready to leave. He put his mobile phone back into his pocket and picked up his jacket that had been neatly folded over the spare chair. Before he stood, he looked Mel directly in the eye.

"I'm really glad I bumped into you. I've been wracking my brains for weeks, since that time I called around to your house to return Sarah's photo frame, in an attempt to recall when we first met. Could it perhaps have been a party? I can't remember exactly when it would have been. If I'm right, it would have been twenty plus years ago, although looking at you now, I can't believe it's that long, so I'm probably mistaken." As he spoke, his eyes never left Mel's. He seemed intent on watching for her reaction, looking for any sign that would jog his memory. At the same time, Mel was equally intent on maintaining a poker face.

Before she had time to answer, one of the counter girls approached the table, looking unusually flustered.

"Boss, sorry to interrupt your lunch. It's just Odette is looking for you and she buzzed through to ask if you were here. She needs a minute, as soon as you're free. Something's cropped up that she thinks you'll want to see before you head home."

"Oh, right. Yes, thanks Becca. Just give me a couple of minutes, please," Mel replied, a little embarrassed by the intrusion. She was unsure whether to feel as if she had been saved by the bell, or disturbed from a pleasurable lunch.

"Boss!" repeated George, as Becca walked away, a wry smile on his face. "So, do you work here then?"

Unsure what else to say, Mel simply replied, "*Just Brewed* is my business. So yes, in a manner, I suppose I do work here. Just not serving coffees anymore. Anyway, enjoy the rest of your day, George. No doubt I'll see you around."

And picking up what was left of her lunch, she walked back to her office, her head held high, allowing a small smile to rest on her face. 'A regular customer,' he had said, leaving Mel with the distinct impression it would not be the last time she saw him.

Chapter 43

As Christmas approached, Jenny's views on her impending 'divorce' continued to vacillate. One minute it was her top priority, the list of solicitors recommended to her carefully stored away in her phone. The next, it was something she needed to give more thought to. Her mind still unsure if it was the right thing to do, or more importantly, how she would cope by herself if she went ahead with it. She knew the process itself of getting a divorce could be relatively straightforward, albeit expensive, with the risks high in terms of what she potentially had to lose if things did not go her way. Weighed up against the advantages of being single again, she questioned was it worth it.

Jason did not make it any easier either. He continued to drop hints each visit about moving back home, although he never came directly out and said it. Little things about Louisa were starting to niggle him. It was nothing significant, just enough to mention whenever the opportunity arose. Jenny noticed how he would wait until Emily and Harry were out of earshot, then try to get the sympathy vote from her. He would attempt to cosy up, as if he was chatting to an old friend, not someone he had chosen to leave for a younger model; a model that was now proving to be both needy and high maintenance. Jenny never chose to bite, preferring to move the subject on, or even better, close the conversation down completely whenever he criticised anything Louisa had said, or done. She had no desire whatsoever to discuss her husband's current living arrangements – regardless of how bizarre or unorthodox they had become.

She sometimes wondered whether Louisa paid her the same courtesy whenever the shoe was on the other foot, and doubted it. Jason would certainly have moaned enough about their marriage to his mistress over the years, of that, she was sure. No, as far as Jenny was concerned, he'd made his choice. If he now chose to moan about it, she certainly had no intention of offering him a shoulder to cry on, or to make life easy for him. She was playing the long game, for the time being at least. Until she had decided what she really wanted.

"Mum," Emily said, sauntering into the kitchen carrying a stack of mail. "Postie's just dropped this lot off for you." Handing the stack of mail to Jenny, before opening the fridge and delving in to see what she could scavenge before lunch. "I saw him dashing off down the drive. He almost landed on his backside when he nearly slipped on that patch of ice near the garage." She laughed as she stuffed a cold slice of pizza into her mouth. Looking at her daughter's slim physique, Jenny wondered where she put all the food. She seemed to eat enough to feed a small village, all by herself.

"He's obviously in a hurry," offered Jenny, showing no interest in what the postman was up to. It was Saturday morning and she was busy. Jason had promised to pick Emily up by noon, after collecting Harry from football practice, and he was already late.

"Looks like mainly Christmas cards, if you ask me," Emily added, once her mouth was empty. "Right, I'll go and find my shoes. Dad should be here any minute," she said, making her way into the hallway where she'd abandoned them the previous evening. He was planning on taking her Christmas shopping to let her chose her present, and said he would help her chose something nice for her mum, even offering to chip in some money if she did not have enough. Given Emily only had the princely sum of just over twenty two pounds left in her savings account, that was good news.

Flicking through the mail, Jenny realised there was nothing particularly interesting among it. The odd Christmas card, a few flyers from local shops and other junk mail, plus a couple of brown envelopes that she suspected were bills. There was however one larger envelope that piqued her interest. It was cream coloured and the paper was shiny, with a printed gilt trim around the edges. It was hand written and obviously far too posh to be a Christmas card, well, certainly not the normal charity ones she seemed to be receiving these days.

"I wonder what this is?" she thought to herself, putting the rest of the mail to one side whilst she surveyed the larger envelope. As soon as she realised what it was, her face fell. "Oh look, Emily. It's the invitation to Craig and JoJo's wedding."

Opening the envelope, she added as lightly as she could, "I wasn't expecting it to arrive for a few weeks," whilst desperately trying to hide the disappointment in her voice. She was already well aware of the date and the venue, but with more than five months to go before their big day, it was something she was trying to keep from the forefront of her mind.

After Craig and JoJo had made their big announcement in Santorini, most of Jenny's initial excitement had wavered, particularly once she got home and reality hit her straight in the face. She was not one for big dos, or fuss in general. Also, the idea of attending a same-sex wedding on the other side of the country was something that really did not appeal to her. In principle she did not have any real problems with JoJo, although he and Craig as a couple was something she still struggled to fully comprehend.

Memories of Amy were always close, and recently they replayed in her mind more than usual. She recalled the look of love on her friend's face whenever Craig was in the room, particularly in those early days, and the happiness they had both displayed when Poppy first came along, doting parents. She struggled to reconcile that with the type of relationship Craig suggested he and Amy had had, one that basically amounted to nothing more than a close and loving friendship.

Whilst on holiday, and for the benefit of everyone else, she had played along, happy to reserve judgement for another day. She had nevertheless remained in two minds about the wedding, secretly hoping that once the arrangements were announced, it would give her an opportunity to politely and diplomatically back out. She could easily argue work, or some other commitment, if need be. Taking time off work during the school term for teachers was generally frowned upon, and as midweek weddings were all the rage now, she was certain the date would clash with her timetable, or her after school commitments.

And, even if she could wangle a day off, what if Emily and Harry were invited too? She could hardly take them out of school and risk the school imposing a fine on her for unapproved absence, could she? Then, if they weren't invited, she could always use them as her excuse not to attend. After all, she could not leave them again, with Jason or her parents, so soon after returning from a three-week holiday. It would be abusing their generosity, surely? Either way, the kids would provide her with the excuse she needed.

But no, that had all backfired when Craig phoned and made it clear they were all invited, and what was more, he'd added, the date would coincide with the spring bank holiday weekend. "What would a wedding be without all my family and friends at it," he had said. "Don't worry, Jen, we've thought of it all!"

Swiftly running out of excuses, she had been forced to accept there was no longer any way of getting out of attending their special day, without appearing rude or coming straight out and saying she was unable to afford it. Spring Bank Holiday it was, a weekend away with the kids now firmly in her calendar.

The downsides remained though, leaving Jenny with no idea how she would address them. No matter how many times she looked at her bank statement, the dilemma was not going away, or the problem getting any easier. She worried that costs for hotels and travel were notoriously higher at that time of year, with rooms at the country house venue Craig and JoJo had chosen well outside her price range. Perhaps she could look into whether there were local budget hotels available nearby; Holiday Inns or Premier Inns perhaps, where breakfast was included. That would cut her costs down further. She might even be able to get a family room, as having to book two rooms would certainly make it more expensive. The kids would not be happy with sharing; that was a bridge she knew she would need to cross nearer the time. She could also drive, and by not drinking she would save a little more money. A glass of champagne with the toast, and thereafter mineral water would be fine by her. Although getting into buying rounds could prove expensive, so she'd need to think carefully about how to avoid that, particularly as Mel liked her drink!

Even ignoring the cost of buying a present, there would be the further expense of clothes for the day itself. They would all need new outfits. Neither Emily nor Harry had anything suitable, or at least anything smart that still fitted them. They both seemed to have shot up during the summer when she'd been away, and what size they would be by next spring was anyone's guess. Harry was a gangly teenager, now nearly as tall as his father, and painfully skinny. He lived in sportswear, so the idea of getting him out of his tracksuit and into anything smart would be a challenge in itself. And in terms of Emily, well, she was maturing into an image conscious teenager, with a liking for designer labels. She no longer wanted clothes purchased from a supermarket, or for that matter anything off the sales rack that Jenny might pick out for her. No, her outfit would be both a challenge and an expense.

Parking what the kids would need, what about her own outfit? What would she be expected to wear? What do you wear to give a groom away, anyway? She had absolutely no idea. And even if she could find something suitable, how would it compare with what Mel or Heather could afford? She would feel like the proverbial poor relation, wearing something off the peg from a high street store no doubt. The day may still be a few months away, but it was proving to be nothing other than one long headache for Jenny. On top of everything else she was having to contend with, she really did not need it.

As she opened the gold embossed invitation, reading the details of the service, a neatly folded piece of paper floated to the floor. Picking it up and reading what she recognised as Craig's handwriting, Jenny's face changed. She allowed a small smile to form on her lips the more she read.

"Oh look, Emily. Craig and JoJo would like you to be an attendant, along with Sarah and Poppy. Craig says he wants all of his goddaughters by his side, looking their best. Harry's been asked to be an usher, too. He's invited you both over in the new year to get a fitting for a dress and shoes, and a suit for Harry. How exciting!" As she continued reading, her smile got broader. "It also says he's reserved accommodation for us at the hotel for the weekend. Two nights, all paid for. Oh, and he's invited me to come over in the new year too, with Mel and Heather so that we can get our outfits sorted. Apparently, there's a theme for the wedding and JoJo wants to help us chose our dresses, as well as pay for them. How generous is all that?"

With a massive sigh of relief, Jenny smiled as she put the letter and the invitation back into the envelope. The wedding arrangements, and the build up to the big day had suddenly got a lot more interesting. Without the worry of the expense hanging over her, or the thought of all the hassle of deciding what to wear, a massive weight had effectively been lifted from her shoulders. The event she had been dreading had taken on a whole new perspective, with the prospect of her actually enjoying herself now a real possibility.

Hearing Jason's car pulling into the driveway provided a sharp reminder that although one set of problems might have been addressed, it did nothing to clarify the other one that continued to hang over her. The dark shadow created by her perplexing relationship still needed to be dealt with. No matter how much she tried to push it to the back of her mind, one way or another it needed sorting, and soon.

Chapter 44

As Heather sat on her balcony, enjoying the mid December sunshine, she stared down at the village square, then out at the Aegean Sea, and sighed. It was a relaxed contented sigh, one that denoted how at peace she felt with herself and her surroundings.

A small cup of black coffee and a bowl of fresh fruit sat on the patio table in front of her, along with the mail she had collected from her mailbox earlier that morning. Although she missed the regularity of the postman calling at home most lunchtimes, she had easily adjusted to walking the short distance to the village store to collect anything that had been left there for her. The postal service in Greece might not be as reliable as back home, but it was certainly no hardship, ambling down to the store in the sunshine to collect any letters or parcels. She rarely made a special trip, simply enquired whenever she called in to buy her fresh produce if anything had been left for her. In fact, there was rarely any mail, most things seemed to be managed impersonally or online these days, she thought, as she glanced over at her iPad, ready to check her emails and messages later in the day.

She enjoyed the short stroll though, as well as the opportunity to test out her language skills on the locals! Greek was not a language that came easily. She laughed as she recalled her attempts to decipher words as she walked around, or practised her pronunciation in front of the mirror. She frequently fumbled to find the appropriate words to greet her neighbours, or buy whatever she needed from the shops. Watching their expressions each time she tried to convey the most basic of sentiments was an education in itself. Living in a small village, and especially outside of the main holiday season, meant there were few English-speaking people around. This increased the pressure to at least try to fit in and converse like a local.

Heather had been in Santorini for almost six weeks, having taken the decision early in November to pack up and follow her dream. After all, what did she have to lose? Jenny had tried to put her off, arguing she was mad to even consider running away, let alone actually going ahead and doing it. Her friend's reaction, once she shared the pictures of the two-bedroom apartment she had decided to rent for three months, was not exactly as supportive as she had hoped.

The apartment was in a relatively remote village, not far from where they had holidayed. There was a regular bus service she could use to get to the more populated areas, or down to the beaches, even out to the airport if she needed it. Heather had visited the village on a couple of occasions during the time they had all been there during the summer, stopping off for the odd drink in the café or the taverna. She had loved the feel of the village square, the pace of life; rustic and largely untouched by commercialism. It was quiet and peaceful, and above all, it felt like a safe harbour for her to moor up in.

The thought of another lonely and gloomy winter in the Highlands had not appealed in the least, and certainly not in the frame of mind she had found herself in over recent months. Once Poppy was off the so-called danger list, she feared there would no longer be any direct role for her in her goddaughter's life. That had been her catalyst to make a move. Heather knew she needed a different dynamic; one that would reignite her creative side, as well as give her a reason to go on. At forty she had to sort herself out. Not wait around, expecting others to do it for her. No, it was time to get out of the widow's weeds she had metaphorically wrapped herself in for too long, and start living. Bruce would not have wanted it any other way.

So far, so good, was Heather's crude assessment of her first few weeks, recognising some of the highs and lows she had experienced, and some of the adjustments she had made along the way. With Christmas looming though, she feared the real challenges were still ahead of her. This year, traditions would have to be reset. No holly, ivy or mistletoe – or even Christmas trees and tinsel. No large family around the table, sharing the turkey or pulling a cracker. And Hogmanay would certainly not be celebrated in the same raucous manner as it was back home. It would be a whole new experience.

Heather kept in regular contact with her sister Ellen, messaging each other most days. There was seldom anything new to say. They had not been particularly close for some time, and now with distance and less in common, their conversations soon became stilted. She did miss her dad, even missed her trips to visit him in his nursing home, although she did not miss the heartache she felt each time she had left. For the last couple of years, she had watched her father gradually drift further away from her; becoming less of the man she remembered. To see him now, barely capable of looking after his most basic needs, was hard. Some days had been especially tough, she now recalled, particularly the times he had failed to recognise her, or even put a name to her face. To hold his slender frame was painful, recalling the bear hugs she had received as a child, the strong man he had once been; the fit, athletic man who had lived an outdoors life, tending his gardens. Now, resigned to living a half-life, reliant on others pushing him from A to B had been heart-breaking for her to witness.

No, the pull back to Scotland had been nowhere near as bad as she had feared it would be. In fact, the loneliness she had experienced at home these past years, surrounded by all her family and friends, appeared to have dissipated recently. It had been replaced by the feeling of warmth she received for a disparate group of people; people she felt a strange affinity to. A group of relative strangers, people who were gradually becoming her new family and friends. Katarina in the grocery store, with her newborn baby Thea, who was usually attached to her with a makeshift sling. Sophia, who worked at the taverna in the evenings and helped out at the café in the daytime. She regularly engaged with Heather whenever she called in for a drink, desperate to learn whatever English she could, in the hope it would help earn her more tips once the tourists came back in the summer. And Nikos, the man who ran the local village workshop.

The workshop, Heather found, doubled as the souvenir shop during the season. It sold whatever wares the locals could produce, as well as some of the more commercial items tourists expected. Its stock was eclectic to say the least, from rustic pottery to earthenware, handmade fabrics to woollens, olive oils to cheeses, and most of all, a fine selection of local wines. The area was renowned for its wine production, with the villagers celebrating that fact at every occasion.

Heather had initially wandered around the workshop during her summer holiday, pleasantly surprised to see the wide variety of stock it carried, and amazed by the garish colours outside the shop, designed no doubt to tempt the tourists in. Trade had been brisk, well, relatively brisk for an out of the way village, in the middle of nowhere. The man who ran the shop had explained that some of the local tour companies included a stop there as part of their sightseeing tour of the island, joking that both the taverna and the workshop did very well out of the trade it generated!

Returning during her first week back, Heather was disappointed to see the outside of the shop looking almost abandoned. The door had been wedged open, so she had walked in. It was cold inside and dark, and looked completely deserted. The shelves were relatively bare, stock now limited to what the locals needed during the winter months, the basics.

Believing the place to be empty, Heather was just about to turn around and walk out when she heard a voice call out from behind an old wooden door.

"Hello, can I help you?" the voice asked.

"Oh, hello," she replied, a little startled.

A middle-aged man walked forward, dressed in faded jeans under a dirty overall, his hair covered by a woollen beanie hat, his face concealed by a straggly dark beard, displaying more than a hint of grey. He was wiping his hands on a rag to remove some of the oil from the door he had been repairing.

Heather thought she recognised him as the man she had briefly spoken to in the summer, but was not certain. He looked older and much more unkempt than the man she remembered. "No, I was just looking, thank you. I remembered calling in to have a mooch around during the summer, and was just passing..." Heather replied, unsure what else she could say to explain her presence. She had hoped to find a few knickknacks to buy to brighten up the apartment, so was feeling a little disappointed to see the shelves empty.

The man removed his safety goggles and looked closely at her, appearing to frown. The way he was staring made Heather feel a little uncomfortable. After a few seconds, his frown was replaced by a smile. A vague recollection came to him.

"I think I remember you coming in. You were all by yourself, if I recall correctly?"

"Yes, that's right." Heather was surprised and a little taken aback it was the same man she had spoken to. "You talked to me for some time, telling me about the village. Then a coachload of tourists arrived, I seem to recall. I could see you were busy, so I left you to it," she replied, feeling more relaxed and pleased he had remembered her.

"Well, no tourists today, sadly. Just me and this old door that's seen better days. A bit like me," he added, smiling as he pointed over to the workbench, where it was obvious some repair work was underway. Passing trade was non-existent at this time of year, so Nikos spent his time repairing items for the village, or helping out with whatever anyone needed doing. He was a handy man and could turn his skills to most things.

"I'm Nikos. I'd offer to shake hands, but as you can see that would not be advisable. How can I help you, by the way?" Although his Greek accent was very pronounced, his English was excellent, and his manners impeccable.

"Oh hello, I'm Heather. No, I was just curious, I suppose. I've moved to the village for a few months, so I'm just getting my bearings. I was hoping there might be a few items I could buy to brighten up the place."

"Oh, that sounds interesting. Whatever brings you here at this time or year, or am I being too impolite to ask a woman that question?" he enquired. Heather liked the way his eyes seemed to light up as he spoke to her, a playfulness about them.

"No, that's fine. It's nothing like that. Nothing mysterious I'm afraid," she laughed, feeling surprisingly relaxed in his company. "I just loved the island so much when I was last here. I simply wanted to recapture some of the beauty and the peace I felt then. I've rented an apartment for a few months, to see how I still feel after living my dream. I need to see whether it works its magic on me again."

"Well, I'm certainly intrigued now." His eyes begged her to continue. "Why don't I open a bottle of wine and some of that cheese? You can then tell me more over a bite to eat, if you have the time, that is?"

Heather had been unsure how to respond. She sensed Nikos was either laughing at her, or flirting with her. For some reason though, she did not feel threatened by him. After all, and if nothing else, it would be good to have a conversation with someone who spoke English. And if he was flirting with her, then was that a problem? It was a long time since anyone had flirted with her, so what the hell! "Yes, that would be lovely," she replied.

Now, a month later and sitting on the balcony, drinking her coffee and taking in the morning view, she turned her attention to the mail she had collected earlier.

As she opened the envelope, she smiled as she read the gold embossed invitation, and especially the small handwritten note that had been inserted into its pages.

"Oh Nikos, come and look at this." She called out to him as he poured more coffee into his cup in the small kitchenette in her apartment. "I've just received that wedding invitation I was telling you about. My friend, Craig, has written to ask me if I'd like to come back to the UK for a few days. He suggests sometime after Christmas, to sort out my outfit. How wonderful."

He strolled out to the balcony and smiled over at Heather, dropping a tender kiss on her head as he did so. Wrapped in nothing but a towel, Heather marvelled at how good he looked, and especially how amazing he smelled. Now clean shaven, with his hair recently trimmed, he was a very attractive man. His olive coloured complexion made an interesting contrast to her pale freckled Scottish skin. Heather had never been blessed with height, or a slender frame, so as he towered over her with his muscular body, toned from all his hard manual work, physically they looked a somewhat odd couple. Nevertheless, she could not keep the silly grin off her face; memories of their previous night's lovemaking still clearly etched on her mind.

In a rash moment, she did wonder about asking Nikos to travel with her; to invite him to fly over to London and meet her friends. On balance though, she decided it was probably too early in their relationship for that. They were still very much finding their feet as a couple, taking tentative steps and anxious to please each other. Taking him out of their environment might pop the bubble they were in, and that was a risk she was unprepared to take, for the time being at least. Whether Jenny still thought she was 'Shirley Valentine' or not, she no longer cared. Although the last thing she wanted was for that discussion to play out in front of him, or for Jenny's cutting remarks to embarrass either of them.

Santorini, or more precisely Nikos, was certainly working his magic on her, and for now she was more than happy to keep him all to herself.

Chapter 45

Mel was enjoying a brief break in her hectic morning, sitting at the front of the café at her favourite table. With a latte in hand, she was staring out of the window, engaged in one of her favourite pastimes – people-watching. Hordes of pedestrians were milling around outside, intent on completing whatever last-minute Christmas shopping they had whilst there was a break in the weather. With only a week to go before the big day, it appeared to be manic outside. The winter sunshine was no doubt boosting people's moods; the rain and sleet from the previous few days having a breather, before no doubt coming back with a vengeance.

It was late morning and their lunchtime regulars would be arriving soon, meaning Mel would feel obliged to vacate her table, and return to her office at the back of the building. Taking the prime table, when there were paying customers around, was simply not her style.

She had arrived at the café before six o'clock that morning, letting herself in before the rest of the team arrived a couple of hours later. She was desperate to get her head around the consultant's latest report on the franchise model that was being developed for *Just Brewed*. One of her legal team had dropped the document off at her home the previous evening, and she needed space to read through it and concentrate on their recommendations.

Sarah and Jake had returned from Yorkshire the previous weekend, both excited their plans were finally taking shape. They were eager to talk her through what they were thinking and to get her advice. Whilst ordinarily she would have encouraged them, grateful to be kept involved, she did not have headspace for that today. So, knowing there was no chance of her getting any peace at home, Mel had trekked into the office before either of them had got out of bed.

Over recent weeks the plans for the franchise had been progressing at a pace, and there was now a real prospect that in the second or third quarter of the following year they could start to roll the model out. There were people actively scouting around for suitable premises, with already a degree of interest being expressed from a few of her contacts that suggested they may be interested in investing. It looked promising, but equally it was starting to look real and that was making Mel nervous. *Just Brewed* was her baby, her concept and until now something she'd had complete control over. Letting it go and getting others involved, however well-managed or overseen the new businesses would be, was a risky prospect. After all, it was still her name, her reputation on the line.

"Penny for your thoughts?" Mel looked round, startled to see George standing by her side. He was wrapped up in his overcoat and scarf, a takeaway coffee in his hand and a freshly made baguette, all bagged and ready to go. "Hope I've not disturbed you."

"Oh, hello again, George. Sorry, I was miles away," she replied, a little flustered to have been caught unawares, automatically smoothing down her hair as she spoke.

"Yes, I can see that," he laughed. "I've been watching you while I was standing in the queue, and you certainly seemed miles away. I've got a meeting later this afternoon, so was planning on eating lunch in the office today. If you don't mind the company though, I'd love to join you. I could do with a break, to be honest. My secretary says I should get out more, even get a life!" he added, with more than a hint of embarrassed laughter.

"No problem. And yes, that would be nice." Mel indicated for him to take the chair opposite her. At least she no longer felt guilty occupying the prime window seats. "So, what's your meeting all about? I'm sorry, I don't think I've ever asked what you do for a living."

"Oh, don't worry about that. It's very boring, I'm afraid." He smiled, hoping that would be sufficient as an answer, but noticing Mel's questioning stare he continued. "I run a small investment company, managing share portfolios and property investments - mainly for private clients. I do have a few corporate accounts, although I tend to try to offload them to my team. I much prefer the smaller, more organic programmes than the huge corporate machines," he explained. "My problem is, I get wrapped up in numbers most days, often failing to leave the office before it's gone dark. My secretary, Tilda, despairs of me! She's regularly trying to fix me up with any manner of social events - anything to get me out from the office and away from my desk, she would argue!"

"Oh, that doesn't sound at all good," Mel laughed, enjoying his self-deprecating tone, whilst sensing a touch of honesty in what he was actually saying, his eyes failing to hide some of the pain he must be feeling. She knew from her brother that George had recently divorced, or at least split from his wife, but she had no other details to hand, or any idea whether there were children involved. It was understandable therefore if he was perhaps having difficulty getting back into the swing of going out, or socialising again. London could be a lonely place. She knew that to her own cost.

Having said that, Mel struggled with the concept of George facing any difficulties securing invitations, or company of any sort for that matter, particularly from the female kind. The closer she looked at him, the more she realised how handsome he was, and how over the years his looks and manner had matured. Although the boyish charm she had first fallen for all those years ago was perhaps not too far from the surface, should the occasion ever present itself, she imagined. "Sounds like she's probably related to Sarah, my daughter. She's forever trying to get me to do the same. Go out Mum, enjoy yourself, she says. And then on the odd occasion I do let my hair down, she's watching my every move. Commenting on what I wear, how I look, to say nothing of the never-ending questions when I return home. I often wonder at what stage the parent-child relationship swapped around. One minute she was my little girl, the next I seem to be hers!"

As Mel allowed herself to relax into the banter, she almost checked herself, mindful of the signs she was probably giving off. What on earth was she doing? Was she flirting with George, even allowing him to do the same with her? She needed to be careful. He was, after all, the man who had broken her impressionable teenage heart, leaving an indelible mark on her life. Getting her pregnant, before scuttling off back into the arms of his fiancée without a second glance, was perhaps not his finest moment. So angry and embarrassed had she been, she had never spoken of the night to anyone. She had even tried, but failed, to convince herself she had been raped, as a way of admonishing his actions. She had vowed she would never allow anyone to take advantage of her again. And now, here she was, guilty of even encouraging him!

George on the other hand had not given her a second thought. She was simply a girl at a party, just another notch on his bedpost. Worse still, he had no recollection of the night they had shared together; the same night that had haunted Mel all these years. A night that had left her mentally scarred, scared of falling for another hopeless man. No, she had put her defences well and truly up, and resigned herself to the fact no man would ever take advantage of her like that again. Taking what he wanted, then going, without so much as a by your leave.

Mel recognised how controlling that had made her in all the relationships she'd had since. She had never allowed anyone to get too close to her, or to Sarah, and had always been the one to dump, rather than risk being dumped.

Now, at forty she was not only wary of men in general, but also lonely and alone. There was no one significant in her life. No one to go home to, no one to cuddle up to or share her thoughts with. And certainly, there was no one she felt comfortable sharing her bed with for longer than the odd hour when she needed sex, or a little excitement. What had life become, she asked herself, and what had fate got in store for her if she continued along this path?

"Sorry, what did you say?" she asked, embarrassed she had been caught out, lost in her thoughts again. Realising George had said something, and was clearly awaiting her answer, she explained, "I was miles away again, sorry."

"Yes, Tilda says I have a tendency to bore people, once I start talking!" He smiled over at her. "No, I was just saying, if you weren't too busy tomorrow evening, would you like to accompany me to a concert? I have two tickets. If you're busy, I will completely understand. It is, after all, the week before Christmas, so I'm sure you'll already have lots of commitments, places to go, people to see." He could feel himself starting to babble, and sensing a rejection, George stood up ready to leave. He placed his business card on the table, imagining it being thrown away with the rest of the rubbish as soon as the waitress cleared the table.

"Anyway, have a think about it. Here's my card, just in case. Give me a ring, or perhaps leave a message with Tilda," the formal tone being employed more as a defence mechanism than anything else. He walked towards the door, before his embarrassment got the better of him.

Without asking the nature of the concert, the time it started, or even the venue, and even before George had time to reach for the door handle, Mel surprised herself by replying.

"George. Thank you. That would be lovely." He turned around and allowed himself a small smile, a smile that instantly lit up his eyes and rendered him almost speechless.

"Let me know what time, and where to meet you," Mel added after a few seconds, finding she was unconsciously returning his smile.

"How about I collect you around seven o'clock." Then added, for the sake of clarity, "in case you're wondering, the tickets are to see the Rat Pack at Canary Wharf. Dinner is included, and served around nine o'clock. There's even dancing afterwards. Just thought you'd like to know, in case you wanted to dress up, that is. I think the dress code is black tie." His last remark was accompanied by a wry smile.

Looking down at the outfit she was wearing; the casual trainers, the mismatched hoodie and stained jeans, her hair sticking up in all directions, and her face devoid of any makeup, she simply laughed in reply. At the same time, she made a mental note. Next time she came into the office at such an early hour, she really needed to look in the mirror before she left home.

Smiling to herself, she stood up and almost floated back to her office.

"You never know what the day's going to throw at you, do you Odette?" she said to her assistant, a silly grin on her face.

As she closed the office door firmly behind her, George's business card still firmly in her grasp, all she now needed to do was concentrate on returning her attentions back to the report she'd been reading, that is before George had turned up and completely discombobulated her thinking!

Chapter 46

It was the third week of January and a bitterly cold Sunday afternoon. The dusk was starting to fall over the capital, the street lights, car lamps and neon signs the only things brightening up the busy roads. Jenny was walking the short distance from Covent Garden to Leicester Square's tube station and was having to be careful where she put her feet, for fear of slipping. The ice and sleet under foot was making it difficult to navigate London's treacherous pavements. Passing cars were splashing dirty water up from the gutters as they sped past, intent on getting to their destinations.

Her journey was not made any easier by having to drag her overnight case behind her. She was feeling a little tipsy from the couple of large glasses of wine she'd had with her lunch, to say nothing of the mild hangover she was still nursing from the previous evening, neither of which did anything to enhance her mood. She was tired and ready for home, and knew that she would be paying for it tomorrow morning when the alarm went off at its usual ungodly hour.

It was still only four o'clock. Jenny, hating to be on the last minute, was glad she had set off in good time, leaving the others to enjoy their cocktails at the trendy bar Mel had taken them to after they had left the bistro. The mainline train from Euston to Manchester Piccadilly was not due to depart for nearly an hour, leaving plenty of time for her to get to the station. There was even time to grab a coffee and a sandwich before it left, if she felt hungry or needed to settle her stomach. After all, by the time she got home she would not feel like eating, and would certainly not fancy cooking anything. Perhaps a slice of toast, if she was desperate.

Jenny was not the most confident of people in unfamiliar surroundings, so trying to cross the city, when people were darting all around her, was proving more difficult than she had imagined. Mel had suggested she get a taxi direct from Covent Garden, but that would have only added extra expense. The weekend had already cost her more than she had budgeted. In fact, had the weather been nicer, she would have walked to Euston. According to Google, it would only take between thirty to forty minutes. In the cold though, with the threat of further snow, and not wearing the most sensible of shoes, she had not wanted to risk it.

As she trudged on, her mind wandered back over the events of the last couple of days. On balance, she felt the weekend had been enjoyable, although it had certainly given her a lot to think about. Plenty of food for thought for the journey home.

It was the first time she had properly met up with Mel and Heather since their holiday the previous summer, so it had been great to have some girly time together. Friday night had been just the three of them, and Mel had cooked a simple, albeit delicious meal at home. Sarah and Jake had gone out for dinner to meet friends, so with the house to themselves they'd had a good catchup, putting the world to rights and swapping whatever gossip they could recall. They had cosily sat tucked up in Mel's sitting room, gentle soothing music playing in the background, the log burner raging in the grate. The combination of the warmth, the food, the wine, to say nothing of the long week of teenage angst Jenny had endured, meant it was not long before she had started to yawn and called time.

Throughout the evening, Heather had been more vociferous than Jenny could ever remember. Gone was her usual reserve and restraint. A bubbly Heather was very much in evidence, displaying a side to her personality that was rarely seen, and certainly not since Bruce's death. She was obviously revelling in her time in Santorini; after finding love, or at least lust, with her Greek Adonis, Nikos. From the photos she passed around he looked almost too good to be true. He was tall, dark and absolutely gorgeous, his Mediterranean looks marking him out from the usual crowd. He was certainly nothing like the lads Heather had typically hung around with at university, and a million miles from Bruce. Bruce, as nice as he was, Jenny had always found more 'paternalistic' than 'love god'. He'd doted on Heather like a prized possession, rather than someone who set his spirits alight. Jenny could tell by the look on Heather's face, as well as her body language that her friend had fallen hard for Nikos and his charms. She simply glowed whenever the conversation moved back onto him. And when she discussed their time together in Santorini, or what they had been up to, a dreamy, faraway look appeared in her eyes.

Jenny had to admit, looking at him, it was not at all surprising. It did leave her wondering uncharitably though, where the catch was. What was he after, with Heather of all people? Her money, she presumed. Bruce had left her a wealthy widow, someone who could easily be preyed upon, or flattered into parting with her fortune. She worried about women like Heather being groomed, knowing how vulnerable they could be. Her fears were not lessened when she learned he managed the tourist shop and worked effectively as the village's odd-job man. Although, looking at those muscles, she would not say no to him doing an odd job for her too, if ever he was around. With a spare hour or two, she could definitely put him to good use, she thought rather suggestively!

And as for Mel, well, that was another story entirely. A mysterious man named George had apparently entered her life, someone who she said she had met in her café. She admitted they had gone on a few dinner dates over recent weeks. There were no photos of George on offer, with Mel failing to share too many details of her new relationship. Mel had never been one to share much on that score, so it was not surprising. As far as Jenny recalled, over the years there had never been any relationships for Mel that had amounted to much. There was the odd passing acquaintance she had mentioned, a few friends with benefits that she called on when the mood took her, but nothing ever serious. Certainly, never any commitment.

So, for Mel to even be mentioning it now left Jenny sensing there was more to it than her friend was letting on, her mind naturally thinking the worst of him too. Mel was a wealthy and extremely successful and independent businesswoman. To say nothing of the glamourous lifestyle she led, and her almost aristocratic connections, with friends in high places. Whilst her fears of grooming were nowhere near the same as they were for Heather, nevertheless, she would still hate to see Mel taken advantage of. Especially not by a man who was nothing more than a passing customer from the café.

On the Saturday morning, Craig and JoJo had joined them. They'd arrived around ten-thirty, in time for a late breakfast, carrying a large cardboard box, full of a selection of delicious fresh pastries from *Just Brewed.* Mel had arranged for her staff to deliver these, but JoJo had insisted the café was en route; secretly, he had told Jenny, he was desperate to sneak a peek at the empire Mel controlled, admitting to having never set foot over the threshold of one of her cafés before. When they arrived, ready for some serious retail therapy, Mel opened the bottle of champagne she had been chilling, to add even more indulgence to what was already planned to be a very indulgent weekend.

He and Craig had stayed over at JoJo's London Docklands apartment the previous evening, catching up with a few of JoJo's friends over dinner, and dealing with some of the issues he was unable to manage online. He was seriously considering letting the property out, so needed to find an appropriate tenant to take it on. His agent had lined up a couple of possibilities and JoJo wanted to interview the prospective tenants, before making any decisions. His main interest was now in the house he was building on the moors, his base these days clearly Yorkshire. Nevertheless, his apartment was a significant investment, and as such it needed to be managed correctly. Keeping it unoccupied was in no one's interest, and on the rare occasions he would be visiting London, either for meetings with clients or to see his staff, he could easily rent a hotel for the night. His office was still operational, regardless of where he based himself, so where he slept, or kept his toothbrush no longer seemed a big deal.

Jenny recalled how Craig and JoJo had been on good form. They were relieved Poppy was now doing well, confirming life had settled back down to normal for them, well, as normal as it could be, given all the plates they had spinning in their lives.

Amelia's was doing well, the restaurant had been fully booked throughout December, with Christmas and New Year proving to be a great success. Takings were up and reviews remained positive. JoJo even joked a Michelin star was surely on the horizon. The staff though, were exhausted. So, Craig had taken the brave decision to close the restaurant during January, allowing his team time to chill, before regrouping in February, ahead of the busy Valentine's Day schedule. It had also given Craig some space to develop a new spring menu, as well as support JoJo with the house. Until then, he had consciously stepped back from the development, allowing JoJo to work his magic. Now though, he needed to get more closely involved. After all, it was going to be his and Poppy's home too. The property was only weeks off completion, with the final fixtures and snagging well underway. Furnishings had been ordered, and they had every intention of moving in before the wedding, fingers well and truly crossed.

The house he and Amy had bought was on the market, the estate agent having already taken a few young couples around for viewings. Boxes had been packed with anything he needed to take with him, sentimental items that he could not bear to part with. Most other items were either being disposed of, or passed onto a local charity shop. Craig admitted how difficult that process had been. Relinquishing some of the pieces of furniture he and Amy had worked so hard to scrape together the money to buy. He had to move on though, move with the times. Their sleek new property had been designed with a different purpose in mind and Craig would have to adjust to that.

Poppy could not wait to have the bedroom she had been promised, as well as the pony – something JoJo insisted every young girl needed. She was so excited and appeared to be taking to her new life as if it had always been her destiny. Sadly, she had no memories of Amy ever being there for her. The role model most children have of a mum was something she had never got used to. Having two loving dads was fast becoming her norm.

Since her health scare, Craig and JoJo were spending more time with Poppy, making her their priority. Her diet and exercise routine were now more normalised, her iron levels had improved, leaving the doctors confident that with regular blood testing and a careful eye, her anaemia could be managed without further concern. There was even the possibility that as she got older, she could grow out of it, meaning the chances of leading a normal, healthy life were high for her.

Saturday afternoon had then been given over to retail therapy, with dresses, headwear and shoes firmly in JoJo's sights. By the end of the day, they had chosen and ordered everything, with minimal fuss and a surprising amount of agreement. JoJo wanted a spring theme, with green being the principal colour, an abundance of spring flowers at the centre of his concept. He had consulted with a personal shopper prior to their trip, even advising on everyone's shapes and sizes before they arrived.

JoJo had insisted he needed a good selection of dresses to be in stock, secretly aware of the challenge he had ahead of him! Mel had short blonde hair and was fair skinned, tall and very slender, almost like a reed at nearly six feet tall. Heather was also fair skinned, but with dark wavy hair and was much shorter and curvaceous, boasting a true hourglass figure. Jenny was in between, her complexion much darker, with mousy brown hair, now starting to show the first signs of grey. Her figure was slightly overweight and between sizes, depending on the fit. It was fair to say, none of them was model material. However, by some stroke of magic individual dresses were chosen that complimented each figure, and at the same time complemented each other. JoJo had ensured shades and contrasts were co-ordinated, with no detail left to chance. To Jenny, one shade of green was not much different to the next, but she clearly did not have his architect's eye, trained on perfection. And as she was not being asked to pay, she was happy to wear whatever she was given.

Emily and Harry had similarly been treated to a makeover when Jenny had driven them to Leeds two weekends previously, meeting with Sarah and Poppy to sort their outfits out. Emily's dress was gorgeous, and the morning suit Harry had been measured up for as one of the ushers had made him appear very grown-up, a proper young man. It had almost brought a lump to Jenny's throat. To see both her children looking so mature had been a very proud moment indeed.

Craig appeared to be going along with the arrangements, happy to sit in the background and let

JoJo take control in the fashion and accessories department. His forte was food, and he was taking control of the menu - working with the venue to devise a seasonal spread for the formal wedding breakfast. He planned on using the best of the local and seasonal products Yorkshire had to offer. And in terms of the wedding cake, well, that was expected to be pure theatre! It was being designed by the cousin of one of the Italian chefs who worked for Craig at *Amelia's*. Luca was a patisserie chef, who had honed his craft whilst working at the renowned Betty's tearooms, and now created spectacular and individual cakes to order. Craig was one of his biggest clients, so he was pulling out all the stops to create a masterpiece.

Throughout the weekend, as Jenny had listened to her friends, happily chatting about their lives and all the developments that had taken place since they had last spoken, a small part of her had felt envious. No longer just the poor relation of the group, she was now officially the unluckiest, especially when it came to love.

Heather was radiant and looked to be finally moving on, having bagged herself a hot Mediterranean stallion to keep her bed warm at night. Mel, she certainly seemed to have finally shed her dating demons, and although she was still being cagey, Jenny would wager there was something going on between her and George. There was definitely an aura of mystery. And in terms of Craig and JoJo, well, where did she start with regards to those two? They were like love's young dream, living in some parallel universe, where unicorns and rainbows seemed to be in abundance. Their world appeared to be covered in sprinkles of fairy dust, with everything they touched recently coming up smelling of roses. Two successful businesses, numerous properties between them, more money than she could ever imagine, and a happy family life to boot, with Poppy the cherry on the top of their cake!

As she finally boarded the train, ready for her long journey back up north, to the grim reality of her nondescript life, a mist of depression descended on Jenny. She thought really hard - what did she have going for her, and where had she gone so wrong in her life? Two children, who barely noticed she was around these days; a teaching job that was driving her crazier by the day; a non-existent social life; a mortgage, with bills coming out of her ears and debts she was struggling to keep on top of; a wardrobe that was long overdue a makeover; and above all else, a relationship that not only defied words, but one she was at pains to do anything about.

When she summed it all up like that, it did not look good, not on any level. And, unless she did something about her life, and soon, what was the point of her going on? This weekend had been a real eye opener. She knew she had no fairy godmother ready to wave her magic wand, suddenly declaring everything was going to be okay. No, she needed to take decisive action herself.

"Plenty of food for thought," she mumbled to herself, as she flopped into her reserved seat in the standard carriage, ready for her long depressing journey home.

Chapter 47

By the time April arrived, Heather had lived on Santorini for over four months. "Where has that time gone?" she reflected, as she sat on the terrace of the taverna, enjoying a cold drink and a well-deserved snack. She had spent the morning working on her latest designs, designs that had been inspired by the scenery around her and the spirit of the island. She was selling the odd piece on the internet and still doing the occasional commission. Largely though she was concentrating on building up her stocks, and importantly her Island Range, ready for Nikos to sell in the shop when the tourists returned, along with the myriad of other local products on offer.

Heather found the light was better in the morning, as were the temperatures, so she generally woke early and sauntered over to the workshop before eight o'clock. Nikos had set up a small space for her in the corner, close to the windows and natural light. It was somewhere she could work peacefully alongside him, content to watch as he applied his skills to whatever repair job had been brought in for him to work his magic on. Sometimes he arrived earlier than her and had the place already opened up. Other days she arrived first using the key he had trusted her with. Increasingly they would arrive together, hand in hand and blissfully happy. The winter rains had now largely gone and the spring days were getting warmer. It would not be long before the tourists returned, Nikos had advised. The idea of her idyll being shattered by an influx of tourists, whilst good for business, was something she tried hard to put to the back of her mind.

Although Heather had renewed the rental agreement on the apartment for another three months, it was now due to expire at the end of May. Her departure date was looming ever closer, and with her plans already in place for travelling home for Craig and JoJo's wedding fixed, they created a stark reminder she needed to give serious thought to her own future.

Her initial plan of staying until the end February had long since been shelved, leaving her with no idea what she intended to do in the short or medium term, let alone the long term. She was living in the moment, with life, as a consequence, taking on a whole new perspective. She felt a real connection here, a peace she had not felt for a long time. The longer she stayed, the more the prospect of returning home haunted her. And where was home these days, anyway? Didn't they say, home was where the heart was? Well, if that was the case, she definitely had no reason to go too far from where she was now.

As she smiled, acknowledging the locals as they bid her good morning or waved over, she realised how much she had fallen in love with this place. This new lifestyle, and more importantly the person she had become, was someone she was totally at ease with. She had time to relax, to enjoy life and no longer felt burdened by the pressures that had haunted her back in Scotland; pressures that had unwittingly held her back. And as she had hoped, the island had reignited her creative juices, with some of the pieces she was now creating feeling totally inspired.

The Godmothers

Heather recognised what a huge catalyst Nikos was for the way she now felt; how settled she had become and how comfortable she was in his company. Over such a relatively short period of time he had become a massive part of her life, instinctively providing her with the inspiration she had been looking for. His approach to life mirrored her own, his values very similar in terms of what was important in life.

Over recent weeks their relationship had gone from strength to strength, and whilst she had never officially asked him to move in with her, his toothbrush had taken residence, with his shaving gear now occupying its own shelf in her small bathroom. They spent their days together, working harmoniously in the workshop, each content to focus on their own projects. Their weekends were spent exploring the surroundings, or taking long walks on the beaches, driving around the island in Nikos' open top sports car when the weather allowed. He was introducing her to his island and the places he loved. They spent most evenings together, sharing a bottle of wine, or cooking a meal in the small kitchenette. Heather was excited to learn Greek recipes, cultural dishes and to discover foods she had never tasted before.

On occasion they would go to the taverna to meet with friends, or around to a friend's home to share a meal. The Greeks were a hospitable nation and Nikos, as a popular man with many friends in the village, received countless invitations. Heather was introduced around and made welcome, many inquisitive to understand what had brought her to their small island, none needing to ask why she stayed.

And at night, well, they were simply consumed with each other, the old creaking bedstead and worn springs leaving nothing to the imagination in terms of how they passed their time. Heather, other than a brief fumble at university, something that had left her both embarrassed and too self-conscious to try again, had limited experience with men. Bruce had been her only real partner. He was very loving, but much older than her, and courteous in all things, particularly in the bedroom. So, time spent between the sheets with Nikos was clearly opening her eyes to some of the delights she had been missing. His physique was indescribable and his stamina something she occasionally struggled to keep up with. No, it was a relationship any woman would be envious of – a lifestyle Heather was at pains to preserve, at any cost.

"Good morning Heather, how are you today?" she heard, as a lady plonked herself down at the table next to her, placing her string shopping bag on the floor. It was full of fresh produce from the local farmers' market that operated twice a week in the village square.

"Alexandria, oh how lovely to see you," she replied, suddenly brought out of her reverie. Alexandria was one of the local women, who over recent weeks had become a good friend. She was also one of the few people who spoke perfect English, meaning Heather enjoyed chatting to her. "I'm very well thank you. I was miles away though, thinking of home."

"Ah, schmuck! Home is where you make it," Alexandria replied, a dismissive tone in her voice. "I've been travelling around so long now I've almost forgotten where my home is! And provided the van remains roadworthy, I'll continue doing so. As long as God allows, that is."

Now in her early seventies, Alexandria lived in an old dilapidated mobile home. It was currently parked on the outskirts of the village, close by the workshop. According to Nikos, it had been there for well over three years, and in the state it was in, in his view there was no prospect of it going very far again. Heather had been introduced to her one morning when she had knocked on the workshop's door, desperate for Nikos to look at the van's heating system. The cooler, winter months were approaching, and try as she might, she could not put off the repairs any longer. The van was very basic and had certainly seen better days, with more miles on the clock than she was prepared to admit. But it was her home and if truth be told, Alexandria had nowhere else to go.

Originally from Greece, she and her husband had toured extensively, setting out in their early forties when a mix of family and political circumstances forced them to flee Athens, with whatever money and possessions they could take limited to what they could carry in the van. They had driven across several continents, crossing seas and oceans to explore new and distant horizons, picking up casual work along the way, whenever the opportunity presented itself. Alexandria had fascinating stories to tell of their travels, tales of times and cultures that predated Nikos and Heather's existence, and occasionally left them spellbound. Other times they listened patiently as she recounted stories she had told previously, many times. Often it would be over a drink in the workshop, when she would come in for a warm, or something to eat, if she managed to time it correctly. She was always happy to rely on Nikos' generosity.

Heather and Nikos were regularly left wondering how much of her ramblings were true, or simply the figment of an old lady's vivid imagination. Fantastical experiences she had perhaps concocted of times past, of memories that continued to fuel her now that she was alone, her travelling days long behind her.

"I know what you're saying, Alexandria," Heather sighed. "You're Greek, and like it or not, despite all your travelling even you've come home. Perhaps not to Athens where you were born, but as close to; well, culturally at least. Here is nowhere like my home, back in Scotland."

"Ah, we travelled around Scotland, back in the day……" As Alexandria began, Heather's mind was already switching off, unable to avoid getting embroiled in another tale; no doubt one where she had seen the Loch Ness Monster, maybe even climbed Ben Nevis. Nothing was impossible, as far as Alexandria was concerned.

After a few minutes, and anxious for her friend to finish her tale, Heather was pleased with the interruption Nikos' arrival provided. Although the flustered way he approached the table, and the worried look so obvious on his face, caused her to feel some concern.

"What on earth's the matter, my love?" Heather questioned as soon as he sat down, indicating to the waiter to bring him over a cold beer.

"I've just had a phone call. My mother is unwell. I need to return home for a few days. I'm flying first thing tomorrow morning. Would you like to come too?" His words cascaded uncontrolled from his mouth, in a manner both unstructured and without explanation.

Heather knew surprisingly little about Nikos' family; other than the odd snippet she'd managed to garner along the way. To her, family was important, but to him it appeared less so. She had gleaned that both his parents were still alive, and he had an elder sister, a brother-in-law and two teenage nieces. She was unaware of any of their names, ages or occupations. From the way he spoke, she estimated his parents must be in their late seventies, and until now he had never mentioned either was in poor health. She knew they lived in Athens. Apparently, his family home was not far from where Alexandria had hailed, a detail he had let slip in a casual comment, although there had been no follow up, or detail added. The fact he rarely spoke about them led her to sense there was some bad blood, or history he would prefer not to talk about. Having lived on Santorini for nearly fifteen years, arriving on the island in his late twenties, and rarely visiting home, suggested to Heather they had perhaps not been close for a long time.

Whilst it had left her curious, she had learned not to pry too closely. His life, outside of what little she knew from what he shared, was not her concern, was it? Thinking this now, made her perplexed. Why the sudden invite to fly back home with him, to see a family she knew nothing about?

"I don't know. Are you sure you want me to come with you?" she questioned, trying to read into his expression or body language for any signs. He was obviously worried, with the look in his eyes one she had never seen before. There was a real sensitivity in it, one she could only describe as hurt. It was reminiscent of how she had felt that last time she'd left her dad at the nursing home, concerned she may never see him again.

She was torn between whether to stay or go, knowing that neither would alter the inevitability of what would happen in time. Did Nikos feel unable to face this visit by himself? Was it something for which he needed her support? And if so, what option did she have, other than to be there for him?

Without waiting for his response, she reached over and took his hand. "Of course I'll come, if that's what you want. What time do we fly?"

Chapter 48

April was proving to be a challenging month for Mel too. The launch of the first phase of the *Just Brewed* franchise was imminent, with the pilot scheme due to launch late May. Seven new premises had been identified in the north of England, with work well underway to outfit the shops. Mel had invested numerous hours with designers and architects to create the look and feel she was aiming for. In addition, her existing premises were scheduled for a similar overhaul in the coming months; the intention was to bring all the cafés up to a similar standard. Having a corporate image and a brand identity was one of the cornerstones of the whole franchise mentality.

An element of Mel was excited to finally be bringing her plans to fruition, although the larger part of her was absolutely terrified. Until now, she had orchestrated everything to do with her business, keeping decisions close to herself and trusting only a small group of people to deliver on what she wanted. She had also personally taken responsibility for any fallout her decisions created, never seeking to find a fall guy, or someone to point the finger at. The service ethos she had established all those years ago, 'friendly, kind and caring', still played out in her cafés. Her teams had fully bought into delivering every coffee with a smile, and providing a warm and polite greeting, regardless of the weather, or the moods of their customers.

Within a few short weeks, a set of franchise owners would be involved – people she barely knew, people she was entrusting to uphold that ethos. That thought was scary and something that kept her up at nights.

The concept of no longer having day to day operational control; having to stand back and allow them to run their businesses, relatively unhindered, was causing her mild anxiety. Regular audits, training and oversight would be established to ensure standards were maintained, but Mel had no expectations this would be heavy handed. Having always favoured the light touch, to do any different now would be going against her better judgement. She had to trust franchisees were investing for the right reasons. As such, she believed they should be incentivised to run their businesses independently, earning themselves a good return for the risks they were taking. Nevertheless, the risk remained. Profit could so easily be put ahead of service, the reputation Mel had worked so hard to establish, ruined overnight.

"Mum, you sound worried. Are you sure you're still okay going ahead with this? It's never too late to pull out, if you're having second thoughts, that is. And if there's something you're not happy with, then don't hold back," Sarah counselled over dinner one evening, the three of them enjoying a rare meal together.

Mel had just finished recounting to Sarah and Jake a meeting she'd had earlier that day with some of her advisors. They had been going through the credit checks and reviewing the due diligence that had been carried out against their potential franchisees. Most investors met the criteria her team had established, raising no red flags. There remained a couple of niggles against some of the applicants though, concerns that meant Mel had still not given her final sign off.

"No, it will be fine, I'm sure." Mel tried to reassure her daughter, although seeing Sarah's reaction, she knew she had not been too convincing. "It's just something George said the other evening, about trusting your gut when it comes to investments and particularly investors. At the time I wasn't sure exactly what point he was making. Today though, when I read some of the reports, his comments resonated." She paused for thought, whilst deciding how much to say. "I have a few concerns - particularly around the couple interested in the premises in Leeds. Do you remember, the shop you looked around for me, last time you were up in Yorkshire? It was something about their application that didn't quite ring true for me. If I'm honest, it's left me in a real quandary."

Jake and Sarah exchange a knowing glance, each raising an eyebrow at the mention of George's name. Recently he was featuring increasingly large in Mel's life, socially and professionally it would now appear. Sarah had known George was involved in something to do with finance in the city, and until recently had not fully understood what. She recalled how he had mentioned it in passing in Australia. At the time, she had paid little, if any, attention. After all, he was simply a passing acquaintance of her uncle's; someone whose company she enjoyed, but nothing more. She never expected to see him again once she returned home, let alone see him grow as close to her mum as he seemingly had.

Within the space of a few months, he was escorting Mel to concerts, inviting her to dine at Michelin starred restaurants, and if Odette's assessment of the number of visits to *Just Brewed* could be relied upon, drinking more coffee than was healthy for a man of his age.

Although her mum was very discreet, Sarah was not naive, and moreover she'd not been born yesterday. She noticed their sly looks whenever George called around to the house to collect Mel for one of their outings. The way Mel touched him as she took his coat, and led him to the sitting room to pour himself a drink whilst she finished getting ready. They had even developed their own language - a kind of shorthand, Sarah noticed, when talking about certain places or events. And what Sarah found most curious was the way Mel giggled, almost like a lovestruck teenager whenever George made a joke, or commented on something in a humorous way. Her mum had never been a giggler. Her behaviour had always been relatively serious and practical, always decisive and focussed, no matter what. No, Mel was not herself and Sarah would wager there was something going on between them. And, what's more, unless she was reading the signs completely wrong, she and Jake surmised the sitting room wasn't the only room in the house George knew his way around!

Nervous about the man who was ingratiating himself into her mum's life, a couple of months previously Sarah had turned detective. With the help of Google, she had started digging, desperate to find anything she could about him. If George was bad news, on the take, or simply messing her mum around, she would uncover it. After all, that's what Google was for, surely?

She recalled how Uncle James had told her George was married, and was going through a separation, and had at least one daughter, although there could be more. He wasn't sure, admitting it was some years since they had been close. Their lives had moved on, certainly since he had emigrated to Australia. Armed with this scant information, plus the business card she had found, casually propped up on her mum's dressing table, she had begun her search. Having grown up without a man around the house, Sarah had always been protective of her mum. They had always looked out for each other, developing a close bond along the way. Men had come and gone, but they always had each other's backs, with none of them ever allowed to come between mother and daughter. And whilst Mel had never directly interfered in Sarah's love life, or vice versa for that matter, neither was afraid to voice an opinion should it ever be needed.

To Sarah's surprise, her search found George was squeaky clean, and no matter which avenue she pursued, she could find nothing untoward, or anything to blight his character. In fact, he was almost a pillar of society, involved in regular charity works and a trustee on the boards of several non-profit making organisations. Sarah turned her attentions to the tabloids and found he turned up infrequently on the social pages, attending the occasional charity function with an attractive lady on his arm, a glamorous addition. More usually he was unaccompanied. There was the odd snippet relating to his divorce the previous year, although nothing salacious, or even gossip worthy. From photographs, Sarah could deduce his ex-wife was probably in her mid-forties and was exceptionally beautiful. As a B-list actress, she had a reasonably high profile of her own. Sarah found various stories about her littering the papers, usually with her latest man in tow, or articles including their daughter Ruby, who was a boisterous teenager, by all accounts. The stories suggested George and his wife had simply grown apart, both having completely different interests, after a rather nondescript marriage lasting fifteen years. There was no suggestion of him having any illicit affairs, or leaving her for another woman. It all felt disappointingly boring, and somewhat flat to Sarah, presuming there must be more to it.

The business papers appeared to contain most about him, and it was clear that was where his attentions were focussed, his dedication and commitment repeatedly reported on. Sarah found he was not simply working in the city, as he had suggested. He was CEO of his own investment company – a respected organisation that was trusted to manage some of the most significant portfolios in the city. Reading one of the finance websites, she found a short bio on him, discussing how he had taken over the business his grandfather started, after Mr Theakston Snr's retirement, ten years earlier. Although it was clear he had been born with the proverbial silver spoon in his mouth, he had nevertheless learnt his trade the hard way, starting on the trading floor and gradually climbing up the corporate ladder. He worked hard, by all accounts, and being the grandson of the boss earned him no special privileges among his peers, or his managers.

After gaining a first in Politics and Economics, his parents had harboured clear expectations he would go into a position in the Government, potentially the diplomatic corps. With their connections, and his charm, there would be no limit to the progress he could make. His mother had her sights set on him becoming Prime

Minister before the age of forty. George however had no long-term interests in politics, or high office. He had seen what it had done to his father, and specifically his parents' relationship, and had no intention of following him into the House of Commons.

So, he had turned his attentions to finance, and specifically the stock exchange. He thrived on the cut and thrust of dealing, the uncertainty and risk of it all. He found he loved the buzz, standing with his sleeves rolled up on the trading floor, watching the screens as the stock values went up or down, barking instructions to buy or sell; fortunes or losses being made at the touch of a button. The feeling it gave him when the deals paid off soon became addictive. He was not driven by money, but it certainly proved to be a lot more lucrative than politics, and a sight more rewarding than a desk job in the Home Office, or some other drab government department.

No, from all Sarah read, it was clear he had earned his reputation the hard way, working solidly and not relying on parental handouts. It was a similar story to her mum's, she noted, even down to the dysfunctional parenting they had both enjoyed! Mel's family had been well connected and extremely wealthy, providing her and her brother James with a privileged upbringing and all that money could buy. It had certainly helped in those early days, with the inheritance from her grandfather coming in handy when buying her first café and getting her first step onto the property ladder. The rest though she too had worked hard for.

The more Sarah considered it, the more she realised they were actually a good match, with George and her mum effectively cut from the same cloth. Their upbringings had been similar and the opportunities comparable in terms of education, wealth and the lifestyle that afforded them. No, she concluded, he was certainly not on the make, or trying to use her, or her networks, as some of her previous boyfriends had attempted. If anything, Sarah recognised, he was perhaps better connected, in the business world at least, with his fingers in many pies. Although when it came to aristocratic connections, then perhaps Mel may have the upper hand there. Sarah laughed at the thought of them playing a game of 'who's who' Top Trumps, or swapping their little black books, to see whose contained the most impressive list of mobile numbers! "I wouldn't mind being a fly on the wall that night," she thought to herself.

"So, George suggests I might want to take them off the list for the moment, or at least until I can address the concerns I have. What's your view?" Mel asked, bringing Sarah out of her reverie and back into reality.

"Sorry Mum, I was miles away. Run that past me again."

"That couple I was mentioning. You know, the ones who want to take over the Leeds franchise. If I take George's advice, I'll need to find someone new to take it on, if I'm to replace them. My problem is, I'm cutting it fine. Especially if we're going to keep to the rollout schedule we've planned."

"Well, how about I take it on? That will save you having to find anyone else, won't it?" Sarah offered, as she looked alternatively at Jake and Mel, in an attempt to gauge their reactions. She was voicing an idea she'd been mulling over in her head for some time; an idea that until now she had not known how to express. This was the perfect opportunity, almost serendipitous, she thought, smiling to herself.

"You know you can trust me, Mum. I know I'm young, but there's not much I don't know about running a café, is there? After all, you took me in when I was still in nappies, and I've always helped out, so it's in my blood. Actually, I'm not far off the same age you were when you started *Just Brewed*, am I? And, if Jake's going to be working for JoJo at the Leeds office, when that opens up in the summer, it makes perfect sense, doesn't it? We can easily buy an apartment up there. And, I can start working for a living, rather than living off you – or going to university, simply to keep Grandpa Lawrence happy!"

Mel looked at her daughter, then across at Jake, unaware exactly what to say to either of them. In that one simple statement, Sarah had not only made it clear she saw Jake as a permanent fixture in her life, but she had made her views on university abundantly clear. Along with her intentions to disobey her grandpa's wish of getting a formal education and making something of herself, saying nothing of her plans to leave home, or buy an apartment. It was a lot to take in.

"Wow, that's a lot to think about!" Mel replied, careful not to jump in, or say something she would later regret. Whilst it would certainly solve a problem, and instinctively she knew Sarah would be able to run a franchise without breaking sweat, was there a danger of it creating a whole new set of issues further down the line?

For the first time in her life, Mel felt a need for parenting advice, and as loathed as she was to admit it, her mind went straight to George. It was time for the talk she had been dreading, but nevertheless knew was inevitable.

Chapter 49

"Hang on, am I hearing that correctly?" Jenny questioned, as she, Heather and Mel were speaking on the phone one evening. It was the beginning of May, only three weeks to the big day and they were having one of their usual monthly chats on the phone, or more accurately on Skype. Wi-Fi reception was not ideal, the summer storm doing its best to play a part in disrupting their conversation. "Did you just say you're bringing Nikos to the wedding, or did I mishear you?"

Over the years, regardless of where they were in the world, or what was going on in their lives, they had all religiously dialled in, usually spending a couple of hours chatting away. Their friendship had always been important, and these calls, more so since Amy's death, were a lifeline for staying in touch and sharing their feelings. At the time, having been hit hard and so unexpectantly by her death, they had vowed they would always be there for each other, and importantly for their godchildren, come what may.

Their conversations meandered, sometimes they reminisced, sometimes they planned and sometimes they simply solved the world's ills – all better achieved with a glass or two of wine in hand. They discussed most things. No subject was deemed off-limits and they were always supportive and non-judgemental towards each other, regardless of the topic. Over the years, there had been countless tears of joy, occasional tears of sorrow, with frustration and anger expressed in equal measure. In fact, the friends had gone through the whole gamut of emotions, in one way or another, as they talked about their families, careers, lives and the lovers who had come and gone.

Recently Jenny struggled more than most when it came to being non-judgemental. She increasingly felt life had dealt her a bad hand, especially when compared with her friends' lives. And, as she aged, she found it harder to bite her tongue, often being accused of engaging mouth before brain. Subtlety had never been one of her fortes.

"Yes, I spoke to Craig and JoJo last week and they said it was no problem. They said they'd love to meet him."

"So, where will that leave Mel and me? I thought we were all coming without partners, not that we've got any anyway," she replied, stating the obvious.

"Yes, I know that was the plan. You'll both have your family there though, won't you? You've got Emily and Harry, and Mel's got Sarah and Jake. I didn't have anyone to bring as my plus one." Heather sighed as she attempted to defend her position. "And after the wedding, we're planning on driving up to Edinburgh to see Dad and Ellen. So, I thought if he's flying over with me anyway, he might as well come to the wedding. It made sense, plus it will give you both a chance to meet him."

"Wow. This sounds like it's getting serious between you two. Am I right, Heather?" Mel enquired, anxious to relieve some of the pressure from the conversation.

"I'd like to think so, but it's still early days. When we went over to Athens last month, he introduced me to his family and some of his old friends. I'd like to do the same."

"Are you sure about this, Heather? You don't really know him that well, other than he's the village's odd-job man. You can't be that serious, can you?" Jenny felt unable to hold her tongue any longer about this whole charade. In her mind, it was high time Heather came to her senses and returned home, before this gigolo, or whatever he termed himself, took advantage of her.

"Yes, I am sure, and I know him a lot better than you'd think. He may be the local odd-job man, but he's also the most sensitive and caring man I could hope to meet. After Bruce died, I thought I'd never get the chance to love again, and Nikos is someone I believe I could be happy with."

"And aren't you at all afraid he's just taking advantage of you, using you? That he's perhaps after you for your money, or your British passport even!" There, she had said it.

Looking at Heather's face on the monitor, Mel could tell Jenny's comment had hit her hard, the tone of it quite harsh. She had cruelly dismissed her relationship and her feelings, assuming Nikos could not love Heather for who she was, rather than what she could bring to the relationship.

"Jenny, I think you've gone too far..." started Mel, determined the conversation would not be allowed to descend any further.

"No Mel, Jenny's right to be concerned for me. However, I would've hoped for you both to have been more supportive, more trusting. What do you take me for?" she asked, a little exasperated. "Nevertheless, I can reassure you, Nikos needs nothing from me. He may just be the odd-job man in the eyes of the village, but that's his business. It has nothing to do with anyone else how he chooses to live his life. However, having met his family and spoken a little more to him about it, that assumption couldn't be further from the truth."

Heather recalled their time in Athens the previous month, an unplanned trip due to his mother's worsening health. A heart scare had left her needing urgent surgery. Fearing the worst, Nikos' sister, Adrianna, had contacted him. She had urged him to come home, before it was too late.

It had been a traumatic time pounding the hospital corridors, waiting for the results of the surgery to become known. Nikos' mother was almost seventy, with the doctors advising her chances of pulling through were above average, although offering no promises. Whilst the family carried out a bedside vigil, Heather was left to wait, often alone in the visitors' room. Although it was a comfortable new private hospital on the outskirts of the city, this did nothing to ease her discomfort. She questioned herself why she had come, why he had begged her to accompany him. Nikos barely saw her for days, and whenever he was around his father the toxic atmosphere was palpable, leaving her to wonder what the cause of it was.

One day, she managed to speak to Adrianna, and casually commented on the father son relationship, or more precisely their lack of any relationship. Adrianna explained how Nikos still held his father partly responsible for the loss of their brother; a brother who had been killed after receiving a fatal gunshot wound to his heart. Heather had been shocked to hear this for the first time, Nikos never having mentioned a brother, let alone the incident.

Adrianna advised it had been an assassination attempt that had gone wrong, with their father the intended target. That night, he had unwittingly sent his son off to meet his fate. Nikos had been close to his older brother; someone he looked up to and worked alongside in the family business, so to lose him so tragically had devastated him, and over what? Money, land, a business deal that had turned sour? No one knew exactly why, and no one was ever brought to justice over it.

When Nikos learned his father had been the intended target and uncovered a little about the nature of the deal that had potentially led to the shooting, he had walked away. He vowed he would never return to Athens whilst his father was around, or benefit from the family's wealth. If there were crooked or illegal elements to the way they earned their money, he wanted none of it. As a young man in his late twenties, he simply left home.

Over the years, the business had turned itself around and was now a hugely successful and legitimate organisation, responsible for shipping tons of cargo in and out of the ports around Greece, and managing their onward distribution around the country. Adrianna and her husband were already working in the business, but given his advancing years, Nikos' father had pleaded with his son to return home in order to pick up the reins. After all, it would be his and Adrianna's one day.

Time, age and maturity had mellowed Nikos, leading him to a reluctant acceptance that his father had not been responsible for the shooting; his brother had just been in the wrong place at the wrong time. Continuing to blame his father was not helping anyone, least of all his father, who still had enough of his own guilt and grief to deal with. He berated himself for not sensing that night that something was wrong; regretting the decision to send his son to his death. And then, for Nikos to react in the way he had, meant the effective loss of both his sons the same evening. His family had been torn apart.

Eventually, and with pressure from his mother, who he adored, Nikos had agreed to help out with the business. His only proviso had been he would support remotely from Santorini, where his home now was. He had no desire to return to Athens, or to test the fragile truce he had reached with his father by working too closely. Time may be a great healer, but some things took more time than others to heal.

No, Heather had certainly gained a greater understanding of Nikos during their few days in Athens, and since their return they had spoken at greater length about it. Nikos had finally opened up to some of the demons that had been haunting him for so long, and the pain of being separated from those he loved. His mother was mercifully recovering, and with time Heather prayed, so too would Nikos' relationships with his family.

"I'm sorry, Heather," Jenny sighed, suitably admonished. "I suppose I'm just jaded by men at the moment. Well, one man in particular. Jason uses me when it's convenient to him, and gives no thought to what I want. I've mentioned divorce again, and he just appears to laugh it off. He thinks I'm not serious, and don't even know my own mind. I've had enough, and quite frankly I'm at the end of my tether with him."

"Jenny, you really need to sort this. You can't continue allowing him to treat you this way." Heather was not usually so forthright with her opinions.

"Heather's right. It's wearing you down, which is not good for your wellbeing, let alone Emily and Harry, who are pawns in his little game. No, you've been suffering with this for over two years, and in anyone's book that alone is grounds for divorce. Go and see a solicitor and get the ball rolling. And, fingers crossed, by this time next year you'll be free of him and his controlling ways for good," Mel recommended. "And, if you need any money to cover the solicitor's costs, I'd be more than happy to chip in!" she added as an afterthought, knowing how much that preyed on her friend's mind.

Chapter 50

Mel was sitting on the settee, nursing a rather large gin and tonic. She had, over recent years, made a conscious effort to try to cut down on her alcohol intake, especially when at home, or alone on an evening. Throughout her twenties, a habit of going straight to the fridge after work and pouring a glass or two of wine to relax had developed. On occasion it stretched to a bottle, with her drinking turning from a social activity to almost a dependence. It was a habit she knew she had to break, knowing the road to addiction was a slippery slope, and one that it was difficult to make a U-turn on. She had a responsibility for a small child, so for Sarah's sake, as well as her own, she had fought to break the habit of drinking alone.

Tonight though, she had made an exception. It was seven o'clock in the evening and George would be arriving any minute. A table had been booked at a swanky new restaurant in Mayfair. It was apparently one of the hottest tickets in town, with people waiting weeks to reserve a table. *Sabor* was the place to be and to be seen, with paparazzi known to hang around for hours on the off chance of snapping a famous face, or a tasty story.

One of George's clients had recommended it, leaving George's secretary, Tilda, tasked with pulling whatever strings she could to secure a quiet table for two. Tilda was quite enjoying this new George, and had become a willing accomplice, happily managing the increasing number of social engagements he asked her to arrange. The restaurant sounded spectacular, with amazing reviews and a select menu. It specialised in Mediterranean cuisine which, according to George, was a favourite of whoever the woman was who was sparking his attentions. Tilda really needed to ask around and find out who she was, do some digging.

Mel had already showered and chosen her outfit, mentally preparing herself for the evening. She had been looking forward to going all week, and had already read the reviews and peeked at the menu online. That was, until she had spoken to her brother earlier that morning. His call had left her completely perturbed about the course of action she needed to take next.

It had started as the usual family catch up, news of the vineyard, of Connie and what the family was doing. In turn, she had chatted about what she had been up to with the franchises, the trips to the theatre, concerts she had attended.

"You and George are certainly getting about a bit, and by the sounds of it you're having fun." James was happy Mel was socialising again, having been concerned for her over recent years, with the lifestyle she was enduring. It was no life, a single mum, working all hours God sent, whilst bringing up a small child. No matter how much money she made. "I'm pleased you've become friends."

"Yes, so far all's going well. It was a real surprise to both of us I think, when we realised we actually liked each other. I'd spent years harbouring bad thoughts about him, almost demonising him for getting me pregnant, before then doing a runner. In fact, he's actually a really nice person, if that doesn't sound too twee."

"No, it doesn't. What did he say when you told him about Sarah; that he's her father? I bet that came as somewhat of a shock, didn't it? Especially after all these years!"

"Well…," Mel paused. "I haven't told him, or Sarah for that matter. Other than you, I haven't told anyone."

"Mel, you can't be serious! You're in a relationship with him now, and he still doesn't know? How on earth is that going to pan out if, or when, he finds out you've been lying to him? Or, were you never intending telling him? Just stringing him along, while the going's good!" James had been infuriated by the end of the call, adamant that if it was him, he would want to know. In his view she had no right withholding the information, adding that the longer it went on, the more difficult it would become for her to hide. To continue living a lie, with the consequences once he found out, was even riskier to predict.

For the remainder of the day, the conversation had repeatedly played out in her mind, almost like a broken record. James' voice, clearly saying she had to say something, her reply that she did not know how, or what to say. It had worn her down, to the extent that she knew she could no longer maintain the pretence. For her own sanity, she had to come clean and suffer the consequences, whatever they may be. How she would deal with Sarah, her parents and her friends thereafter was a whole new question, and one that she would have to beg George to work with her on. The last thing she wanted was for him to broadcast anything before she'd had chance to say something herself; to get her own ducks in a row first.

Mel could hear a taxi pulling up outside and could hear George asking the driver to wait a moment, expecting Mel to be ready. He had phoned earlier to let her know he would be on the last minute.

As she opened the front door to him, still wearing her dressing gown, the glass now empty in her hand, she looked deep into his eyes.

"Oh, I see you're not ready yet, Mel. Is everything alright, you don't look too well?" he had enquired, in his typically concerned manner.

"George, you may want to cancel the taxi. I think we need to talk."

Chapter 51

What felt like the wedding of the century was only two days off and Jenny was starting to panic. She had an appointment at the hair salon later that afternoon to get her hair cut and her roots done, and had even booked a manicure at the same time. Makeup and hair would be done the morning of the wedding, by a makeup artist JoJo had found locally, she had been advised. It seemed a lot of fuss and expense, and coupled with the dress she was wearing, the whole experience was taking Jenny well outside her comfort zone. She was not usually one to dress up, or make much of an effort with her appearance, if truth be told. Why should she, when she rarely went anywhere these days? And on the rare occasion she did venture out, the furthest she got was to the local pub, conveniently situated across the road from school. A quick drink with colleagues, and a bag of pork scratchings if she was lucky, was usually the extent of her excitement.

In fact, she could not remember the last time she had taken this much trouble over her appearance. Her own wedding perhaps, but that had been so low key and had certainly not been themed, or required wedding planners!

Heather and Mel would both be glamorous, their figures accentuated by their choice of gowns, as they floated in on the arms of their current lovers. Mel had casually dropped into a text the previous week the fact that she had asked George to accompany her, which had left Jenny even more disheartened. She, by comparison, would fade into the background, the proverbial wallflower, sitting alone, or worse still, placed on the table at the back with all the kids or the misfit relatives!

She was determined to look her best though and not let the side down. It was Craig and JoJo's big day and a lot of thought and preparation, to say nothing of the cost, had gone into it. She had even tried on her dress and shoes the previous evening, in a desperate attempt to build up some excitement, before they were carefully wrapped in tissue paper. Her bag was almost packed with the rest of the things she would require for the weekend. It was sitting on the bedroom floor, just waiting for those last-minute essentials to be added in the morning, before they all set off.

"Mum, can you drop me off in town," Harry shouted from upstairs. "I forgot to get my hair gel. I can't go to the wedding without it!"

"I'll take you when I go to the hairdressers in an hour, so be ready," she shouted back, mildly amused at his first world problem. "When did my son get so image conscious?" she thought to herself, as she munched away on her egg mayonnaise sandwich? She'd noticed the tracksuits and sportwear he'd lived in were gradually being replaced by smarter, more trendy clothes. She had even noticed he'd started wearing shoes that were no longer caked in mud. These new clothes, unlike sportswear that could be smoothed and folded, added to the mountain of ironing she needed to do each weekend. She had also noticed the aftershave he'd started to wear whenever he left the house to meet friends – even though at fifteen, he still had not actually started shaving! It was a familiar smell; a bottle of Hugo Boss Jason had left behind. It was an expensive one she had bought him the Christmas before he'd left. For some reason she could not bear to clear it out of the bathroom cabinet, believing as long as it stayed there, there was hope he would return.

How foolish had she been in those early days? To think he would be coming home and would resume their happily married life, without missing a beat. His affair a little blip, swept under the carpet for appearances. She had been almost delusional. And then, two years later, how stupid to still entertain the thought of having him back, after all that time playing happy families with Louisa and her son. To think he had suggested moving back home, and she had just stood there, unable to utter a word. No, it may have taken a while, but she had finally come to her senses.

Now, more than comfortable with her decision, she had instructed a family solicitor to file for divorce on her behalf. Enough was enough, and whether he liked it, or not, then that would soon no longer be her problem.

Since making her decision, the concerns about money, the house, the children and above all her self-respect, had not gone away. Her solicitor, Mrs Jessop, had reassured her those feelings were natural when going through a divorce. She had gone on to outline a series of further points Jenny had not even thought about, none of which did anything to ease her anxiety.

"Try not to worry, Mrs Lennon," she had said sympathetically. "All those matters will be addressed once the proceedings get underway. Financial agreements, custody provisions and providing a stable home for your children will be my top priorities. And, as you appear to be the injured party in this marriage, I'm sure the courts will look favourably on that. They, and I, will not allow your husband to take more than he's entitled to. I can assure you of that."

Whilst Jenny had attempted a smile to reassure Mrs Jessop, it had done nothing to convince either party.

"We probably need to schedule a meeting with Mr Lennon and his solicitor at the earliest point, because in my experience the more we can achieve through sensible discussion, then the easier it will be on everyone," Mrs Jessop had added, returning Jenny's smile. Her client's nerves were no different to those displayed by the hundreds of clients she had dealt with over her many years of practising. "Now if you can give me some more details, I will get on with filing the paperwork for you. After which, we can get that meeting scheduled."

Good luck with that, Jenny had thought ruefully as she left the solicitor's office thirty minutes later, knowing Jason would be caught out when the envelope eventually landed on his doormat in a few weeks' time. He would no longer be calling the shots, and how he reacted to that state of affairs was frankly something Jenny was not entirely sure she was prepared for.

"Oh well, let's get the weekend over with first, and not get ahead of ourselves. We can cross that particular bridge when we come to it," she thought to herself, knowing that it was not only Jason, but Emily and Harry who would be hit hard when the news eventually broke. They were certainly not ignorant to the fact their parents no longer saw eye to eye. Presumably they had friends whose parents had gone through similar separations, so divorce was not unheard of. And they were both sensible kids, so it must have been something that had crossed their minds. Nevertheless, that did not mean it would make it any easier. Throughout their separation, Jenny and Jason had been at pains to protect their children from any fallout. How they would survive this final stage though was anyone's guess.

As she finished her lunch and walked the dirty crockery over to the sink, ready to join the mounting pile of dishes she needed to attend to, she muttered to herself, sighing, "I suppose I should get this washing up done. After all, if I'm forking out for a manicure, I wouldn't want to ruin my nails and spoil the whole effect, would I?"

Chapter 52

Mel had woken around six o'clock to the sound of birdsong. The sun was slowly rising in the distance, with the sky appearing to be completely cloudless. Well, the bit that was just visible from her position, propped up in the huge four poster bed she'd been allocated in the Pickwick Suite. Overall, it looked like it was going to be a beautiful day, which augured well, she thought, for the forthcoming nuptials. Now, all she needed to do was focus on getting herself out of bed, making her way to the shower and getting presentable before the makeup artist and hairdresser arrived. Armed with a couple of painkillers, to deal with the mild headache she was feeling from the previous evening's pre-wedding celebrations, she attempted to make her way to the bathroom. The promise of a glass of cold water, before a well-deserved shower, should be enough to waken her up!

Their hotel was an old country house, located in the heart of North Yorkshire, close to Malton, a historic market town, easily accessible from the M1 motorway. They had driven up the previous morning, keen to avoid the Friday afternoon traffic, arriving in the village in time for a late lunch. Malton was not a town she was familiar with, so was interested to learn it had recently been christened Yorkshire's Food Capital by a renowned chef, given the wealth of artisan shops, cafés and restaurants it boasted. Mel had been intrigued to investigate how well their cafés matched up to *Just Brewed,* and equally whether she could get any tips!

Craig and JoJo had discovered the town whilst touring the area the previous summer and had attended one of the famous food festivals it hosted. They had sampled the local ingredients and enjoyed the atmosphere of the quaint old town, staying overnight in one of the historic coaching houses, after partaking of one too many glasses of wine to drive home. Thankfully, Poppy had been staying over at her grandparents' house that evening, so there had been no rush to get back.

So, when they started their search for a wedding venue, Craig had instantly been drawn back to that area; the wealth of local produce that could be sourced to complement his menu, an obvious attraction. The area boasted a plethora of venues, some that had featured in magazines, or been used as locations for films or TV series over the years. However, they were looking for somewhere unique and bespoke; more intimate, charming, accessible for their friends, and above all, off the beaten track.

When they saw Old Dickens, a country house situated in over fifty acres of managed parklands, it instantly ticked all their boxes. It had been named after Charles Dickens, who had apparently been a regular visitor to Malton and the surrounding area. He had even reputedly based some of his characters and the plots behind his novels on people and premises in the village.

JoJo instantly fell in love with the weathered stonework of the extensive two storey Georgian property. Its huge sash windows and sweeping driveway, lined with trees, shrubs and a variety of seasonal flowers, provided a feast for his professional eye. Once inside, he was equally captivated by the architectural aspects, both old and new. The property had recently benefited from a major redevelopment; a huge investment to transform it into the bespoke and luxurious property it was today. JoJo was impressed by the modernisation, noting how tastefully it had been completed. None of the old charm had been lost at the expense of transforming it into a comfortable and contemporary private hotel. The reception rooms and dining areas were light and airy, and with twelve double bedrooms in the main hotel, plus a further ten housed in small cottages located in the grounds, it was perfect. There was also a separate cottage that acted as the bridal suite, located at the end of a private driveway. It boasted one of the largest four poster beds in the land, plus an outdoor jacuzzi and a private terrace, shielded from prying eyes.

Craig had toured the property alongside JoJo; his eyes more focussed on the kitchen, the cleanliness of the property and the overall service ethos of the management team. Hospitality was his speciality, and under no circumstances would he entertain his family and friends in less than the standard he could provide himself. A series of probing questions prompted answers he was comfortable with. The chef assured him he would welcome Craig's menu and source produce both locally and ethically, with the general manager reassuring him of the professionalism of the front of house and service staff they employed. JoJo smiled when Craig eventually signalled he was happy, at the same time feeling a little sorry for the staff who had been on the receiving end of Craig's inquisition. His standards would not be compromised on such an important occasion.

"Where are you off to?" questioned George sleepily, as he rolled over when he felt Mel move. He had slept better than he had done in years, contented in Mel's arms.

"Just to get a shower, I won't be long. We've a long day ahead," she replied, dragging one leg from under the quilt.

"Not so fast, young lady." He reached over and pulled her close. "The shower can wait a few minutes, surely?" The unspoken question clear in his eyes.

In the Copperfield Suite, just down the corridor, Jenny was just about stirring. She too had slept well and enjoyed the previous evening, drinking and chatting with her friends. She'd also finally had the opportunity to meet both Nikos and George in person, along with some of the other guests who were staying over.

She found Nikos, about whom she admitted she still had some reservations, exceptionally charming and well mannered, if a little reserved and quiet. It was not surprising though, given he'd effectively been thrown to the wolves! Attending a same-sex wedding and meeting Heather's friends was one thing, but to follow that with an immediate trip to Scotland, to meet the prospective family must be daunting. She had to applaud him and give him credit for staying the course. As well as his charm, the physical attraction was not entirely lost on her, and the more she watched him, the more she could see the attraction was mutual. This was not just about Heather being infatuated by an Adonis of a man, he appeared equally smitten. His eyes were never far from her, his smile lighting up whenever she spoke to him, or included him in the conversation. He looked like the proverbial cat who had got the cream; having not only snaffled a woman who was clearly besotted with him, but someone with a figure which most men could only dream of holding. Heather appeared to have lost weight in all the right places; her complexion was flawless and she was clearly blossoming from all the attention she was receiving, to say nothing of the sex she must be enjoying! The relationship and the island had certainly worked its magic on her, and Jenny was forced to regret her unkind comments, comparing her to a latter-day Shirley Valentine.

And George, well, what could she say about him? He was totally dreamy and she struggled to take her eyes off him all night. Mel had described him as looking similar to a middle-aged George Clooney, and in doing so had done him a huge injustice. He was an extremely handsome man with an innate sense of style; someone who exuded confidence, and had a certain X factor that set him apart from other men. It was clear he felt comfortable in social environments and was used to meeting new people and putting them at ease. What's more, the chemistry between him and Mel was electric. It was almost as if they had a fabulous secret, just one they were keeping closely guarded. Leaving Jenny more than a little intrigued.

Mel mentioned George's charity work at one part of the evening, describing some of the fundraising events he had attended, and the various trustee boards he supported. "I bet he doesn't go short of donations," Jenny had thought to herself, convinced he could charm his way into persuading anyone to part with anything, if he asked nicely!

To think, George was a similar age to Jason. As far as any other comparisons could be made, she shuddered at the thought. No, there was no competition. Not in any department!

As Jenny lay in bed, willing herself to get up and face the day, she had to admit to feeling more than a little envious of her friends. It was a depressing thought. Approaching middle age fast, without anyone significant in her life, other than two teenagers who hardly noticed she was there, and a career that she would happily throw away tomorrow, if she was not so desperate for the money. "Pass me the razor blades, now!" she thought despondently. If only there was anyone there to pass them to her!

By nine o'clock, Heather and Nikos had already had breakfast and were relaxing downstairs, waiting in reception for the others to surface. They were taking in the flurry of activity all around them. They had watched the flowers being delivered; huge arrangements of spring blooms, in various shades of pinks and yellows, to contrast with the swathes of greenery that had already been set up in the marriage room the previous evening. Five minutes earlier, they had watched as armfuls of multicoloured balloons had been carried in, gingerly, by an extremely slight woman. There were so many balloons, she was struggling to control them. She transferred them to the function room, where the guests would later dine, before dancing the night away. Thankfully it was not too breezy a day, although Heather laughed to herself, as she imaged the woman taking off in a good gust of wind. A bit like Mary Poppins, but without the umbrella.

A man had also wheeled in some disco lights, and what looked like an old-fashioned sound system, presumably for the music later. JoJo had promised there would be a real 80's disco vibe to the evening's proceedings, with no one allowed to slope off to bed early! The wedding might not be until later that afternoon, but it was clear the hotel was readying itself.

The girls were having hair and makeup done from ten o'clock onwards. With so many, a rota had been drawn up to avoid everyone hanging around, or made to feel like a spare part as they waited their turn. Mel had offered to go first with Sarah, then Jenny and Emily would be next, followed by Heather and Poppy bringing up the rear. Poppy was overly excited, declaring it was her first time of being a bridesmaid to anyone who cared to listen; no one prepared to contradict her by pointing out there was actually no bride! She had run around the hotel the previous evening, determined to open every door and take everything in. She would not miss a thing, desperate to remember everything, so she could share it with her new best friend when she went back to school after the holidays.

Poppy was staying in her grandparents' room overnight and would remain with them for the following week, leaving Craig and JoJo to the privacy of their honeymoon suite and a few days alone afterwards. Their honeymoon plans were being kept secret, although reading between the lines Mel believed a few days alone in their new home was what was being planned. The house had finally been completed the previous week, but with all the preparations for the wedding, neither JoJo nor Craig had had a moment to think about moving in. No, she would bet they were planning on holing themselves up in their love nest, just the two of them. And who could blame them?

Heather had offered to keep her eye out for Poppy during the day, watch what she was eating, as well as offering to get her dressed, when the time was right. "No sooner than is strictly necessary, please," Craig had begged, careful to avoid any catastrophises to either her hair or dress! He knew his daughter well, and as delighted as he was that her natural boisterousness had returned, today was not the day for Poppy to be given free rein to gorge herself on chocolate, or create havoc at the ceremony. Well, not until after the cake had been cut and the speeches were over, at least.

"Good morning, did you sleep well?" Sarah asked Heather and Nikos as she and Jake came into reception. They were followed closely by Emily and Harry, still half asleep by the looks of them. They were all staying in one of the two-bedroom cottages in the grounds, with Emily and Harry sharing the twin room next door to theirs. Craig had thought it would be good for Jenny to have some time to herself, so had allocated her a room in the main hotel. It would also make Emily and Harry feel more grown-up, not having to share a room with their mum. Now teenagers, he knew better than anyone the value they would put on their independence. Jenny had initially been reluctant to be separated, however reassured by Sarah that they would be fine, she had agreed. After all, they were not babies anymore, were they? Also, a couple of nights luxuriating in that huge bed and enormous whirlpool bath, with no screeching kids to disturb her, would surely not go amiss, would it?

"Yes, we slept okay, thanks. We're in the Nickleby Suite and it's a lot more luxurious than the

Premier Inn we stayed in at the airport when we arrived," Heather laughed. "Our room overlooks the car park at the rear of the hotel, and the views over the Moors are amazing. It was lovely and quiet, well, until the birds started their dawn chorus, at least. We were awake and exploring the grounds by six this morning, weren't we Nikos?" She reached over to squeeze his hand as she spoke.

"I know what you mean. One of the attractions of the English countryside, I've found," Jake laughed. "It's so different here to Australia, but I'm loving it," he added, smiling over at Sarah, his grin as wide as the Cheshire cat's. Since arriving in England, and enjoying all the country had to offer, he could honestly say he had no desires to return home to his family, or his old life Down Under. And now, securing an internship with JoJo, and working towards his final architect's qualifications, had given him the perfect excuse to stay around; to say nothing of the little lady, whose hand he was tightly holding. Finding Sarah, and being made to feel welcome among her family and friends, made him feel as if all his birthdays had come at once. He had well and truly landed on his feet. Although he was not sure his parents saw it quite the same way, when he'd discussed his ideas for staying in the UK longer than he'd originally planned.

"Right, we'd best go and find some breakfast, before the kitchen clears it all away," Sarah said. "I'm starving!"

"Well, if you hurry, you should still be okay. I'm not sure your mum and George are down yet, and there's been no sighting of Craig and JoJo, or Jenny for that matter," she added, looking across at Emily and Harry.

They continued to remain awkwardly behind Sarah, feeling no doubt a little out of place in such surroundings.

"No, I'm sure they'll all be down when they're ready." Sarah had a knowing glint in her eyes. She suspected George was getting increasingly serious about her mum, and she did not know quite what to think about that. Mel, and long-term relationships did not normally go together.   She feared for her mum, should things not go to plan, given this time the relationship felt decidedly different.

"Right, let's go and hit the buffet...as I've said, I'm starving!" Sarah led the way to the restaurant, with Jake, Emily and Harry following in her wake.

Chapter 53

At two-thirty that afternoon the wedding guests were assembling in the hotel's bar, adjacent to the room where the ceremony was taking place. They were having a quick drink to settle their nerves before proceedings began. Those who had travelled up that morning were mingling with old friends, excited to hear what was planned for the rest of the day and to chat about how the dinner the previous evening had gone. There was a whole array of glamorous outfits on display and some interesting characters, from the nature of the chatter going on.

Craig's mother, Mavis, and his three sisters, with their respective partners and children, had arrived earlier that morning, already dressed in their wedding clothes, creased from the journey. They had opted to hire a minibus and travel together, rather than stay at the hotel the previous evening, or attend the pre-wedding meal. They had also intended travelling back home that evening, as soon as the meal was over. Craig had argued he really would like them to stay, and to let their hair down. He wanted them to celebrate with him and JoJo, to share in their happiness. His mum had eventually relented, albeit reluctantly.

Although known to be outspoken at times, Mavis had never been particularly outgoing or sociable, and in truth was still struggling to get her mind around her son's new relationship. She had nothing against JoJo, or his parents per se, she simply preferred to keep her own company. She had never been one to enjoy small talk or fuss, so was mindful of saying the wrong thing, or offering up an unwelcomed opinion. She was a plain talking Yorkshire woman, and it was clear from which parent Craig had inherited his pride and his natural reserve.

His three sisters were a little livelier, although it was equally obvious they were overawed by the event. However, they loved their brother and would support him, come what may. None of them had been remotely surprised when he'd told them he was gay, or that he was in a serious relationship with another man. They even made light of it, declaring it was almost inevitable, given that he'd been brought up in a household full of women. They also liked JoJo. It was just everything else that was so far removed from their working-class backgrounds, or the types of places they would usually frequent that caused them to feel unease. As they sat in the bar, nursing their half empty glasses of wine, and waiting for proceedings to begin, it was not surprising the sisters felt on edge.

Ron and Jean Rawcliffe, Amy's parents, Poppy's grandparents, also sat awkwardly in the bar, occupying the corner, furthest from the entrance. They were unsure what to say, or who to talk to. Other than JoJo and Mavis, there was no one else they recognised enough to spark up a conversation with. Poppy was with her dad, so even she was not there to provide a distraction. They felt like fish out of water, dressed in their Sunday best, in a hotel that was well beyond their usual budget. Ron was wearing a suit that had seen better days but still fitted him, and a crisp white shirt and matching tie that had been bought as a boxed set. He had clearly made an effort. Jean had bought a new dress from Marks and Spencer's, having toured Sheffield's Meadowhall shopping centre for hours, trying to find a suitable outfit. Nothing in her wardrobe had seemed appropriate for the occasion.

It felt strange for them to be attending the wedding of their son-in-law to another man, a circumstance they would never have dreamed possible. They had resigned themselves to the fact that after their daughter's death, Craig would move on. They expected that he would probably remarry and have more children, siblings for Poppy. He was still young and had his life ahead of him. Above all, Craig was a kind man, a generous son-in-law, and someone for whom they always wished the best. Memories of the day he married Amy flooded back; the day Ron proudly walked his daughter down the aisle, the happiness so evident on everyone's face as he gave her away. How times change.

When Craig first introduced them to JoJo and explained his feelings, they were shell-shocked. Words could not describe how surprised, or stunned they had been, or how they would ever explain it to their wider family or friends. They soon realised they had a simple choice to make. They could either embrace this new relationship, or not. The consequences of the latter though were unimaginable, with the risk of being left behind, or worse, being left out of Poppy's life. A consequence that was too awful to contemplate. Above all, they sensed the happiness Craig felt, and it was as clear as day that Poppy was adored by both her daddies. So, in truth, what option did they have?

"Hello Ron, Jean. Lovely to see you here. You're looking well." Heather walked over to them, Nikos in tow.

"Lovely to see you too, love," Jean replied, the relief in her voice evident. "We were hoping you were coming, as we wouldn't have known many people otherwise. Are Mel and Jenny here too?"

"Yes, we all arrived yesterday afternoon. I'm sure they'll both be down shortly. In the meantime, let me introduce you to my friend, Nikos. Nikos is from Greece, and we met in Santorini, where I'm living for the time being."

"Yes, I've heard all about that, love. Craig gives me a running commentary on what you girls are up to, whenever he calls around or drops Poppy off." Jean smiled over, whilst Ron offered his hand. "Nice to meet you, lad. You'll look after our Heather, see now't goes wrong, won't you lad?"

Nikos smiled and shook his hand, unsure exactly what the correct answer was to such a question. His ear was gradually becoming attuned to Heather's broad Scottish accent, whereas the Yorkshire dialect was proving a little more challenging.

"Oh, here's Mel now. She's with her new partner, George. And Sarah and Jake are right behind them. I presume you've heard about them too, Jean?"

"Yes, he's a proper looker isn't he, as is your young man, I might add Heather," she added quietly, with a glint in her eye after giving George the once over. She might be getting on in years, but Jean could still appreciate a good-looking man.

As the conversations continued and noise levels started to build, along with the excitement as more people joined, Jenny was slowly making her way down the staircase. She was careful not to wobble off her heels, holding tightly onto the banister rail for extra support. She had deliberately waited as late as she could before joining the party. Her intention was to sneak in without anyone noticing and simply blend into the background. She felt completely outside of her comfort zone; looking ridiculous in her fancy frock, that incidentally felt too big for her now! Her hair was arranged in an Audrey Hepburn styled beehive, with makeup that probably made her look more like Coco the Clown, with her bright red lips and heavily made-up eyes. "Why on earth did I ever agree to this?" she thought to herself, seriously considering whether it was too late to turn around.

As Jenny hovered by the doorway deliberating her next move, she could just make out the back of JoJo standing at the bar. His white, tailed morning suit fitted him perfectly, accentuating his tall, athletic frame. He was talking to someone she did not recognise. The two of them were obviously laughing at a joke; clearly something had amused them. In the distance, she could see Mel and Heather with the rest of the gang, including her two children, who were appearing to be talking to Amy's parents. Other than that, it was simply a sea of faces, leaving her almost too nervous to step forward.

"Wow, who's the hotty in the doorway?" As he and his best man had completely different definitions of what classed as hot, JoJo swivelled around to see who he could possibly be talking about. "Oh, that's Jenny," he replied with a smile on his face when he saw her standing in the doorway, looking more glamorous than he would ever have imagined possible. Any reservations he may have had about her dress, believing it might have been a tad tight for her at the fitting, simply dissipated away. She had obviously lost some weight, and the way she was standing, probably due to the height of the heels, helped her stature. She looked stunning. "She's one of Craig's oldest friends, and she's lovely – if a little forthright sometimes, as she rarely minces her words! They all met at university, over twenty years ago. Mel and Heather are the other two, they're standing over there, with Amy's parents," he added, pointing in the general direction of the others. "They're not a bad bunch really. Not when you get to know them."

Callum's eyes did not leave Jenny. There was something about her eyes that was mesmerising him, making her appear both vulnerable and enigmatic at the same time.

"Mum, everyone's over here, come and join us." Emily waved, calling her over. Jenny smiled, noticing how lovely her daughter looked in her ballerina length cream dress, her hair nicely styled, in curls that framed her face and her pretty smile, wearing the slightest hint of makeup. At fourteen the puppy fat was long gone, with clear signs of the beginnings of a womanly figure developing.

Noticing her smile as she turned towards the girl, Callum asked JoJo "Who's she with?"

"Oh, that's Emily, her daughter. And the young man next to Emily is Harry, her son. They seem lovely kids." His reply failed to hit the mark, in terms of replying to the question Callum was actually seeking an answer to.

"And what about her husband? Has he been invited too?"

"No, and that's a long story, and one we haven't got time for now. Although, if I remember rightly, you're sitting next to her at the meal, so you should have plenty of time to ask her yourself," he replied, finally understanding where his best man's interest lay. "Right, get that drink down you, it's showtime, my friend. Time for me to go and make an honest man of myself!"

Chapter 54

Jenny was starting to stir the following morning, still snuggled up in her king sized bed, afraid to open her eyes, for fear the dream she'd been having would suddenly dissolve away as soon as she did. It was a similar dream to one that had played over in her mind countless times before – the type of dream where she is whisked away by a handsome stranger, carried to her bed, and made love to the whole night long.

As she opened one eye, she could just about make out her dress, neatly folded over the back of the bedroom chair, the diamanté on the shoulder straps glinting in the morning sunlight. And her shoes, with those killer heels, that she had even surprised herself by keeping on all evening, dancing until to the early hours, were placed next to her overnight bag. The bag acted as a gentle reminder that it would soon be time to pack up, check out of the hotel, gather the kids and return to reality. A reality she had done her best to put on hold for the past forty-eight hours. It was the end of this particular fairy story, the end of her dream. But what a great dream it had been. And what an amazing weekend, given it was one she had, if truth be told, been dreading.

Everything had gone to plan, and Jenny could not have picked a single fault with the whole proceedings. Poppy held Craig's hand as they walked down the makeshift aisle, Emily just ahead strewing petals, to where she, Mel and Heather were waiting. Their task was to give him away, which thankfully had not involved much more than them each giving him a kiss, before wishing him well. The vows Craig and JoJo had then exchanged had left everyone in tears, as had the speeches delivered by the best man and both grooms.

Craig's life before JoJo, was acknowledged, and the love he had shared with Amy was not shied away from. It had all been very emotional, the start of a new chapter for both of them, well, all three of them. Poppy had certainly not been shy in making her presence known throughout the day, and by JoJo's reaction it was clear how much he doted on her. Craig had excelled himself on the choice of menu. The food had been spectacular, as had the copious bottles of wine and champagne that had flowed all evening from the free bar. And the wedding cake was the true masterpiece that had been promised, with Luca, the patisserie chef even turning up for the cutting ceremony, in order to judge people's reactions.

After the meal had been cleared away and the speeches and toasts delivered, guests had been invited to rest while the room was reset for the evening party. Everyone was advised to reserve their energies for the dancing, and the DJ did not disappoint. He played a constant stream of hit after hit; his selection of dance music, pure genius.

Jenny remembered dancing as if her life depended on it, her usual inhibitions parked for the night, as she let her hair down and partied with her friends. She had received so many compliments on her outfit and her hair, so rather than continuing to feel self-conscious, she had embraced her new look and revelled in the attention she had attracted.

JoJo's best man, Callum, had paid her particular attention. They had been sat together at the top table, and not at the back of the room where she had imagined she would be placed. Throughout the meal he had taken a real interest in her, and their conversation had flowed effortlessly. He had been good company, regaling her with tales of him and JoJo growing up together in London. Jenny learned they had been friends since high school, so he easily identified with the bond she and the others girls had with Craig. He talked about how similar it was for him and JoJo – even going as far as discussing some of the difficulties JoJo had faced in accepting his own sexuality when he was only sixteen. Callum spoke of standing up to some of the bullies JoJo had encountered and helping him deal with the fears and prejudices he'd been forced to overcome over the years. They obviously shared a close friendship.

He also listened attentively as she explained about Jason, and the impending divorce, never being judgemental or offering an unsolicited opinion. He simply listened and took an interest in what she was saying. He drew the occasional parallel to his own divorce four years earlier to show empathy.

As the evening progressed, Jenny noticed his eyes rarely left her. On several occasions he turned up at her side, asking for a dance or bringing her a fresh drink, or simply joining in the conversations she was having. As the night wore on, and the slower dances began, Jenny noticed Mel and Heather exchange a knowing smile, even an encouraging nod. Callum had definitely caught their attention too, and looking at him it was not at all surprising. He was as tall as JoJo, slightly broader in build perhaps, with dark hair and an attractive, well-trimmed stubble beard. He was a builder by trade, and from his physique it was clear that he liked to get stuck in. There did not look to be an ounce of unwanted flesh on him, with hands that knew honest labour.

When the clock struck midnight, and the DJ announced it was time for the last dance, Mel appeared at Jenny's side. "Sarah's said she and Jake will keep Emily and Harry occupied for you in the morning. So, don't worry about being disturbed, or coming down too early - should the mood take you, that is!" she whispered knowingly, nodding in Callum's direction, before moving into George's arms and joining the others for the last dance.

And as the DJ played the classic from Dirty Dancing, 'I've had The Time of My Life', Callum sidled over to her and said cheesily, "Come on, nobody puts baby in the corner," before leading her to the dancefloor. The perfect end to a perfect evening.

As she turned over, still not fully awake, she could hear a slight noise in the bathroom, and noticed the light had been switched on. Panicking that someone was in the room, and hoping it was one of the children and not a maid, she called out, almost in a whisper. "Hello, is anyone there?" How embarrassing if she had overslept, and they needed her to check out of the room fast.

"Oh, good morning, sleepyhead. Back in the land of the living, are we?" Callum replied, as he came out of the bathroom and walked over to the bed, wearing nothing but a pair of tight-fitting boxer shorts. "I've been trying my best to sneak about quietly, so that I wouldn't wake you. You looked so peaceful, lying there. And you were clearly enjoying your dream, whatever it was," he said, continuing to smile over at her.

Jenny did not know what to say in response to that, completely flabbergasted at seeing him standing there, in all his glory, in her bedroom. She was now fully awake, and frantically looking around, trying to get her bearings.

"I've been awake for nearly an hour, and have just about tidied up the mess we created last night. Your dress is folded over there, with your shoes." Callum observed casually, pointing to the chair. "I'm sorry, I think you might need to invest in some new lingerie though, as these panties look beyond repair." He grinned as he held up a piece of frilly black lace. The image instantly brought back memories of what had happened after he had walked her back to her room after midnight, and she had invited him in for a nightcap.

"Oh my god. I must have been in a deep sleep, and an even deeper dream!" Jenny replied, mortified to learn he had stayed the night, without her even realising. "Have you slept here all night, and what time is it anyway?"

"It's just after seven, so it's still quite early. And yes, I've been here all night. Although, if I recall correctly, there wasn't much sleeping going on." The contented smirk did not leave his face.

"Oh, no. I hope I didn't embarrass myself too much, and I hope I didn't talk in my sleep, or worse still snore! I probably drank too much, which isn't good either. God, what must you think of me!" Jenny was now starting to panic about what she may, or may not have said, or done. Or worse still, wondering what a nightmare she must look, first thing in the morning, before her hair was brushed or her teeth cleaned. Her mouth tasted dry, like the bottom of the proverbial budgie cage, so she had a sense of what her breath must smell like too. Jason had always said it wasn't her finest hour. "And I haven't a clue what I was dreaming about!" she lied, not too convincingly.

Sitting on the bed, and pulling the duvet back, he reached over and gently stroked her thigh, close to where some of her stretch marks were clearly on display, she was embarrassed to notice. "Was it something along these lines, or perhaps when I touched you here, or even here?" he asked suggestively, as he slowly moved his hand further up her body. "Or perhaps when I did this, and you made that strange squeal? Oh yes, that's the one I remember." He was amused as Jenny let out a groan of pure pleasure as she responded to his touch. "Would a quick replay of last night's activities help with your recall, do you think?" He was unable to take his eyes off her naked body, his look clearly indicating he liked what he saw.

Jenny returned his stare, unsure how to respond now that she was sober(ish); the party and the flirting of the night before firmly behind her. She was technically a married woman, one who had obviously spent the night with another man. A man she barely knew. What on earth was she thinking? Then again, she was separated and in the throes of getting a divorce. So, who could blame her, or even judge her? Especially after what she had put up with from Jason these last few years. If she did have some meaningless fun, or find a little fleeting pleasure, then wasn't she entitled to that? "What the heck," she thought. "Life is for living, and even if he's not Mr Right, he's certainly Mr Right for now."

"Sounds like a brilliant idea," Jenny replied, a mischievous glint in her eyes. Looking over at the clock, she added with a sense of growing confidence, "and who says it needs to be quick? I think we've plenty of time before we have to check out, don't you? So, there's no need to hurry on my account."

Chapter 55

The drive back from Malton to London the morning after the wedding, with Sarah and Jake in the back of the car, was proving to be more than a little uncomfortable for Mel. They had waved Heather and Nikos off, as their taxi arrived to take them to the railway station to catch the train to Edinburgh, before doing the same to Jenny, as she packed Emily and Harry into her car, her mood noticeably lighter than when she had first arrived. They arranged to have a catch up call the following week, to rake over the embers of the weekend. In truth though, Mel and Heather were just desperate to hear more about what had put such a huge smile on their friend's face.

Now, as George drove down the motorway, she stared out of the window. She focussed on passing road signs, other vehicles, animals or crops in the fields. In fact, anything to keep her mind off what was really troubling her. There were some difficult discussions ahead, discussions she could not afford to put off any longer; discussions she was frankly at a loss to know how to even broach. Coming clean after all these years was going to be a real challenge, and one she did not relish.

Sarah and Jake were chatting excitedly behind her. They were returning to Yorkshire the following weekend, with plans for starting their new life together all they could talk about. Mel had eventually agreed to Sarah taking over the Leeds branch of *Just Brewed,* although as a manager rather than a franchise holder, for now at least. She still remained uncertain if that was the role she wanted Sarah to take in the company, but accepted that until she decided, it was not a bad stopgap.

The couple who had previously been interested in becoming franchisees had been formally turned down. Shortly after Mel had mentioned it to George, it transpired their funding was not in place, with some of their references not stacking up. Mel's instincts had been sound and she had been right to trust them. The slight delay however had meant the shop would not be opened until the beginning of July, with Sarah still needing to finalise staffing and training before then. Odette had stepped in and offered to spend a few days in Leeds, to give Sarah the support she needed. Mel had accepted her offer, almost biting her hand off at the suggestion.

Jake was also due to start his new role with JoJo the following Monday, once the newlyweds had returned from their brief honeymoon. He had been looking at some of JoJo's existing clients, to get a feel for the nature of work the business took on, and was excited at the prospect of getting himself more involved. Whilst there were only a couple of projects in the North, it was a growing market, and one JoJo was keen to expand into. This all added to Jake's mounting excitement.

He and Sarah had secured a small, furnished apartment in the city centre, in one of the new high-rise developments. Being centrally located it meant it was convenient for both the nightlife and the social side, moreover they would not need to buy a car. It was also low maintenance, so until they got more settled, it would serve them well. Mel liked the fact Jake appeared to be pragmatic and mature in his thinking; his head was clearly screwed on. He was a good balance for her daughter, who as much as she loved her, knew could be quite scatty and impetuous. Sarah still had a lot of growing up to do, but the signs were promising. Mel could also see the sense in renting, as it was clearly risk free and did not tie either of them into anything permanent. Although she sensed neither of them saw any risks in what they were doing, nor in their relationship. It was as if they were love's young dream – completely oblivious to any problems that might be lurking around the corner.

Their plan was to pack up their things from the London house, and drive to Leeds the following Saturday, in a self-drive van Jake had found to rent. In the meantime, they planned on fitting in a brief visit to Devon, as Jake wanted to see his grandparents before they went north. He knew he was not going far, and if he needed to get back to see them for any reason, it was completely manageable. After all, the three hundred or so miles between Devon and Leeds, was a whole lot easier to navigate than the ten thousand miles between there and Australia!

She and George had eventually spoken about the night they had first met, all those years ago. It was almost as if the penny finally dropped, when Mel confirmed it had been the millennium New Year's Eve party. She reminded him she had accompanied her brother, James, to be abandoned as soon as they had entered the building, adding how he had swept in and taken pity on her. How he kept her amused throughout the evening, with his jokes, funny stories and copious amounts of drugs and alcohol.

As more of the memory resurfaced, George began to feel a little embarrassed. Whilst he suspected they had probably slept together he was unsure, and did not want to presume. By his own admission, he had been a 'bit of a lad' in his youth; someone who liked to party and enjoy the finer things in life, especially the company of attractive girls. He had certainly sowed his wild oats back in the day, never short of a partner. By the start of the millennium though, he had been engaged, so perhaps not.

"I do remember that night, now you mention it. It was wild, if I recall, with fireworks as midnight struck. There was a lot of partying in those days, wasn't there?" he asked, almost rhetorically. He was still unclear why Mel had chosen to cancel the meal they had both been excited about, to go down memory lane. Or why she looked so nervous, as she sat in her dressing gown, clearly not ready to go out. They had built a close friendship over recent months, although something about her manner suggested she was building up to giving him the big heave-ho!

"So, do you not recall what happened after the fireworks, at all?" She was still finding it difficult to appreciate that whilst that night had haunted her for more than twenty years, for him it had not even featured in his consciousness.

"I know I had to leave quite early the following morning, to go back to London. I think I'd arranged to attend a lunch with my then fiancée's parents. Other than that, no. I fear it's all a blur. Did I embarrass myself perhaps? I know I had a tendency to do that in those days, especially if I'd had too much to drink," he added, quite sheepishly.

Mel realised the discussion was not going to plan. So, rather than use the subtle approach she had been planning, decided it was time to be a little more direct.

"Yes, you're right you did have to leave rather early. You left before I'd even had time to wake up, or get dressed for that matter. That is, after our drunken one-night stand!"

"Oh dear." The shock on George's face was an absolute picture; Mel confirming one of his worst fears. From the point of his engagement, George had tried desperately hard to curb his habit of sleeping around, and once married was proud to say he had remained faithful. Over the years he had faced endless temptations, with women throwing themselves at him. He knew money and power acted as aphrodisiacs, and coupled with looks that he could not deny, he understandably was often targeted.

To learn now that he had failed was tough. But it was not the end of the world, surely? And, even so, he was still at a loss to understand why Mel was bringing it up. They were enjoying each other's company. The last few months had been fun, so why rake over twenty-year-old coals?

"George, I can clearly see you're still not getting where this conversation is going, are you?" Mel was starting to get frustrated she was having to spell everything out.

"No, I'm sorry Mel, I'm not. Would it be easier if I just got my coat and left, as clearly we're not going out tonight." He had obviously upset her, so was resigned to the end of their relationship. It had been lovely whilst it lasted, and he was wise enough to know all good things had to come to an end.

"George, if I really have to spell it out to you. then so be it." Mel's frustration was building. "When you left me that morning, you left me pregnant. At the time I was furious with myself for being used, but more so with you for using me. You left me without a second glance, to go off and play happy families. Whilst I was left to bring up my daughter, our daughter, single handed. Over the years, what happened has haunted me, and I can't continue like this, any longer. I'm sorry if I've strung you along these last few weeks." Mel struggled to disguise the quiver in her voice.

"Our daughter? What do you mean?" The shock was evident on his face. George was unable to utter another word, or properly take in what Mel was saying.

"Yes, Sarah is yours. She doesn't know that yet, in fact she doesn't know anything about you." Mel allowed what she had said to sink in for a minute. "It's just I've started to develop feelings for you, and if our relationship is to go any further, I can't continue to lie to you, or to her. So, at the risk of what you may say or do, I needed you to know."

As there was still no response from George, Mel continued. "I'm not asking you for anything, and if it's too much, you're free to leave. Although I would ask you please not to say anything to Sarah, or anyone else for that matter, until such time as I'm ready. And if this is the end of our relationship, then so be it. At least I'll have been honest with you." As Mel delivered her last line, she burst into tears, unable to bottle up her emotions any longer. She had said what she needed to say. Now she could only face the consequences.

Seeing her break down, George reached out and brought her into his arms. Whilst he still did not know what to say, he knew that his next words could be life defining, so he had better choose carefully. Sarah, his daughter. Wow. He had certainly not seen that coming.

"Shall I order in some pizzas, because I fear they'll have probably given away our table by now?" he asked, gently stroking her back as the sobbing subsided. They were not possibly the most momentous words he could have chosen, under the circumstances, but he was struggling. "And then, I'll pour us both a drink, and you can tell me a little more about my daughter. It looks like I've got twenty years of catching up to do. To say nothing of the rest of her life to look forward to." His response signalling he was more than happy with how things had panned out.

It was not exactly the night they had planned, although in the scheme of things it turned out much better than Mel could ever have hoped. Over a bottle of wine, they had talked, with Mel being honest about how his actions had coloured her views of men and relationships over the years. She had felt let down, used, disappointed and so alone, vowing never to be put in that position again. Above all, she had been afraid to speak about it to anyone. For years, unable to voice her feelings, or deal with other people's reactions.

In time she had built a protective wall around her and Sarah, a wall that only became threatened once she learned he had met Sarah in Australia; more so, on hearing they had got on so well. She had opened up to James, with James then being the catalyst for knocking the wall down entirely.

George had listened as Mel poured out her heart, ashamed at how his boyish actions had made her feel – and concerned about how many other women he had similarly treated in his youth. He apologised, leading to even more tears, this time from him. By the end of the evening, they were emotionally drained. As she led him to her bedroom a questioning look in his eyes, he followed. Tonight, it was not about sex, it was about healing. And, as George spent the night holding her, allowing her emotions to express themselves in any way she chose, they both felt their relationship move to another level.

Now, with George at her side, Mel finally felt able to face the discussion with Sarah – together. It was just a matter of choosing the right moment when they eventually got home, and listening to the endless list of jobs she and Jake needed to do before their departure, that in itself would be a challenge!

Chapter 56

Three months later

It was a baking hot day in late August, with temperatures already in their high twenties, and a gentle breeze the only thing keeping the early afternoon heat bearable. Nearly everyone had travelled north again. This time for a BBQ and a housewarming party, to christen Craig and JoJo's new home. It was also the opportunity to finally expose the project JoJo had poured his heart and soul into over recent months, to say nothing of the money he had spent to bring his dream alive. Now finished, it was time for inspection by their nearest and dearest.

Poppy was the most excited of them all, keen to show off her own pony, Treacle – so named after its brown colour that in the sunlight turned to almost orange. It was happily grazing in the meadow that was attached to the converted barn, along with a small herd of sheep Craig had recently acquired, to say nothing of the brood of chickens and geese that roamed freely around the courtyard in front of the old stable block. It was clear Craig was embracing the good life, with plans to turn over part of an adjoining field to grow fresh vegetables and plant fruit trees. JoJo was not sure what would grow out in the wilds, but knew better than to interfere with Craig's plans, especially where food was concerned.

To say it was simply a converted barn was a stretch! There was little left of the original structure. It had been replaced by a modern state of the art building, complete with floor to ceiling windows and bifold doors that ensured an almost uninterrupted view of the landscape and the rolling moors. With so much glass, there had been a fear the building could either overheat in the hot weather, creating a greenhouse effect, or be too cold in the winter, when the gales whistled across the heathlands. Consequently, the heating and air-con system that was installed was second to none; a feature that had certainly not come cheap.

In reality nothing had come cheap, with JoJo investing heavily in the build, to say nothing of the quality of the fixtures and fittings he had used. The kitchen was restaurant standard, custom built, but with none of the industrial feel about it. The rooms were spacious and airy, with clever lighting, the furniture tasteful and homely. It was not a showhouse, or one simply to look at through the covers of a magazine. It was a home and the overall effect was truly stunning.

Jenny and Mel made a series of appreciative noises as they toured the property, as JoJo proudly pointed out its features. Their oohs and aahs as they went from room to room did not go unnoticed, and when they saw the walk-in wardrobes and the ensuite bathroom in the master bedroom, Jenny almost fell over. "This wardrobe is bigger than my bedroom, all by itself. I think I could put my whole house in your front lounge! And what I'd give to have a rainfall shower like that. Actually, any shower that worked would be a bonus at the moment." There was a lightness about her comment that Mel noticed was new. None of the usual acidity or jealousy that she could sometimes default to was there.

"Yes, it's great, isn't it?" JoJo replied. "Can you see, the shower head is sunk into a panel in the ceiling, with the controls all working automatically through a series of sensors, on an LED panel in the wall. We've programmed different settings for mornings, evenings or after a workout, depending on the mood or the temperature you require."

Mel bit her tongue to avoid making an obvious comment about it not getting too hot or too steamy, and simply smiled as they moved on. It was giving her a lot of food for thought. Living in London had many advantages, with the house she lived in valued between four to five million pounds, after the recent upturn in property prices. But her house was nowhere near as spacious, or as modern as this. Perhaps it was time to think about moving to the countryside too. After all, what was keeping her in London, now that her business was more dispersed? With additional franchises springing up around the country, and more people taking over the general operational side, she could step back and manage from a distance. The idea of being a lady of leisure had a certain ring to it, and was becoming more appealing the more she toured around.

"Well, I think it's a masterpiece. You should be extremely proud of what you've accomplished here, JoJo. I hope you and Craig will be very happy." Mel was genuinely touched by what they had achieved as a couple, and although it had come as a huge surprise, in just over twelve months she had seen a different person in Craig. He was a happy, contented man, comfortable in his own skin, with a large part of that obviously down to the man standing in front of her now.

"I think we are, now that we're more settled. And more so given that Poppy's happy in the local school and has made friends. That was a big thing for both of us. It wasn't just our lives that were changing by moving out into the countryside, but Poppy's too. She will remain at the forefront of all our thinking, and won't miss out by being here. Ron and Jean have already stayed over, and it's not a long drive to theirs, if we ever need babysitters," he added, reassuringly.

They had gradually moved in after the wedding, eventually selling Craig's old house and investing the proceeds from that into a trust fund for Poppy. The old house, to an extent, had represented Amy, so by transferring the money to Poppy, it felt like neither of them had taken away a part of her heritage, or her inheritance. That money would be there for her, should she need it. No, it had been time to move on and Craig was sure the memories would remain with him and Poppy, regardless of where they lived. They had a new life, and a chance of happiness with JoJo, of that he was sure. He never regretted the day he had poured his heart out to him, or the subsequent chain of events that had created. He was gay, and that was something he was not only comfortable with, but proud to shout from the rooftops, should he ever be required to!

"Right, can I tempt anyone to one of Craig's sausages, they're a treat not to be missed!" None of the innuendo was lost on the adults. He smiled over at Craig, who had been standing at the BBQ for the last hour, politely refusing any help from the band of willing commis chefs. The meat was almost cooked, the table was set for the meal and by the looks of it most people's glasses were full. So it was time to relax and enjoy the company. It may only be a select little gathering, but for now it was all they needed.

As Sarah took her seat around the garden table, ready to tuck into the spread Craig had created, and careful to keep herself out of the sun for fear of burning, she looked around, soaking up the atmosphere.

Next to her sat Jake. The man who, less than two years ago, had appeared in her life and was already making himself almost indispensable. She had never been in love before, and with Jake, if this wasn't love, well it was the closest she had ever been. For the last few months living together in their apartment, they had found a harmonious rhythm and a routine for their lives. They both worked long hours, she at the café and Jake at his office five miles away from where she worked. She started early each morning, and remained on call most of the day, even at weekends when staff covered her shifts. Jake started later, and had to travel more, occasionally staying overnight when visiting clients. Their time together became more precious, so they had made a commitment to enjoy their social life and any downtime they could get. Leeds may not be as glamorous as Australia or even London, and city living was not always as great as it was cracked up to be, but they were enjoying themselves. There was a real vibe around the city. It was young and vibrant, and the Yorkshire hospitality made them feel welcomed.

Above all, she was enjoying her independence. Living at home, with her mum, was all she had ever really known. So, now to be running her own household, with responsibility for paying the bills, to say nothing of doing the shopping and the laundry, was a real challenge. At twenty though, her mum had been doing all that, with a baby in tow and a new business to run – so who was she to moan? And anyway, even if it did all go pear-shaped, she knew where home was, if ever she needed it. No, her mum was a real hero in her eyes, and that would never change.

She was watching her now, completely relaxed and at ease, sitting opposite Jake and looking years younger than her age. She was chatting away to George – or should she say, her father. That had been a real bombshell, and in truth she was still trying to come to terms with it, and the impact of having a father figure in her life. She had managed for twenty years without one, so what could he bring to the party? For the moment, at least, she was happy to see him as her mum's boyfriend. She would process the rest when she was ready. It was not that she did not like him, and she could see how much he cared for her mum, but there was something in the story, and the way they were telling it that did not add up in her book. Her mum mentioned they had known each other previously, and that it simply hadn't worked out. She was missing a piece, because if that was the case, why had her uncle or George never mentioned it when he came calling at the vineyard? And why had it taken her mum so many months to get round to telling her since they had got back together? George had an ex-wife and a daughter of his own, and she wasn't ready yet to add to that. In time, perhaps, but for now the jury was still out.

"Poppy, why don't you come and sit here, next to me?" Sarah asked, as Poppy walked past, looking to find a place to sit. "At least I only have the idea of one dad to worry about," she thought to herself as she cleared a place for Poppy, wondering how the child must feel finding she now had two dads to contend with!

"Hello, is anyone at home?" They could hear a male voice coming from inside the house.

Jenny looked around wondering who it could be. She knew Heather and Nikos could not make it over from Santorini, so was mentally working her way around the table, and struggling to determine who was missing. On seeing Callum emerge through the bifold doors though, a couple of bottles of wine in his hands, and wearing cut-off denims and a tight-fitting T-shirt, a smile soon came to her face. She had not seen him since the wedding, and although they had exchanged details and agreed to keep in touch, the odd text had been the extent of their contact. She had certainly had no warning he would be turning up today.

Jenny had taken their night together for what it was. Great sex, a feel-good factor, but nothing more. She had moved on. Her divorce from Jason was progressing, with discussions so far, around splitting their assets and custody arrangements, being conducted amicably. Her lawyer, Mrs Jessop, advised it was going as well as could be expected, under the circumstances, advising by Christmas her decree nisi should be through. If anything, the weekend of the wedding had strengthened Jenny's resolve to get her life in order, and made her see what she needed to do.

Being with Callum, although fleetingly, had given her back some self-esteem, some self-worth. The new and improved Jenny was someone who took more time for herself and knew the value of her own wellbeing. And in terms of Emily and Harry, well, the news of their parents' impending divorce had come as no surprise. Their response had been priceless; they simply shrugged as if to say "tell us something we don't already know", before going up to their rooms, as if it was just a normal day.

"Hope you don't mind that I let myself in, mate," Callum said approaching JoJo and handing over the bottles. "And I'm sorry I'm late. The traffic on the M1 was horrendous. At one stage, I thought of detouring and coming up the A1, but satnav said that was as bad. Anyway, I'm here now."

"I'll grab you a beer. You get a plate, and find somewhere to sit," JoJo offered, after embracing his best mate.

As JoJo went to get more beers, Callum made his way to the BBQ to shake hands with Craig. He did not know him particularly well, but he knew enough to know that he made his best mate happy, and in his book that was enough. And Callum, as a builder with a hearty appetite, believed anyone who could cook as well as Craig was a winner, as far as he was concerned.

Coming over to the table, he greeted each of them with either a kiss or a handshake, before going over and kissing Jenny on the lips, adding "hello, beautiful," quietly in her ear. The glint in his eye made Jenny blush, something that did not go unnoticed by Mel.

"It's good to see you all again," he said after sitting down. "Although isn't someone's missing?" he asked, glancing around the table. "Where's Heather? I thought you three were joined at the hip." As he laughed, he directed his comment at Mel and Jenny.

"Oh, no. Heather and Nikos couldn't make it over this time. They're sorry to be missing out, though," Mel advised, before adding for Callum's benefit, "I'm not sure if you know, Heather and Nikos are expecting a baby at Christmas, and given her age the risks are considered higher. Apparently, the doctor suggested, in her condition, it would be safer not to fly."

"No, I didn't know, but what brilliant news." Callum seemed genuinely delighted. "I believe that deserves a toast. To Heather and Nikos, and the patter of tiny feet."

"Cheers!" they all chorused.

"Yes, we're delighted for them. We're already planning a flight over in the new year to visit once the baby's born, aren't we George?" Mel added, raising her glass too, whilst squeezing George's hand. "They've moved in together, into Nikos' home. They want to get everything prepared before the baby arrives. I think there's some renovations needed though to make it fully comfortable. I understand it's a large property on the outskirts of the village, so there's plenty of room for expansion. And room to hang a swing alongside the swimming pool, according to Heather."

"Well, if renovation's what's required, then I'm your man. Well, my company is. I could easily get a team over there tomorrow, if they needed any help, that is," Callum offered. "We deal with quite a few international projects. In fact, I have a gang that travels out on assignment whenever it's needed, specifically for that type of work. Quite a few people buy property overseas and want British workmen, so it would be no sweat at all."

"Right, Callum. Enough business talk for today. I'm sure Mel can let Heather know you're available, should there be no dishy Greek builders to hand," JoJo laughed. "And now that we've wet the baby's head, so to speak, and as none of you are driving home tonight, I'd say it's time to get this party started. My husband hasn't been slaving over a hot BBQ all day for nothing. So, let's eat and get drunk!"

On learning everyone was staying over, Jenny could not hide her silly smile. Her stomach was doing somersaults at the potential of another night with Callum. Any qualms about being branded a scarlet woman were now firmly behind her. So what, if she was forty and naughty, she was loving the person she had become these last few months. And for once, she was relieved it was Jason's weekend to have Emily and Harry to sleep over, ensuring no interruptions, should she be lucky enough to have another good dream!

Chapter 57

Whilst everyone was enjoying Craig and JoJo's BBQ in Yorkshire, Heather and Nikos were sitting next to their swimming pool in the grounds of Nikos' villa. They were relaxing under the shade of the old umbrella and enjoying a cool drink after a busy day. Scaffolding was up all around them, with workmen's tools littering the walkways, empty paint containers strewn around. It was exceptionally hot, and at five months pregnant the heat and the ongoing building work was starting to take its toll on Heather. After all, she was not in the first flush of youth, at least not as far as motherhood was concerned.

To Nikos, however she was 'blooming', her little bump now clearly visible, her ample breasts in his opinion more appealing than ever. He adored her and the child she was bringing into the world; a child neither of them had ever planned, nor imagined possible.

Heather, discovering she was pregnant at the age of forty had been in total shock; initially believing the symptoms she began experiencing when her periods stopped were due to early menopause, rather than anything else. It was a condition her mother and sister had suffered from; a condition she understood could be carried through her genes. So, to return to Santorini after the trip to the UK for the wedding and find she was already two months pregnant had taken some getting used to. Children and motherhood was a concept she had long since given up on, her chance she believed lost after Bruce's untimely death.

Nikos similarly had never considered fatherhood as something he would experience. And given his terse and often uncomfortable relationship with his own father, he did not feel that was a great loss to humanity. They were resigned to it just being the two of them. However, once the shock had worn off and reality hit home, they were absolutely delighted at the prospect of parenthood. It gave them something positive to focus on.

Since Nikos' mother's health scare earlier that year, he had spent an increasing amount of time supporting his family's business, operating from the makeshift office he had constructed in the villa, or occasionally flying over to Athens if the need arose. He experienced first-hand the scale of the business his father had developed, the number of people it employed and the livelihoods it supported. He allowed himself a moment of pride at what the family's name meant in the area. Equally, he discovered areas where his father had potentially lost focus, even taken his eye off the ball. He felt able to offer suggestions. Simple actions that could be taken to reduce the risk, or better manage the profitability, without jeopardising the integrity of the business, or the family's reputation. It started to draw him in, almost as if he was an insect, caught in a spider's web.

Consequently, he found less time to work as the village's odd-job man or run the store. Even tinkering around in the workshop and helping the locals in whatever manner he could became a problem. As far as managing his time was concerned, there never seemed enough hours in the day. It had never been a job he did for money, just the satisfaction and appreciation of the people who most needed his help was enough. Payment, more often than not was a beer, or a bag of fresh groceries dropped on the doorstep. Even an invite to share a meal at the home of a grateful neighbour, by way of demonstrating their gratitude.

However, throughout the year, as the demands on his time grew, he found the number of hours he was able to open up the workshop significantly reducing. By mid-June, with the peak holiday season fast approaching, and the need to stock the shop ready for the summer trade, a crunch point came. It forced Nikos to seriously think about his life. Until then he had enjoyed his independence, with the freedom to simply please himself and go where life took him. All at once, responsibility seemed to be being heaped on his shoulders, from all directions. It was shortly after he and Heather had returned home from the wedding, around the same time as the pregnancy was confirmed, and their emotions were running high.

"You're going to have a nervous breakdown if you continue like this. You need to sort something out, Nikos." Heather had warned him late one evening, after Nikos returned back to her apartment from the workshop, exhausted. He had worked all morning on his father's business at his villa, before doing a few hours work in the afternoon on the villa itself, to get it ready for them to move into. Transforming it into a home, rather than somewhere he had simply existed, was a much bigger task than he'd imagined.

He had then gone directly to the workshop to repair a window frame that needed some attention. The repair jobs were stacking up, and with summer coming, the workshop activity needed to be scaled back, to give more space for the touristy items to be displayed.

"You can't do everything. The villa, the shop, the workshop, your family's business – they're all demanding your time. And now with me and the baby, and the need to get us moved into the villa before it's too late – it's all getting too much. Something has got to give!"

Whilst he knew Heather was right, it created a real conflict for Nikos. Not least because he believed the ties to his homeland had long since been broken. So, why were they still pulling on his heartstrings so much? Why was he allowing his father's business to demand so much of his time? But at the same time, the villagers needed him. Who else would repair their things when they broke, or be there to service whatever needed maintaining?

He was being forced to choose between doing what he loved most, or doing what he felt was his duty – not only to Heather, but to his family too. His duty had to come first. After all, he was to become a father himself soon. He had to accept that responsibility came with the territory, and if that meant a little less tinkering in the short term, then so be it.

A local couple, on hearing of his dilemma offered to run the shop for him during the busy periods, with Heather volunteering to help out occasionally if needed, especially as they were stocking a selection of her jewellery. She was keen to see how her Island Range would sell, as well as get feedback from the tourists that she could work on for the coming year's designs. She also believed it would give her an occupation while she awaited the baby's arrival. She was not prepared to simply sit around at the villa and twiddle her thumbs, whilst Nikos worked away in his office, or supervised the workmen he had eventually agreed to employ as they managed the renovations. No, the shop was a lifeline to the village and it needed to survive. And if she could support that in any way, then even better. The workshop on the other hand would need to take a back seat for the time being; she could not see herself with a screwdriver under any circumstances, let alone in her pregnant state!

Now, having made some adjustments, Nikos was a little more relaxed. His priority was clearly to Heather and their baby, and creating a home for them. Making the suggestion to move into his villa, once the news of her pregnancy was confirmed, had become the obvious first solution. It would give them more space, and once the modifications were complete, they would have a real home. A place to which they would be comfortable to invite their family and friends to stay. He could afford to get professionals in, so why had he been killing himself, trying to do it alone? With a team of workmen now on hand, things had begun to move at a real pace.

In the early days, Nikos had regularly stayed over at Heather's apartment and had rarely returned to the villa. In fact, Heather had never visited it, or really known of its existence until after her pregnancy was discovered. She knew Nikos lived somewhere locally, it had just never been important for her to establish precisely where, or what his accommodation was like. She had presumed it was an apartment, similar to the one she was renting herself. So, when Nikos mentioned it and suggested it may be somewhere she could consider living, initially it had thrown her.

"Come and look at the property first, before you dismiss it," he had suggested, sensing her reluctance. "If you don't fall in love with it, then we will find somewhere else."

He went on to explain that it was a property he had bought on instinct some years previously, shortly after moving to the island. A project to throw himself into, using his natural DIY skills. Something that would distract him from the troubles of home, back in Athens. It was old and in need of repair, but without a purpose, he had not found his heart to be in it. Whilst jobs had begun, nothing had ever been finished. It was habitable, but only just. He had simply stayed there, when he didn't bed down at the workshop, never particularly comfortable within its four walls. Now with their impending new arrival, he had a clear goal, a strong purpose, and with some renovations he could make it into a proper home for his family.

When Heather saw it, she had fallen in love with it, immediately realising the potential it offered them. Nikos set his hand to the renovations and Christmas became a milestone to work towards. Now, with the professionals on board, and only four short months and counting left to go, there was still a lot of work left to be done. But at least they were living in it and it was starting to take shape. Their vision was becoming a reality.

Plans beyond that remained sketchy, with Heather and Nikos having plenty that needed thinking through, before decisions about their longer-term future could be made. Nikos' parents regularly hinted at him returning to Athens, those hints getting more frequent since news of their next grandchild was received.

For Heather, there was still her home in the Scottish Highlands to consider, and her family there. The cottage, for now, was rented out to tenants, so that was at least one less worry, with Misty happily rehoused with her neighbour, Mrs McNally. And her father was comfortable, albeit in his care home. He was being looked after, content in his own little world. As sad as it made Heather to see his deterioration, she was realistic enough to accept that moving back to Scotland would alter nothing, as far as her father was concerned.

Her home now was with Nikos and their baby, and whatever shape that took, or wherever they eventual decided to settle, then she would be happy with that. She was no longer the widow, vicariously living her life through others. She had met a man who had turned her life around, and far from it being over, as she had once feared, that could not be further from the truth.

She had so much to live for, so much to love. For now where better to spend her time than in a place surrounded by such beauty? Santorini had certainly worked its magic on her these last few months.

As Nikos came over, placing his hand gently on her stomach as she felt the baby kick, she smiled contentedly. She sensed the next chapter of her life was just about to begin, and she could not wait.

"I was wondering, do you think on top of everything else, we'd have time to fit a wedding in, between now and December? Or would you prefer to wait until next year?" Nikos asked, as he knelt next to her.

"Is that a proposal, by any chance?" she questioned, a smile crossing her face. They had never really spoken of marriage before, simply happy with the commitment they already had.

"I believe it might be," he laughed. "What would you say if it was?"

"I'd probably say yes," she replied, laughing back at him. She reached over to kiss him. "Perhaps though, it might be better if we wait until after the baby arrives. I think we've enough on our plate at the moment, don't you, my love? And I quite like the idea of a combined christening and wedding. What would you think to that? I'm sure Mel and Jenny would love that. Whoever this little bump turns out to be, he or she is going to need her godmothers around, and I'd hate to arrange a wedding without my best friends here!"

"That sounds perfect, my darling," Nikos replied, completely content with Heather's suggestion. "I suppose though, I probably should get some more work done. I can't sit down resting anymore. Not if we've a wedding and a christening to plan for. There's no time to waste."

"Bring it on," thought Heather excitedly, as her stomach fluttered once more; the little life inside her gently reminding her of its presence.

THE END.

If you enjoyed The Godmothers, I would be delighted if you could leave a positive review on Amazon, and perhaps recommend it to your family and friends.
Equally, if you haven't yet discovered my other novels, please check these out.
Finding Home and its sequel Forever Home were published in 2022 and After the Rain in 2023.
Thanks, Angela

Printed in Great Britain
by Amazon

30843236R00202